what you do in the dark . . .

by

Deborah Marbury

This book is a work of fiction. Places, events, and situations in this story are purely fictional. Any resemblance to actual persons, living or dead, is coincidental.

© 2002 by Deborah Marbury. All rights reserved.

No part of this book may be reproduced, stored in a retrieval system, or transmitted by any means, electronic, mechanical, photocopying, recording, or otherwise, without written consent from the author.

ISBN: 0-7596-9701-9

Library of Congress Control Number: 2002100612

Printed in the United States of America
Bloomington, IN

This book is printed on acid free paper.

1stBooks - rev. 05/14/02

acknowledgments

I give the highest honor, glory, and praise to God who is the head of my life, and in whom I have entrusted the success of this novel. (Proverb 16:3).

Special thanks to my Pastor, Larry L. Harris Sr. of Mt. Olive Missionary Baptist Church and Rev. John Harris of Cincinnati, Ohio who inspired the sermons in the church scenes.

Many thanks to Cleveland State University's Imagination Conference, CSU Professors Dan Chaon, Sheila Schwartz and Stephanie Byrd, friends Gregory Dotson and Frederick Burton, and to the many other friends, classmates and professionals who have helped contribute to the quality of this novel.

dedication

*To God, who is my **Provider**, Jesus Christ, who is my **Savior**, and the Holy Spirit, who is my **Comforter** and **Counselor**—please allow this story to touch the hearts of women everywhere so that they may know that you can supply all their needs (Philippians 4:19), and that they may also know that what you are for me, you can also be for them*

To my son, Calvin Darnell Kelly, who is the motivation for every good thing that I do. I love you!

To my mother, Inez Marbury, who has always encouraged met to do my best.

To the memory of my father, Clinton Marbury, who always believed in me and supported me in all my endevours.

For there is nothing covered, that shall not be revealed; neither hid, that shall not be known.

Therefore whatsoever ye have spoken in darkness shall be heard in the light; and that which ye have spoken in the ear in closet that shall be proclaimed upon the housetops (Luke 12:2-, KJV).

what you do in the dark...

sweet november

*But maybe sweet November will tell us a story
That will bring us back the love that we once knew*

Friday, November 7, 1989 @ 6:30 p.m. (T.G.I.F.)
Maybe it's because he's boring. Or . . . maybe it's because he's been unfaithful. I guess it's because I'm tired of being alone. All I know is that I'm excited about the date I have tonight with my new friend. My new friend is sexy, exciting and handsome. He makes me feel like I got it goin' on! **He** makes me feel like a woman and everybody knows that men are just like jobs. You don't leave the one you have until you find another one.

Friday, June 11, 1999 @ 10:30 p.m.
I had written that journal entry almost ten years ago. Tonight, I dug it out of a box of old diaries to amuse myself. I wanted to see where my head had been in those days. I also wanted some answers. I read somewhere that if you were constantly finding yourself in unfulfilling relationships, it was a sign that you may need to break some patterns. I've kept a journal since I was fifteen, so I know if there are any patterns to break, I have enough material to spot them.

Deborah Marbury

So, here I am, ten years later, fifty pounds heavier, lying in my bed surrounded with plenty of late night snacks and old notebooks that serve as journals. Almost immediately, I decided that this was the journal entry that had ruined my life. It caused me to be almost 35 years old and still single. I had planned to get married in June of 1990. As I reflect on the events of that year November 1989 to October of 1990, I'm sure, it was that journal entry, that night, and that year, which had changed my life **forever.**

I had gotten my hair and nails done earlier that day. Then, after taking a long, relaxing, scented bubble bath, I sprayed on some of my favorite perfume. I remember putting on the sexiest outfit in my wardrobe while I listened to one of my favorite R&B male artists, Johnny Gill. It was 7:00. My date was supposed to pick me up at 7:30. I sat at the desk in my bedroom and added to my journal:

Tonight, my new friend won't be able to resist me. I will finally feel appreciated again. Even though I'm engaged and should have no intention of making love with him tonight, I don't see anything wrong with making him want me. I need to know somebody wants me even if my fiancé doesn't.

His constant excuses were readily doled out to my subtle, but desperate pleas for companionship. "Do you wanna go to the movies tonight?" "Can we go pick up a bite to eat?" "You know, I sure wouldn't mind going away for the weekend."

"I can't tonight, Red. I gotta do somethin' with my family." "No not today. Me and my boys, Craig and Tyrone, are goin' out." "You know I got that fraternity meeting out of town this weekend. I'll see you when I get back. I'll bring you somethin' special." His low, bass voice, which matched his strong, rugged appearance, was always matter of fact. *My* needs were never up for discussion. I *longed* for my short, stocky fiancé. When his arms were around me, I loved the feel of his hard muscles tightly covered with smooth, plum-colored skin that made small threats to burst the seams of his postal uniform like the Incredible Hulk. He made me feel safe.

what you do in the dark...

Our dates had dwindled to only once a month since we'd set our wedding date this past June for the following year. I should have known that something was going on with him, especially when we stopped making love, but instead I rushed to make wedding plans, ignoring all the signs. It will get better once we're married, I told myself. I thought I'd have something small and intimate at Jackie's church.

"I'm getting married Jackie," I told my childhood friend and co-worker a few days after we set the date. "I'd like for you to be my matron of honor."

"Congratulations! It's about time! I would love to be your matron of honor! I'd have an attitude if you chose anyone else. So what happened? How did he propose? Give me the scoop! I can't wait to tell Bernard!"

"I'll have to tell you more at work tomorrow, 'cause I have some more calls to make, but I wanted to know if you could get Reverend Peoples to marry us?"

She let out an exasperated sigh. "I'll see," she grunted. "He usually likes to counsel the people he marries, *and* he likes for them to be members of the church if at all possible."

"Later for that!" I smirked and sucked my teeth.

"Lord! Pleeeze! Help her!" Jackie laughed. I pictured her raising a hand high to the heavens.

I laughed too. "You so crazy!"

"I'll see what I can do," she promised.

"Okay, I'll talk to you later."

"Hey!" she called to catch me. "What about Michelle?"

"Maid of honor." I said it quickly and hung up.

"Girl, come on. Let's go out. Don't just sit at home waitin' for him to call. Stop bein' available all the time. Get out! Do somethin'! Ain't nothin' to it, but to do it!" The voice of my best friend, Michelle, rang in my head, taunting me as I contemplated the night ahead of me.

"Dag Auntie, do you ever go anywhere?" I pictured my niece, Sheila, looking at me with pity in her big brown thirteen year old eyes.

"Can I have the pleasure of your company at the dinner dance tonight?" His voice was smooth and seductive when he called me that morning at my job.

You most certainly can! I thought. I'm not gonna just sit here waitin' for my man to call, and I won't be starin' at the walls in this box of an apartment tonight either! I refuse to be lonely anymore. A handsome, *influential* man wants the pleasure of *my* company and tonight, *he's* gonna get it!

"Hi. What time did you say you'd be picking me up?" I called him back that afternoon to reassure myself that I really had a date with him.

"How about 7:30? The food will be served at 8."

"That's fine."

"I can't wait to see you. What are you wearing?"

"I don't know. I'm still trying to decide."

"You got anything red?"

"I think so."

"Wear that. You'd look great in red. Throw in some black here and there too, to set if off, okay?"

"Okay. See you at 7:30."

"Don't worry I'll be there."

I wasn't dreaming. I had a date! And with *him* of all people.

I left the seat at my desk and my journal writing to turn on my stereo. I began to critique myself in the full-length mirror on my bedroom closet door for at least fifteen or twenty minutes to the crooning of Johnny Gill singing, **My, My, My**. As I let it play over and over again, I paid meticulous attention to every detail I believed a man appreciated in a woman.

I wanted my hair, face, body, and outfit to look perfect like a Jet Magazine beauty of the week. I combed and re-combed my Cleopatra-style pageboy. Shook it to make sure my jet-black locks fell softly to my shoulders. I admired its body and sprayed it with oil sheen. My stylist was a genius, I thought. How she could take a sister's hair from Africa to Europe in two hours was a miracle right up there with the parting of the Red Sea from that movie, **The Ten Commandments**.

Michelle had advised me over the years how to dress so that I accentuated my figure just the way a man likes. I pictured her jiggling her apple-sized breasts in the mirror to make sure her blouse did them justice.

"Do these jeans make my butt look flat?" she often asked me before we went out to a nightclub. "Men hate flat butts, you know. You think I should change?"

I never thought Michelle should change. She looked great in everything. Tall, slender, well-proportioned, and slightly bow-legged. Her silky, sandy brown hair in a short, but jazzy precision cut framed her flawless banana-colored face perfectly. She could have been a model.

what you do in the dark...

She looked like Halle Berry, and she knew just how to get a man's attention. Yet, she never seemed satisfied with the way she looked. When we got dressed to go out on the town, she would fuss over her appearance long after I'd settled for however I looked.

But tonight, I knew I had to look my best. I let Michelle's voice coach me as I kept smoothing my red suede mini skirt. I turned and twisted in the mirror to make sure the skirt fell smoothly over my 38" hips. Frustrated, I raised the skirt above my breasts to tug down my sheer, low-cut, black blouse showing off my 26" waistline. I pulled the skirt down and smoothed it again. I didn't want the imprint from my blouse or my underwear to show.

"You shouldn't wear panties." Michelle's feisty voice interjected. "That's why your pantyhose have that cotton liner. Duh!" she teased.

I couldn't imagine not wearing underwear.

"Make sure you have on clean bloomers." My mother would warn as most mothers do. "You never know when you might get in an accident and have to go to the hospital."

Somewhere in American history, somebody went to the hospital with dirty underwear on, and kids have been warned about it ever since! Lord forbid if my mother found out that I was brought to the hospital with no underwear on at all!

I tugged the lapels of my suede jacket that matched my skirt, fixed the collar, and decided to leave it open in the front revealing a peek at the cleavage of 38" C cup breasts. If I wasn't confident about anything else, I knew I had a great body. I moved in closer to the mirror to apply a little makeup.

"Am I pretty?" I heard myself ask my fiancé for the millionth time after lovemaking, during dinner, or while driving.

"You know you are," his tired response. "Stop fishing for compliments."

As I applied apple red lipstick to the perfectly curved female version of my father's thin lips, I tried to ignore my lazy eye, which peered out of an almond-shaped, cream-filled hollow and turned in toward my nose. I hated that about myself. A woman needed her eyes. It was part of the seduction. How would I ever keep a man if I couldn't look straight into his eyes? I knew my body would get him, but I needed my eyes to keep him. I could feel myself starting to get anxious and nervous.

"It's not that noticeable," I tried to convince myself, but I could hear that familiar question coming at me like a well-aimed dart to the heart.

"Are you looking at *me*?"

Neither of them ever asked it, but I was sure the question was always there stifled only by politeness.

What if he doesn't like women who wear mini-skirts? I wondered. My fiancé once told me that women who show too much of their bodies seem easy.

"I'm not easy," I answered his insinuation. Maybe I should wear something more formal...elegant perhaps, I told myself.

I looked down at my long legs showcased in sheer off black pantyhose until my eyes met red, high-heeled pumps. I compared myself to the mirror's image, and decided I looked like a whore. I felt myself sweating. My hair would be ruined if I kept this up. Those bouncy, black locks were threatening to go back to Africa. I turned the volume up on Johnny, and let his sensuous baritone voice croon seductive lyrics to soothe me.

> *Put on your red dress*
> *And slide on your high heels*
> *And some of that sweet perfume*
> *It sure smells good on you*
> *Put on your lipstick*
> *And let all your hair down*
> *I just wanna take some time.*
> *I just wanna look at you*

My door buzzer rang. I walked into the living room, which led straight from my bedroom with no door. I buzzed him into the apartment building, then ran back to check the geographical location of my hair, and to practice how I would open the door to greet him.

"Hello Robert." A professional greeting.

"Hi Robert." A casual greeting.

"Hey Robert." A sexy greeting.

When I heard his knock, I took another look at myself in the mirror to gauge how I should hold my head so that my eye looked straight. I turned the light off my reflection, walked slowly into the living room, and opened the door.

Cool Water cologne gushed forth, and filled the apartment like air freshener, not strong, but obvious and refreshing. I looked up at him. He was slightly taller than my 5'6" frame even in my 2" heels. His full

what you do in the dark . . .

brown lips topped with a faint moustache eased out a pearly white smile that brought out a small dimple in his slightly pointed chin, which was accentuated by a goatee. My eyes followed his slim physique down to his black wing-tipped shoes. He had on the same colors as I did, a black sports jacket and matching slacks with a red, round-collared silk shirt. His jet-black, processed waves complemented his smooth brown skin like chocolate chips on a chocolate sundae. He could have been an S-curl man.

"Oh, now I see why you wanted me to wear red," I said grinning, blushing really.

"I want everybody to know that the prettiest lady in the house is with me." His voice was smooth, confident, and sexy.

He called me pretty. I rejoiced. He pulled me close and kissed my lips gently. His presence was overwhelming, and I felt like a caramel sundae in his hot fudge embrace. I backed away from him after a few moments. I needed to lower my body temperature in order to preserve my 'do'. I realized that this was the first time we'd kissed. This *was* a date. I took a deep breath, smiled nervously, and invited him in for a drink. We drank a glass of wine and talked about how each of our days had been.

I had met Robert Turner over a year earlier during an interview for the newspaper I worked for, **The African American Times Weekly**. He was a Cleveland councilman, and I had been assigned to cover his plans to build a community center.

"Hi, I'm Caren," I said as I walked into his office. I deliberately neglected to mention my last name. "I'm here to interview you about your community center project for the **AA Times**."

I held out my hand to shake his. I usually take a quick look around the office of my subject to get clued in on personality and background, but when he looked up from his work, I had to do a double take of the most beautiful Colgate smile I'd ever seen. He stood up, and looked directly into my eyes straight through to my soul. I looked away quickly before he noticed it, and asked that question.

"Hello Caren," he said taking my hand and holding it for longer than it took to complete a business handshake. "It's very nice to meet you," he told me trying to hold a steady gaze with me.

I felt embarrassed because I knew my grip was not the firm one that was appropriate between professionals. His hand felt hot. His gaze was hypnotizing. I couldn't return it. When he asked me to have a seat, I stumbled and fell into the chair behind me across from where he sat at a neatly organized, large desk with a rich dark oak finish.

I could feel beads of perspiration developing in my armpits onto my new royal blue silk blouse. And as the grandmother in Eddie Murphy's **Nutty Professor** would say, he was making me moist.

"What was your last name again, Sweetheart?" His penetrating gaze burned through me, and his smile mesmerized me.

I looked around at the pictures and plaques on the brown, paneled walls to keep from having eye conversation and also to keep from answering his question. The office was immaculate and spacious, but warmed by aged oak furniture that blended with the walls and the brown, slightly worn, but exceptionally clean carpet. There was a dedicated wall of well-aligned pictures of him and the Mayor accepting awards together or of the Mayor giving some commendation to the Councilman. I noticed his bachelor's degree from Florida A&M and a law degree from Ohio State University.

Pictures of different sections of his ward reminded me of why I was so interested in the community center project. There was a big map pinned to a corkboard, which sat on an isolated easel. The map outlined the neighborhoods that made up Ward One. A big red dot with large black letters read, "**WARD ONE COMMUNITY CENTER.**" It marked an area most familiar to me, my mother's neighborhood, the place where I grew up. A special set of streets nicknamed, The Island.

I think it got its name because it's set apart, in a world all its own. People who don't live there rarely pass through its streets because they lead to dead ends. It used to be a close-knit neighborhood because everybody knew everybody's business as if they needed each other to survive like castaways shipwrecked on a deserted island.

I can remember our parents sending us to each other's houses like the Skipper, the Howell's, the Professor, Mary Ann, and Ginger would send Gilligan running from hut to hut with messages.

"Caren, what you doin' eatin' them crab apples? You know they make you sick. You go home and tell Mary to call me."

"Jackie, you and Caren run down to Mark's house and get that package Gladys has for me."

"Mark, run over there to the Village and put my numbers in. Caren and Jackie, y'all go with'em."

And the children of most of the families grew up and became lovers, but hardly ever husbands and wives. Yet, the place bred lots of mothers.

Bold, single teenage mothers on welfare. And a new generation of siblings sprang forth with the same mothers and different fathers or the same father and different mothers. I never became one of those teenage mothers because of *my* mother's strict discipline, my sister's example, and my own strong will not to be like any of the girls in my neighborhood.

Although moral decay permeates the Island, the neighborhood is still quite special. I think I will always love it. The people mind their own business now. My mother hardly knows anyone who lives on her street not to mention in the neighborhood. I don't know many of the people who live there now either.

"Ma, what happened to Miss Blackfoot?" I asked my mother when I came home one year from college for summer break.

"Dead."

"What about the Jones family?"

"Moved."

"The Townsends? Mark and his mother?"

"They live in Bedford Heights now. Gladys calls me from time to time. She still goes to church out here. Over there at Matthias. That church is growin' too. Done added on somethin' new every year. Pastor Peoples' son is the preacher now. They say he's young and handsome. Jackie and her husband still go there, you know."

I'd ask my mother about somebody each summer vacation from college until I grew disinterested. Some of the older citizens whose adult children have gone on to college, military, career, drugs, the streets, prison or death are still scattered about on the various streets in the neighborhood. They talk through rumors and hearsay from their grown children—The Island's rumor mill.

"I saw Lucille, Hattie's daughter, at the grocery store the other day. 'Said Thomas Jr. strung out on drugs. I think that Mark is sellin' them ol' reefers too."

A lot has changed in the Island, but the young guys and girls sittin' on porches and hangin' out at the neighborhood store hint that the children are still becoming lovers. Some things never change.

That following August morning after our first meeting, Robert and I walked through the streets of the Island so he could show me the vacant lot where they were planning to break ground for the community center.

We visited the store that has always been run by the same family. We waved at the retired neighbors that remembered me from my childhood years and recognized the Councilman as they watched us stroll by from their now broken down porches. All the while Robert talked of his plans to redeem the neighborhood. He claimed he would restore it to the splendor it once knew when it was inhabited by whites.

There would be new houses, a playground, grants or loans for business and residential rehabs, and of course, the community center. The center would house a daycare, senior citizen programs, and recreational facilities for the youth, and meeting rooms for area churches and businesses. He even had plans to plant more trees on the tree lawns to give the streets more shade and that quiet, suburban quality. I was grateful and hopeful.

"Did you go to this church when you were growing up?" he asked as we approached a beautiful, red brick church. Matthias Fellowship Christian Church. It was the only building that didn't look run down in the whole area. The Island's bright spot.

"Yeah, I got baptized here when I was fifteen." Memories of Jackie and I attending Sunday school classes together came back to me. We got baptized together too. I was a long way from that girl now, I thought. I stopped praying when I went to college. My roommate didn't pray, and I didn't want her to think I was weird. I stopped professing Christ after my first 'Intro to Sociology' class. I had no idea that there were other religions. How could you possibly know which one was right?

"You ever come back to visit?" Robert's voice interrupted my thoughts.

"What for? I'm not a hypocrite. I'm not gonna live the way church people say you should live. So why bother?"

"Yeah, I know what you mean." His response felt like it betrayed his true feelings.

"Do you belong to a church?"

"Most politicians belong to a church," he stated matter-of-factly. "I belong to Matthias. I grew up in Pensacola, Florida, but I was born here in Cleveland. My parents moved away because of some fight my mother had with her brother over my grandmother. My uncle's still here, but I don't know him or remember him. They used to live here in Ward One, but they must have moved because I haven't seen their names listed as residents on my roster."

We visited my mother. She was usually home watching the morning game shows like all the other retired people who weren't tending to their

what you do in the dark . . .

yards or sitting on their front porches like the ones we'd just waved to. Robert and my mother were already well acquainted with each other.

"I try to know all my residents," Robert bragged as we entered the side door, which led to my mother's kitchen. "I helped your mother with some property tax issues just after your father died. You must have been away at school."

"Hey there, Councilman Turner. I see you workin' with my daughter now," my mother greeted him as she offered him a kitchen chair and a cup of coffee. Her presence was always warm, but domineering. She stood 5'6" like me, straight and firm with ample bosom, smooth dark brown skin, and medium length black hair streaked with gray that she wore in lots of curls.

"Yeah, she's doing a great job. She's a lot like you Mrs. ---."

"Hellooo!" Robert's call jolted me back to his office. That day I had been very distracted by problems my fiancé and I were having. "Your last name, Sweetheart. Do you mind telling me what it is?"

"Boogerton," I said. "Caren Boogerton." I faked indifference, but I heard my young schoolmates yelling in my head. "Caren is the booger girl! Caren is the booger girl! How many boogers she got? Booger-ton! Ten boogers! But she sees twenty!" I couldn't wait to get married and rid myself of that hideous last name.

"Did you say, Bookerton?"

"No. Boogerton."

"You know Mary Boogerton?"

"Yes, she's my mother."

He smiled approvingly, leaned back in his chair and rubbed his palms together.

"Okay Caren," Robert said smoothly. "Where do you want to start?"

I loved the way he ignored my imperfections. He didn't make any jokes about my name. Although, I couldn't help but picture him rolling on the floor with laughter after I'd left. I suppose it was easy for him to keep a straight face this time since he'd already heard the name when he met my mother.

After that initial interview, we exchanged numbers. He called me everyday both at work and at home to discuss new ideas about the community center. He invited me to every business meeting, social function and fundraiser connected to the project. I worked on stories about Robert and his community center almost to the exclusion of other assignments. As I got to know him better, and my fiancé started spending less time with me and more time with his friends (or so he said), I became more attracted to councilman Turner.

Jackie, as secretary to **AA Times** publisher, Mr. Caldwell, saw it all coming. She often made comments when I wrote "Robert Turner's office" on the reporters' log kept at her desk.

"That's the third time this week you've been to Councilman Turner's office." She tossed her extension braids behind her shoulder, stood up to use the copier and tugged the lapels of yet another gray business suit. "You're only supposed to see him once a week. You better be careful, Girl. Watch yourself now. I think the councilman wants to make you a notch on his belt. I know those player types, Girlfriend. And he is the ultimate player!"

Jackie and I had been friends since elementary school, and even though we're the same age, she's always acted as if she were my mother. I cherish her friendship, but she gets on my nerves sometimes. Not only because of her motherly ways, but also because she was everything that I wasn't.

Men admired and respected her. They hounded and whistled at me. I was pretty, red and sexy. She was beautiful, black and graceful. She liked neutral, conservative clothes and Afro centric hairstyles. I liked bright, colorful clothes and Euro centric hairstyles. I did everything wrong according to her. I lost my virginity on prom night and dated the same man for ten years.

First, our parents thought we needed to go to college. We agreed. Including high school, that was the first seven or eight years of our courtship. He went to the Air Force and joined me at Central State two years later. He dropped out of college a year after I graduated. Next, he had to find the right job, two more years. Year ten, engaged. Next year, marriage aborted.

Jackie told me to wait until I got married before having sex, but that would have been ten years of waiting. No way I was going to wait that long. Yet, I often wonder if that's why she's happily married while Michelle and I were desperately single?

"Girl, don't you do it! Wait on the Lord," Jackie urged one night when she and Michelle were at my house for a sleepover.

"Wait on the Lord for what?" Michelle demanded.

"Confirmation. If he's *the one*, he'll wait."

Michelle busted out laughing. "Now Jackie, please! Give me a break. Waitin' for marriage went out with the fifties and sixties. She gon' be

what you do in the dark...

waitin' on the Lord all alone! Listen Girl, if you wanna keep a man, you gotta give him some. It's just that simple. Just make it good so he'll keep comin' back for more. Ain't nothin' to it, but to do it!"

"That's fine talk from somebody who can't even keep a man," Jackie retorted.

"You right! I can't keep *a* man. I get as many as I want, and I don't want to *keep* none of 'em. I'm tellin' you, Girl. Give him some, and you won't be able to get rid of him."

"He won't respect you," Jackie urged.

"He'll worship the ground you walk on," Michelle insisted.

"He'll just use you," Jackie implored.

"And if it feels that good getting used, then let him use you 'til he use you up!" Michelle quipped.

"You're such a tramp!" Jackie kidded Michelle.

"Yo' mama!" Michelle shot back, then stiffened her body and spoke in her 'proper' voice, "And you are such a prude!"

We all laughed and changed the subject.

I took Michelle's advice and gave it up to a man I never married while Jackie remained a virgin until she married Bernard shortly after high school graduation and had two kids.

It seems sometimes that the few girls I went to high school or college with who did wait were all married now, except for Cheryl Brooks. She was still waiting when I saw her at the five year high school reunion. Michelle and I, still single. But, at least we're not like Cheryl.

Jackie's husband, Bernard introduced my fiancé and me. They had been best friends. They were from an area called the Village which was separated from the Island by a big woodsy field that had lots of creeks running through it and a trail that connected the two neighborhoods. We met them during our sophomore year at John F. Kennedy High School. They would follow the trail that led to the Island to meet us, then we would cross the railroad tracks to exit the Island at Miles Avenue, then walk from Miles Avenue past our junior high school, Charles W. Eliot on 160th and Lotus Avenue, up Lotus Avenue to Lee Road, through the Lee-Harvard Shopping Center to Harvard Avenue where Kennedy was located. It was about a mile walk.

Bernard walked Jackie to school once when I was sick. The next day, when I tried to resume my place as Jackie's walking companion, I became the proverbial third wheel. Bernard brought his best friend along a few days later. We knew what we were supposed to do, so we fell right in. Crossing the tracks and walking that mile as couples.

You can fall in love on a daily mile-long walk. I wasn't attracted to him at first, but he treated me like a queen. I loved how special he made me feel. No one had ever made me feel like he did.

We used to go to the movies, skating, or just hangin' out at the new Randall Park Mall. The four of us became inseparable until we met Michelle in our junior year. Then, Michelle and her date of the day, hour, or minute became part of our group as well. Michelle had recently moved into the Lee-Harvard area on Judson one block up from Lotus Avenue. All these areas made up Robert's ward and our connections to one another.

My fiancé's entry into the Air Force broke his connection to Bernard after high school graduation. Jackie and I remained in touch, but our friendship lost something when she married and I went away to college. Besides, I think I preferred to hang out with Michelle because she was more fun. We went to Central State together and had a ball! Just one big party after another. It seems, however, that there was a time when I had more in common with Jackie. Yet, sometimes I longed for that time and that person to return.

Jackie helped me get hired at the **AA Times Weekly**, initially as a summer intern when I was home for vacation. She recommended me highly to Mr. Caldwell and the editor, Margaret Daniels. I did three summer internships there and was hired as a staff reporter upon college graduation. I made minimum wage as an intern and a whopping $250 a week as a staff reporter. I knew I would not retire there.

Thank God my fiancé got hired at the Postal Service the following year and started paying the note on a '88 Ford Tempo as well as the rent on my new apartment. He even paid for my beauty salon visits. I bought groceries, paid the utility bills and all my high interest credit cards, which purchased my always stylish wardrobe.

Jackie started at the **AA Times** when it was launched in 1981, the year we graduated, and she's been there ever since. I was sure she'd never leave. Jackie was like that. Stable, dependable, sensible, and moral—very moral. I didn't tell her when I accepted Robert's request to attend the dinner dance as his date.

After we finished our wine, Robert asked if I was ready to go. I was. So we left my apartment, and went outside to his car. It was a warm, November night. I remember looking up at the full moon and noticing

what you do in the dark . . .

what a very dark night it was in spite of that moon. It was following us, watching us just like when my sister, Carla and I were kids. We would be on our knees in the backseat of Daddy's car looking out the back window.

"Look Daddy! The moon is following us!" I shouted.

Talking to a woman he had offered a ride home, he just responded, "Yeah, that's nice."

I marveled at how it was always there no matter how fast Daddy drove or how many turns he made.

It took us about fifteen minutes to get from my Bedford Heights apartment complex to The Chique Nightclub on Lee Road right across the street from the Lee-Harvard Shopping Plaza. He helped me out of the car and we headed along with other guests to the hall's entrance. The approving glances we got from everyone told me that we looked great together. The Jet Magazine beauty of the week and the S-Curl man. I knew we had it goin' on! My tension eased and my confidence returned.

He treated me just like a lady. He opened the door for me when we entered the dance hall. He helped me with my coat and checked it for me. He also pulled the chair out for me when we reached our reserved table for two. My fiancé hadn't taken me out to a setting like this in years. He never tried to make me feel special anymore.

The dinner dance guests included a few dignitaries, people from the Mayor's office. Mostly, there were a lot of Ward One residents in attendance. I didn't recognize many of them. They'd probably moved into the area after I went to college. Besides, Ward One had so many neighborhoods, it was impossible to know all the residents. There was a podium by the DJ booth that Robert used occasionally to make announcements, but there was no formal program. Guests had bought tickets to eat, drink, dance and know that the money was going to improve their ward and build their community center.

We enjoyed a buffet-style dinner. Fried, baked, and barbecued chicken, roast beef, ham, cornbread, dinner rolls, macaroni and cheese, corn, greens, green beans, pasta salad, fruit salad, cakes, pies and peach cobbler. We went through the line quickly filling our plates with just about everything on the menu. Contemporary jazz played in the background creating an intimate ambience, and I felt myself getting comfortable with Robert.

"You look great," he told me. His sparkling, dark brown eyes resumed their familiar gaze and promised intense interest to every move I made. I instinctively crossed my leg to give him a look at my thigh.

"Thanks. So do you," I said. "I thought this outfit might not be appropriate for tonight."

"Oh, it's better than appropriate." He smiled generously nodding his head as his eyes explored me without inhibition or apology. Michelle had taught me well. I was working this man. The tension eased some more.

"How are things going with your fiancé?" he asked earnestly. I had complained to him several times before.

"The same."

"Shame," he sighed. Then, he looked down at his plate and picked up a forkful of macaroni and cheese. I took a bite of my fried chicken while he wasn't looking and quickly dabbed the grease from my lips.

"He just doesn't realize what he has."

"I suppose." I looked down at my plate now. I didn't want to talk about it.

"Anybody ever told you that you have beautiful brown eyes?"

I tilted my head. "Yes," I answered quietly, truthfully.

"You have a nice smile, too. Use it." The command was gentle and quiet. Then, he touched my hand and started that gaze thing again.

I blushed.

"We won't talk about him anymore." His words were like a gentle hug. "Let's just enjoy ourselves, okay?"

"Okay."

The DJ announced it was time to get the party started. Time for the line dance set. The new line dance song, "The Electric Slide" bumped out of large black speakers. Guests from all over the room raced to the dance floor. I felt great now. The dance floor was my territory. I was ready to jam! I knew all the line dances, except this one.

"Let's dance." Robert motioned me to the floor.

"I don't know this one," I pouted.

"Come on. I'll teach you. It's easy."

"Okay!" I jumped to my feet.

We carved out our position in the crowd. Robert put his arm around my waist to guide me as he coached me on the appropriate foot movements. I caught on after a couple of minutes. We were jammin'! We did "The Monorail," "The Trans-Europe Express" and many more of our line dance favorites.

what you do in the dark...

As I danced, I made sure I gyrated my hips to keep Robert's eyes only on me just like Michelle and I always practiced at home. We hitchhiked, dogged it out and put our booty in it! When it really got good, the DJ and the crowd started to shout back and forth, "Repeat that mutha! Party right where? Party over here! Who jams the most? Us Black folks! Ain't no party like a Ward One party, 'cause a Ward One party don't stop!"

The call and response between the DJ and the crowd continued non-stop as the big black speakers pumped out strong, bass-filled beats. I admired Robert's smooth moves that preserved his dignity as the councilman, but showed he was no 'stuffed shirt.' We had a great time. I couldn't remember ever having that much fun with my fiancé. *We* never went dancing. Whenever he did take me out, we went to the movies, bowling or out to eat. A night of dancing felt romantic, like foreplay.

The DJ eventually slowed the pace and my man, Johnny Gill sang ***My, My, My*** as my, my, my new forbidden love sang along with him softly in my ear:

Tonight will be a special night
No matter where we go
And I'm so proud to be with you
I just wanna let you know
You got me singing, 'My, my, my'
You sure look good tonight
And you're so damned fine
I gotta say, 'My, my, my'
You sure look good tonight
After all this time

"Lord have mercy on my soul!" I said to myself. "This man has got it goin' on! It's one thing to look good, ignore my imperfections and treat me like a lady, but when you start singing Johnny Gill in my ear, now you're messin' with my emotions!"

He pulled me closer and I inhaled the fresh aroma of Cool Water cologne and spearmint gum. He smelled shower fresh as if he hadn't just worked out for the past two hours on the dance floor. I was star struck, like a groupie. That's probably why I became a reporter. It gave me an excuse to be around exciting, celebrated people. I would have never thought I had what it took to interest someone like Robert. He could have any woman he wanted. Why would he want me, a nobody?

Deborah Marbury

I believe my fascination with celebrated personalities must have started as a young girl growing up watching soaps with my mother during the week, and playing songs of love and happiness on the weekends. My mother got so involved with the soap operas, it was if these people were real to her. She got mad at them for immoral behavior. Loved them when they did the right thing. Cursed them. Praised them. Cried when they were killed off. Laughed when they came back to life. She was the same way about singers. She always related their lyrics to real life and she cared about her favorite singers as if they were personal friends.

"That's just how Sam got killed," she'd tell me for the millionth time while we listened to **Frankie and Johnny**, a song about a woman who killed her cheatin' lover. "Just like when Al got them grits on his back. Need to quit bein' so damned whorish. Sam would still be alive and Al would still be singin' love songs if they woulda quit all that whore-hoppin'!"

Sometimes when we watched the soaps, she would run to the bathroom during a commercial and demand that I keep her informed on what was happening if she couldn't get back before the commercial ended. It seemed that the phone would always ring at the same time.

"Tell me what Erica said when Tom asked her 'bout them birth control pills!" she yelled from the bathroom. "She ain't gon' do nothin' but lie. I hate a liar! Answer that phone! If it's Mabeline, tell her I ain't here. She don't want nothin', but to talk about her ol' crazy husband. I don't know what make her think I wanna hear that sh--!"

"Ma! It's back on! Tom is pissed!"

"What you say Girl?"

"Tom is mad."

"You feel so good," Robert whispered softly in my ear and squeezed me tightly. The hot, sweet-smelling air of his breath made my knees weak. I was sure he had to hold me up through the rest of the song.

Soon Johnny's song ended, and the DJ mixed in the mellow sound of the Deele's, **Sweet November**. I listened to the lyrics intently as Robert and I held each other close.

When autumn first arrived
You were my lady
And love was hidden in the wind to show....

what you do in the dark . . .

Something about that song reminded me of the year in high school when I met my fiancé. The feel of the music made me think about how we used to cut classes just to be together. We would talk about our dreams and hopes for the future. Those were the days when he didn't have time for anyone or anything else but me. He would just look at me sometimes as if I alone completed him.

Then with the change of month
There came October
And now, I wonder where the love did go. . . .

He hadn't even taken me out for Sweetest Day this past October. He, Craig, and Tyrone went to a bowling tournament out of town.

It was the second rain of autumn
We shared our feelings
And it was such a glorious autumn dream
Yes it was. . . .

I thought back to the first time when he told me he loved me. It was at Kennedy's homecoming dance. We slow danced to "I Do Love You" by GQ. He didn't really say it. He said that's how I feel about you, referring to the song as the lead singer sang the title lyrics.

But like kids, we were too shy to say to each other
That together we would always like to be
Someday soon I know we'll come together
Even though our feelings change as seasons do
But maybe sweet November will tell us a story
That will bring us back the love that we both knew.

It was this part of the song that sent a chill up my spine and a twinge of regret that this November night was telling a story that might mean the end of whatever love my fiancé and I had left. I held Robert closer, and fought back tears as I willed myself to concentrate on the man I was holding. Feeling his arms around me brought the only salvation from the never-ending ache of loneliness that had taken residence in my heart. Now, if he could only hold me forever.

Deborah Marbury

Robert and I stayed until all the guests left and supervised the clean up. Robert took care of some financial matters with ticket takers. I sat alone at our table, waiting. Red, high-heeled pumps decorated the tabletop taking the place of the centerpiece candle that had just been collected. I propped my aching feet on Robert's chair and blankly surveyed the quiet room filled with intimate round tables topped with upside down pairs of chairs.

"Tired?" he asked when he returned.

"Exhausted."

He took my feet in his hands as he sat in the chair, resting my feet on his lap. He massaged them gently and asked "How's that feel?"

"Real good," I oozed out in a sleepy, sexy voice.

"How 'bout you let me take you home to finish this massage at your apartment?"

I guess he knew that I was about to protest, make some excuse about being too tired because he leaned in to me quickly, pulled my chin toward him and kissed me. His tongue was probing my mouth slowly and my body was heating up liked he'd pushed some automatic button. I was speechless when he gently pulled his lips from mine, picked me up, grabbed my shoes with his fingers and carried me to the car. I rested my head on his shoulder and surrendered.

"I really enjoyed your company tonight," he told me after we'd been driving for about five minutes. "You have to be the most fascinating woman I've met in a long time. I've loved your articles about me, the Ward and the community center. They've generated so much interest that I may have to get an additional secretary just to field the calls. Smart and beautiful. What an amazing combination! You deserve so much better than your fiancé. I hope you know that."

"I guess," I muttered.

"If you were my woman, I'd cherish the ground you walked on. But, I'll settle for pampering you, at least for tonight, if you'll let me. I could tell you were sad tonight. I know you were thinking about him. I wish you would just concentrate on me. Just for a little while. I think you'd feel better. I know I can't concentrate on anything else but you."

He put in a cassette tape and LTD's **Concentrate on You** started to play. He leaned into me once again and gave me a soft, lingering kiss. He sang along with Jeffery Osborne playfully as we drove along. He had told me many times that Jeffery, Johnny, and Peabo were his favorite singers. We pulled into my parking lot.

what you do in the dark...

He parked the car. I put my shoes on, and went for the car door.
"No, let me get that for you."

He jumped out of the car and hurried to the passenger side to let me out. He extended his hand to help me. I hobbled along with him as we headed toward the building entrance. I unlocked the door, and we stepped into the foyer. The lonely ache was returning fast as I tried to convince myself to say goodbye. He took me into his arms and hugged me.

"You want me to stay?" He leaned back, trying to look into my eyes for the answer. "Can we just talk for a little while? I'm not ready to end this night. Are you?"

His eyes searched mine. I wouldn't look at him.

"No," I said quietly.

"Good."

I could hear him breathe a little easier. Then, he kissed me again. A sweet, passionate, lingering kiss that thanked me, worshipped me, and praised me for giving him just a little more *time*. He wanted more time, with me. It felt so good. To be appreciated. To be wanted. To be needed. To be touched. To be held. To be kissed. I wanted more.

He was undressing me in the elevator as he kissed each part of my body that he uncovered as if he treasured what he found. I hoped I would make it to my apartment before I was naked just in case some other late night partygoer was roaming the dimly lit hallways. I was down to my underwear when we made it inside the apartment. We stopped long enough for me to turn on my stereo. I let Johnny play again in the background as we made love, and it was unlike anything I had ever experienced.

Slip on your nightgown
And step in my bedroom
I just wanna take some time
I just wanna look at you
Girl, you are so fine
I can't believe my eyes
And all that I wanna do
I wanna make love to you
Tonight will be a special night
Of many more to come
And I'm so proud to be with you

Deborah Marbury

So proud to share your love. . . .

The only man I had ever been with was my fiancé, and he made love to me like I was his car that he was giving a tune-up. He knew instinctively where everything was and what adjustments were necessary to make things run smoothly. And our lovemaking did run smoothly, like a well-planned routine! There wasn't any romance in our lovemaking anymore. Just two people reporting for their assigned duties until one day we both went AWOL.

But Robert made love to me with a sort of sweet apprehension that touched the depths of my soul. He seemed to ask, no beg, permission to give each kiss, to touch each part of my body as if he wanted to assure me that he didn't want to do anything to me that I didn't want done. He seemed acutely aware of each and every one of my desires. He touched and kissed me hundreds of times in thousands of places in millions of ways. He whispered gentle assurances of heartfelt desires and promises of sexual fulfillment in my ear that made my body tense and relax intermittently in response to each gentle request from his hands and lips.

My fiancé didn't talk to me anymore when we made love. Whisperings of sweet nothings had just become nothing, but making love with Robert was even more than just the act of two people fulfilling their desire for one another. It felt like we needed each other so intensely that we were compelled to experience each other thoroughly.

I was totally drained by the pleasure we shared in the darkness of my bedroom with that threatening moonlight peering through my window shade still watching us and knowing our secret. So, after praising the lover of my body, I passed out into a deep slumber that left me sprawled across the bed not the least bit concerned about being in his arms or making sure I slept in the right position so that I didn't snore.

When the light of the bright sun awakened me that morning, I reached for my new lover, but he was gone. There was a note on the pillow where I had hoped his head would be.

"Good morning Sexy," it read. "Sorry I couldn't be here when you woke up, but I had some work to do this morning. I'll call you soon."

I smiled and turned toward the window, and the sun's light pouring into my room and my eyes startled me back to reality and to the fact that I was engaged to someone other than the man who had put this big Kool-aid smile on my face.

what you do in the dark . . .

I held my hand in the air to examine my modest engagement ring. I'm supposed to be in love. How could I do something like this? I had never been unfaithful to my fiancé before in all the years we'd been together. I felt a little ashamed. I rationalized that he hadn't always been faithful to me. I had caught him two or three times with other women, but he always assured me that they meant nothing. He truly loved me. Moments of weakness. Mistakes. That's what they were. And I forgave him because I was committed to him, like my mother was committed to my father. She never left my father when he cheated. But then again, she never retaliated with her own infidelities either, at least not to my knowledge. My mother deplored most immoral behavior, except cursing and lying, and she didn't too much care for *those* immoral acts if they were committed by someone other than herself.

I got out of bed to make myself some breakfast, hoping that would make me feel better. As soon as I started for the kitchen, the phone rang. It was my fiancé.

"Hello, Mrs. Jennings," he said to impress me.

"Hi Darnell," I replied with a sigh.

"I'm not going to be able to make the movie tonight. I forgot I had already made plans with Craig and Tyrone. That okay?"

"Oh yeah, sure. It's more than okay," I answered sarcastically.

"Is something wrong, Red?"

"No. Why would something be wrong?"

"No reason I guess. Well, I gotta go. I'll call you tomorrow. Maybe we can do something then."

"Yeah, maybe," I said already hanging up.

I didn't protest Darnell's breaking our date because I had learned through the years that it wouldn't do any good. He always did exactly what he wanted no matter what I thought about it. I was tired of arguing with him about the same old issues anyway. Besides, he had agreed to marry me. He paid my bills and he gave me everything I wanted, except him.

Anyway, now there was Robert. Robert paid attention to me. He complimented me. He talked to me. He listened to me. He seemed to have lots of time to spend with me, too. My days were filled with barely anything else but spending time working on articles about Councilman Robert Turner and his plans to build a community center. Now that we had made love, I was sure that we'd spend even more time together.

It was Saturday, so I busied myself running errands and constantly checking my answering machine for messages from Robert. There were none. I returned to my apartment late that evening, but there were still no messages from Mr. Turner. I thought about calling Michelle. Maybe we could go to a club or something. Then, I remembered that she had gone out of town for a weekend getaway with her current lover. I never called Jackie to hang out. She did family things. My sister, Carla, ditto. So, I waited.

I turned on Nick-at-Nite to watch old sitcoms, and I laughed much too hard at them. Hard enough to keep from crying. Wanting to cry because of the ache of loneliness that had returned and was overwhelming me. I topped the night off with Saturday Night Live, and I laughed at some of those corny skits so hard, I made myself sick. But, it was better than staring at the phone all night. I just glanced at it occasionally during commercials. Finally, it rang! I almost knocked it on the floor trying to answer it.

"Hey Bae, how ya doin'?" My heart sank with disappointment when I recognized the voice on the other end.

"Oh, hey Mark."

"What's a lovely lady like you doin' at home *this* Saturday night?" I could hear my mother playing Sam Cooke.

Another Saturday night, and I ain't got nobody!

Mark's voice was low, soft, and sexy. He always spoke slowly and slurred his words. Mark was an old friend I grew up with from the Island who has always had a crush on me.

"Girl, Mark Townsend wanna get wit' you!" Michelle would tease me.

"Ain't nobody thinkin' 'bout Mark Townsend. He's not my type."

"I know that's right. He ain't got no class, no style, and no rap!"

"He don't even go to church no more!" Jackie interjected.

"But, he is cute," Michelle admitted.

I liked to think of Mark as my 'comforter,' like in that song by Shai. He was always there for me when Darnell neglected me. We'd just gotten reacquainted a couple of years ago when I leased my apartment. He used to do maintenance work for the people who managed the place. He became my personal fix-it man. Anytime that anything was broken, my plumbing, my attitude, my heart, Mark was always right there to fix it.

what you do in the dark...

"Oh, just watching TV," I answered him. "Darnell went out with Craig and Tyrone, and so I'm home alone."

"Girl, you need to drop that zero, and get with this hero!" he told me as if he were the first person to ever use that tired line.

"Yeah, whatever Mark. So, what's up?"

"Well, I thought you'd be home by yo'self, seein' how yo' man ain't never got no time for you, and I ain't doin' nothin', so, I thought you might want some company. I picked up a couple of movies from the video sto', and I could be at yo' place in about fifteen minutes if you game."

I looked at the clock. It was two o'clock in the morning.

"Mark, it's late. I'm about to go to sleep."

"Bae, I know you. You lonely. You can't sleep. You wishin' yo' man was there. I just wanna give you a shoulder to cry on. I know you need it. A little companionship to cure yo' lonely heart. Besides, you gon' be 25 years old on Monday. If you ain't gon' party this weekend, you should at least be with somebody."

I smiled. He remembered. Mark was so sweet. He was everything I wanted in a man, except he didn't have a car, a job, and he lived with his mother. He had absolutely no ambition. His main goal in life seemed to be to win my heart on that glorious day when I would realize how much better off I'd be with him instead of Darnell.

Yeah right!

But, his offer for a couple hours of companionship was tempting. I *could* use some company.

"Look Mark," I answered finally, "I'll watch one movie with you, and then you'll have to go."

"Okay that's cool, Bae. I'll be over in fifteen minutes."

Mark lived only a few blocks away in a cozy, ranch-style home in Bedford Heights. So, he usually walked over to my apartment to visit me on nights like this. I never really told anyone about my late night rendezvous' with Mark. I didn't want anyone to read anything into our arrangement. I only let him visit at night and I never mentioned him to any of my friends or family, except for Michelle, and only vague reports to her.

cold december

*If you can't be with the one you love,
you gotta love the one you're with!*

Weeks went by, and I hadn't heard from Robert. So, I began to recommit myself to my future husband. Maybe he didn't give me all the attention I needed, but he was better than nothing. So I went to bed every night with fond memories of my dark secret and woke up every morning with elaborate plans for my bright future with Darnell.

Until one morning, I awoke with an acute case of nausea two weeks after a missed period. I knew I was in trouble. I left work early and went to see my doctor that afternoon.

It was a cold, December day and the daylight seemed to last a shorter time than usual. It was getting dark as I arrived in the parking lot at my doctor's office. I walked inside the medical building and proceeded to the reception area, which was brightly lit as if purposely intending to illuminate my secret.

I told the woman at the front desk why I was there as I looked around to see if I knew anybody. There were only two other women in the waiting area. I didn't recognize either of them. The receptionist instructed me to have a seat to wait for my name to be called. I did as she asked. After about fifteen minutes, a nurse called my name and I went to be positive about what I already knew in my heart.

I was examined, asked some questions about my feminine health and cycle, and then instructed to provide a urine sample. It was time to wait, think and pray. I thought about Darnell. He called me his angel, his queen. He'd never suspect I'd been unfaithful. He trusted me. He believed me to be virtuous. He'd always been sure that he was my only lover. He treasured that about me and so did I.

What would he think of me if he discovered that I was carrying another man's child? He certainly wouldn't think it was his own. We hadn't made love in months! What would my mother think? What would his mother think? My friends? His friends? This couldn't be happening to me! It was just too scandalous! It just couldn't be true! So, I resigned that it just wasn't true. I prayed a quick prayer. "Lord, please don't let it be true."

Nevertheless, the nurse met me in the examination room with a smile. "You're going to be a Mommy!" She beamed luminously. I just held my head down in shame, in deep contemplation of my dark predicament. The nurse nervously gathered up the papers from my file and told me I could get dressed. She was obviously disturbed by my less than enthusiastic reaction. I really wanted to be happy about her news. I had never carried a child inside me before and it just seemed like I should have been happy.

She hurried out of the examination room, leaving me alone with my thoughts again. I knew I couldn't bring this child into the world. It would end my life. Darnell would leave me. My family would be disappointed in me. My co-workers would talk about me behind my back. It just wouldn't look right at all. I knew what I had to do. I went home and called Michelle.

Michelle regarded my confidential discussions with her about my dilemmas with men and life over the years as if we were involved in a soap opera. She didn't take any of my problems seriously. Like the time in college when I was thinking about cheating on Darnell while he was away in the Air Force. She just said, "Do it! I bet you he ain't sittin' around worryin' about right and wrong when he's doin' his thang!" As far as she was concerned, there was nothing to think about. Her favorite line was, "Ain't nothin' to it, but to do it!"

Michelle just didn't take life as seriously as I did. She didn't believe in getting emotionally vexed about anything, but *I* got worked up about almost everything. So, I found myself in the habit of sharing all my problems with her with the high intensity and emotional level that characterized our conversations as teenagers. Everything that caused the least bit of difficulty in our lives was dramatized like a daytime serial. That was our way and we were both okay with it because I think we both understood how we really felt.

"Michelle!" I exclaimed when I heard her voice. "I'm so upset! You won't believe what happened!"

"What Girl? What's up? What's goin' on? What's the problem?" She rattled off questions playfully. "Come on, Girl, tell me! Wait! First, let me get a cigarette."

I laughed because she always had to get a cigarette when she knew I was about to drop some heavy drama.

"Yeah, I can hear it in your voice. I know I'm gonna need a cigarette for this. Hold on."

"Alright! Hurry up tho'! This is big!" I urged as I sat on my bed holding the phone as if it were sustaining my life.

I rocked back and forth in anticipation for Michelle to return to the phone. My mind was racing. I still hadn't heard from Robert. I wondered if I should try to contact him at his office tomorrow or just call him at home.

"Yeah, Girl, so what's up?" Michelle's voice startled me. "What happened? Girl, come on now. Talk to me quick!"

"I'm pregnant!" I blurted out.

"Pregnant! Now I need a drink! Hold on!"

Michelle left the phone again and I started to rock even harder. I wasn't as amused this time, but Michelle was serious about needing her smokes and drinks in order to listen to my stories. I had to talk this through! Why did she have to keep putting me on hold? If I didn't talk to someone about this soon, I felt like I would explode.

"Okay Girl, I'm back. Now, when did this happen? I thought you and Darnell haven't been doing anything lately?"

"We haven't, Michelle! It's not Darnell's baby!" I heard her blowing smoke and taking another drag of her cigarette.

"You kiddin'! Girl, who you been getting yo' groove on with?" Michelle's voice was now two octaves higher. "You ain't told me 'bout nobody else!"

"It's the councilman that I've been working with."

"Councilman! What councilman? Councilman who?"

"Councilman Turner. Councilman Robert Turner!"

what you do in the dark . . .

"Girl, you talkin' 'bout that fine man you've been writin' those articles about for the past year?"

She was taking loud, long swigs of her drink now. I'm sure it was a beer. She loved ice-cold beer to relax her after work. Michelle was a CPA at a large accounting firm. I hated numbers so I never took much interest in her work. I couldn't even remember the name of the place.

"Yes, Michelle. He's the one."

"I thought you two were just friends."

"Things changed a little quicker than I anticipated. I've been meaning to tell you about us, but you've been leaving town so much I haven't had a chance."

"Girl, you go! I thought you had a thing for him. He's got it goin' on too, for real tho'!"

I was encouraged by Michelle's approval. I wanted to tell her all about what a great lover he was, but now wasn't the time. I put it out of my mind.

"Michelle! I'm pregnant and I haven't heard from him since the night we slept together!"

"The dog! He ain't all that! That's why my mother and father didn't vote for his sorry butt!"

"Michelle, please! What should I do? Should I tell him? What about Darnell? Should I tell him? Should I keep it? Should I have an abortion? Come on Michelle, tell me what you think I should do?"

"Girl, I don't know! Why don't you start by tellin' Councilman Butthead, and see what he has to say."

"Yeah, maybe you're right."

"Well, how do you feel Caren? Do you love this Councilman Turner? Do you love Darnell?"

"I love Darnell. My future is with Darnell. Darnell loves me, and Robert, obviously, could care less about me. I mean Robert does have it goin' on, but you know how it goes Michelle. If you can't be with the one you love, you gotta love the one you're with."

"Yeah, I heard that," she mumbled softly as if she were processing whether she really agreed with me or not, then she came out of it. "Okay Girl, so give the councilman a call, and let me know what he says, the old dog. Then, I think you know what your next step needs to be."

"Yeah, I think I do. I know Robert has already pretty much kicked me to the curb. I'm afraid to hear his reaction to this pregnancy."

"Girl, quit trippin'! Ain't nothin' to it, but to do it! Just call the man! But Caren, whatever you do, don't tell Darnell. You don't have to be so damned honest with everybody. Darnell don't tell you everything he does. Believe that!"

"I'll keep that in mind Michelle. I'll talk to you later."

"Alright, Girlfriend. Peace."

I hung up the phone and lay on my bed for a while, thinking. Thinking about appearances. Thinking about what would *look* best rather than what would *be* best in this situation. It would be nice if Robert were happy about my news and ask me to marry him so that we could raise the child together. People have done it before. We've known each other for a year. If we'd just be committed, it could work. My mother would love the idea of my being married to a politician. She wasn't that crazy about Darnell anyway. She liked Robert too, especially since he'd helped her and had all those plans to improve her neighborhood.

My mother always did want us to marry well and Robert was about as well as it was going to get for me, unlike my sister who had a history of dating men of means. She was married to a successful lawyer. However, that still hasn't made up for her getting pregnant at age fourteen. I can still remember overhearing my father say how disappointed he was about Carla's pregnancy. My mother was livid. She called Carla and her boyfriend every name but a child of God. My father wasn't around anymore to be disappointed. He was killed in a car accident during my third year of college. Still I didn't want to shame his memory. Then, there was still the raft of Mary Boogerton to face, which wasn't going to be easy even at age twenty-five. Not under *these* circumstances anyway. I was engaged to be married to Darnell, but pregnant with Councilman Robert Turner's baby.

"Whore!"

That's what my mother would think of me. She'd think I'd been sleeping around like a common whore! How could I explain it? I couldn't pass this child off as Darnell's. We hadn't made love in months! Maybe I could sleep with Darnell and then tell him that the child was his. That is, if I could get him to spend a good five minutes alone with me. But, it wouldn't be fair to the child to rob him of his true identity. How could I live with myself if I had to lie to my child for the rest of his life about who he really was?

what you do in the dark . . .

I'd have to have an abortion I decided. Make the whole situation just go away like it never happened. Unless Robert agreed to marry and help me raise the child, I'd have to terminate the pregnancy. If I kept it, Darnell would leave me and I'd be alone for sure. I was afraid to have an abortion. I knew I had made some bad choices after leaving the church, but I didn't want to *really* get on God's bad side. My mother had always berated women who had abortions. She said it was a sin and they were going straight to hell.

I remember how she trashed Brooke and Erica on **All My Children** when they had abortions. I didn't want to have to carry the knowledge of having committed this sin on my conscience for the rest of my life if I didn't have to. Because even if I could keep the abortion a secret from my mother and Darnell, I knew God would know.

I dialed Robert's number and I hung onto the receiver for dear life again as I said a short prayer. I reasoned that if God did not want me to commit this sin, He would make it easy for me to keep this baby. He would give Robert the mind to support the right decision. What did I know about freewill? I thought God just did whatever He wanted, no matter what *we* wanted.

"Hello." His voice was soothing.

"Hi, eh Robert? Is that you?"

"Yes. This is Robert speaking. Who's this?"

"It's Caren."

"Oh, hello Sweetheart. I've been hoping to hear from you. How are you? Why haven't you called?"

"You left me that note saying you'd call me. Remember?"

"Yeah, I did, didn't I? I got a little nervous I guess. I was hoping you'd call me. I wanted to take things at your pace, considering your fiancé and all. I didn't want you to feel pressured. I just wanted to ease your pain that night."

"Well, you did. I just thought . . .well, that maybe we'd see more of each other."

"I want to see more of you too. The night we spent together was great. You're just so sexy!"

"Thanks." I paused, "Eh, Robert?"

"Yeah?"

"I have something to tell you."

"Yeah. What is it?"

I contemplated how to tell him. Finding no easy way to put it, I decided to just say it.

"I'm pregnant."

Dead silence.

"Robert?"

"Yeah, I'm here. What did you say?"

"I'm pregnant."

"Your fiancé's?"

"Yours."

"You're sure."

"Sure about being pregnant or sure about it being yours?"

"Both."

"Positive. I saw a doctor today, and you know I haven't been with my fiancé in months. It's your baby."

"So, what are you going to do?"

"What am *I* gonna do?"

"Yes, Sweetheart. It's your body and your decision. What are *you* going to do?"

"But it's *our* child! What do *you* want for *us* to do?"

"Well, I don't think I'm ready to start a family right now. I don't think I'd be much help to you."

"Robert, I think I want to have this baby. I know this isn't an ideal situation, but from the moment the nurse told me I was going to be a mother, I think I've wanted to be one. I'm just afraid to do it alone."

I took a deep breath. The truth was I was terrified to do it alone. It would look better if I had this baby with the father as my husband. Also, I knew that if I had the baby, Darnell and I would be over and I just didn't want to be alone. I wasn't going to take any chances that having the baby would change Robert's mind. I'd seen far too many women lose that game and end up single mothers.

"Robert," I continued, "the neighborhood where I grew up, the ward you represent, is full of unwed mothers raising kids by themselves on welfare. My sister used to be one of them and even though she eventually got married, those first few years were rough for her even with my parents helping. I want this baby, but I need you too. I'm not sure if it's right to have an abortion. I'm afraid that I might earn myself a permanent place in hell. Can't you just think about it?"

"Caren, I can't tell you what to do, but I'm not going to marry you. It's not a good time right now. I mean you're definitely something

what you do in the dark...

special. If I were going to have a family right now, you'd be the ideal person to start a family with, but I'm just not ready. Besides, we barely know each other. We don't know if we'd make good parents together. Is that what you really want for your child? Would it be right to bring a child into the world with parents that don't love each other enough? I don't think that's how God intended children to be raised. He'll forgive us."

"We loved each other enough to make this baby. Why can't we love each other enough to raise it, to be a family? Don't we owe it to our child to at least try? Robert, nobody has ever made me feel the way you do. I know we could be happy together."

"I just can't do it Caren. I'm not ready."

"So, you're saying to just have an abortion. Kill our child. Just like that. And to think I believed you when you said you'd treat me better than my fiancé."

"Caren, we made love once. We've had a year long friendship, a business relationship really. You're engaged to someone else. How can we just become a family just like that? We're not ready Caren. We're just not ready."

"I'm afraid to have an abortion."

"Sweetheart, I'm afraid to get married. We can get over an abortion. We can't get over ruining three lives, possibly even four if you include your fiancé. You can't just switch partners like we're on the dance floor or something. This is life, Caren! Real life! I can't marry you. Baby or no baby."

I slammed down the phone, and thrust myself into my pillow to have a good long cry. I cried for about ten minutes, then the phone rang. I wiped the tears from my eyes as quickly as possible causing them to burn and put on my most composed voice before the phone hit the third ring.

"Hello."

"Hey Bae. What's goin' on?"

"Hey Mark. I'm so glad it's you. I need you. Can you come over?"

"I'm already there. What's wrong?"

"Well, if you're already here, why do I still hear you asking questions that could better be answered in person?"

"Alright. In a minute."

We both hung up, and I began to feel relieved that I didn't have to be alone. It started to set in that I *was* pregnant and I had some serious thinking to do. I felt like I didn't mean anything to Robert. I just couldn't understand how we could have shared all that passion and he didn't want to have the child we created. Wasn't it obvious to him that I wouldn't have spent the night with him, if I wasn't at least *contemplating* leaving Darnell for him? The night seemed so warm and beautiful, but now everything was cold and impersonal. Could I have been so wrong about Robert? I thought he really felt something for me and now he was acting like a jerk!

I took a quick shower and put on something comfortable, but sexy. My black stretch pants and an oversized, but low-cut sheer black blouse. The blouse hung loosely over my hips, but its sheerness showed the flawless caramel-colored skin of my flat stomach and back, only my breasts were hidden from view by two black silk pockets on the front of the blouse. Underneath, I wore no bra.

I wanted to feel beautiful, needed and desired. I knew Mark was just the person to boost my deflated ego. I lay on my bed and practiced ways I could look alluring, but not too inviting. I just wanted my femininity to be appreciated and men usually only take notice when you wear something sexy. As I lay there, my mind began to wander to thoughts of Robert and fantasies about the birth of our child. I imagined him coaching me in the delivery room like I had seen couples do on TV. His eyes and smile lighting up when the doctor said, "It's a boy!" I immersed myself in the fantasy and found it comforting.

I was startled back to the reality by my door buzzer. I jumped up and ran to answer it. "Yes!" I said into the intercom.

"What's up, Sis? Buzz me up!"

"Oh no!" I panicked. It was Carla.

What could she want? How could I get rid of her before Mark arrived? I hit the buzzer and ran to get my big white terrycloth robe. Moments later, my sister was knocking at my door. I gave the apartment a quick once-over, looking to see if there was anything I needed to hide. I let Carla in. "What's up?" I greeted her. A shorter, more voluptuous version of me with a short finger-waved hairstyle strutted through my door.

"Nothing. I just stopped by to see if you wanted to go Christmas shopping for the kids with me. Only four more shopping days, you know."

Her eyes were surveying my apartment critically as usual and my eyes were following hers with the usual fearfulness that there was something

what you do in the dark . . .

out in the open that she could tell Mama about. My work clothes I had shed a few hours ago were in the middle of living room floor. I picked them up quickly and tossed them into my bedroom closet.

"You didn't clean up today?" she asked.

I ignored her question. Mama had raised us to keep our houses neat and orderly, but I was the one who always fell a little short in the area of housekeeping. Carla had taken my mother's insistence on a well-kept house to a new level and I wasn't going there with her, especially not today.

I picked up the remote control to my television, plopped into my recliner and began to flick through the stations absently while trying to look intent. Carla started to say something to break the silence, but suddenly I felt ill. I rushed to the bathroom to throw up. I splashed cold water on my face and wrapped a cold hand towel around my neck to dab my face. I started to return to the living room when I bumped into Carla who had followed me.

"Are you pregnant?"

"Naw!" I answered defiantly.

I was terrified. Carla had been pregnant three times. I believed all women knew when another woman was pregnant, especially if that woman was their daughter or sister.

"Please Lord," I prayed silently, "please let her leave before Mark gets here and before I give myself away."

I walked around her and headed back to my recliner. She resumed her seat on the sofa.

"I think I must have eaten something that didn't agree with me," I explained.

"Well, can you go with me?" she whined.

"No Carla!" I snapped. "I'm not feeling well and I want to get some rest so I'll be able to make it to work tomorrow."

"Alright!" She sounded dejected.

She got up and pulled her car keys from her purse to indicate she was leaving.

"I can't stay. I have to get this shopping done before John brings the kids back."

She and her husband of five years had two boys together; one was four, the other, three. And, of course, there was her thirteen-year-old love child, Sheila.

"Okay," I responded trying to conceal my relief that she was leaving.

I pulled the belt on my robe tight and held the collar closed at the neck as I walked her to the door.

"Maybe I can do some shopping with you this weekend. I still have some things to get the kids too."

Carla looked really sad when she turned to say good-bye as she stood in the corridor, but I didn't care. I just wanted her to leave. I assumed her sad expression had something to do with her soon-to-be ex-husband. My mother had confided in me about a week earlier that John had decided to leave Carla for some reason. Whatever it was, I knew my mother would call soon to report it. I let out a deep sigh of relief when I closed the door. I headed to my bedroom where I intended to rejoin my fantasies, but the door buzzer turned me back.

I buzzed Mark up and met him at the door by engaging him in a huge embrace. He held me tightly, but tenderly while gently massaging my back as we stood there, *forever*.

Finally, he whispered in my ear, "What's wrong, Bae?"

I just held him tighter, not sure if I wanted him to know. I didn't know what he would think if he knew I had been unfaithful to Darnell, especially if it hadn't been with him.

"Come on, Bae," he said holding my face in his hands. "Tell me, it can't be that bad."

I felt cold without his arms around me, holding me.

"Is it cold outside?" I asked.

"It's getting there. It's supposed to snow tonight."

"Can you just hold me?"

Mark walked me to my bed, sat down with me and took off his jacket and shoes. He lay down on my bed and pulled me down beside him. Then, without saying a word more, he held me just like I asked. Why couldn't Robert do this? Why couldn't Robert comfort me?

Mark Townsend had been my friend since kindergarten, but our lives had certainly taken different paths. He was a thug. He drank lots of beer, smoked lots of cigarettes and made his money selling marijuana. I didn't smoke, rarely drank, and would have absolutely nothing to do with any drugs. I made my money selling words.

He didn't sell or use drugs around me, but I remember Mrs. Bagley's eighteen-year-old son from across the hall asking him for some 'bud' one night after I'd let Mark out of my apartment. He always had money even though he didn't have a job. And of course, there was the Island's

what you do in the dark . . .

rumor mill. Mark and I had lost touch when I went away to college, but the day he came to fix my garbage disposal easily erased our time apart.

"Hey Bae, heard you had some problems with your disposal, so here I am *at your disposal.*" He often used corny lines like that, but he had a certain sex appeal that helped you forgive him.

"Mark Townsend! What are you doing here?"

"I work here."

"It's so good to see you. How've you been?"

"I'm doin' alright now that I've found you again."

"You so crazy!"

"How's your Mom?"

"She's alright. But, enough about me. You still with that loser Darryl, Derrick or whatever his name is?"

"Darnell. Yes, we're still together."

"So, when you gon' be my woman? I'm never gonna give up on you. I've loved you since kindergarten."

"Mark, quit playin' and fix my disposal!"

I gave him a hug and watched him work. He was so fine. Reddish brown complexion, sandy hair, tight muscular slim physique and the most gorgeous hazel eyes I'd ever seen. He'd always been handsome, but he looked better now than he did growing up. He always wore baggy jeans or work pants, old T-shirts and expensive tennis shoes. He kept his hair braided in about ten neat cornrows starting from his forehead and dangling at the nape of his neck. When he smiled, his eyes flashed and sparkled like a pinball machine.

"I tell you somethin', Bae. If that Negro ever messes up, you call me. And he better not ever hurt you or I'll take care of him personally."

Mark lost his job as the apartment maintenance man a few months earlier when management changed. He acted like it was no big deal, but I knew he'd been wanting to get out of the dope game and do some honest work. He knew he couldn't even hope to have a chance with someone like me unless he did.

We fell asleep for about an hour after we lay there silently holding each other in my bed and then awoke simultaneously when in the relaxed state of sleeping we got a little too close.

"Are you ready to talk to me?" he asked quietly.

The room was very dark. I assumed Mark had turned off the television that had been providing the only source of light from the living room into the bedroom. My eyes had adjusted to the darkness, but

I could still barely see Mark's face. I felt very cold even though I was still wearing my terrycloth robe. I pulled the collar up tight around my neck, and nestled close to Mark for warmth.

"I'm afraid," I answered finally.

"Afraid. Why? Of what?"

"Afraid of what you'll think of me when I tell you."

"Bae, I could never think bad of you."

"Don't speak too soon. You haven't heard what I have to say yet."

"Well, whatever it is, I thank God for it because I don't think I've ever been this close to you before and I'm in heaven! Whatever it is, it's okay. Come on. Just talk to me."

I lay my head on his chest. I felt more at ease, but still fearful.

"I'm pregnant," I whispered.

I closed my eyes tight as if waiting for an explosion. I felt something go limp inside Mark. He didn't respond to my announcement for several minutes.

"Mark?" I raised my head from his chest to get a glimpse of his face.

"Well, what's so bad about that Caren?" he responded finally releasing me from his embrace. He sat up straight on the bed. "You're engaged. It's the eighties. So, the order of things ain't quite right. God will forgive you."

"It's not Darnell's baby. We haven't had sex in months. I've barely seen him since we set our wedding date."

"Not Darnell's. What are you tryin' to tell me, Bae?"

"I slept with someone else, Mark."

"Who?"

"A councilman that I've been interviewing for the paper."

"You don't even know this man?"

"Yes, I know him. I know him very well. I've known him for a year. I know what this must look like, but I just got caught up!" I started to get hysterical.

"Sssh, don't get upset. It's okay. So, what you gon' do?"

"He wants me to have an abortion." Tears started to flow again.

"And what do you want?"

"He doesn't love me, Mark." I sobbed.

"He don't know you!" Mark yelled. "I mean," he continued softly, "he don't know you like me. If he knew like I know, he'd be the happiest man in the world."

"Well, he's not, Mark."

what you do in the dark...

"You don't have to have no abortion if you don't want to, Bae."

"I know Mark, but I don't want to be alone. If I have this baby, Robert won't be there for me and Darnell will leave me. My mother will be ashamed of me. My co-workers will laugh behind my back. My friends will pity me. I don't even think *our* relationship would be the same if I had a baby, Mark."

"Oh, I ain't gonna change. I'll be here for you, Bae." He took me in his arms again. "I am surprised you'd do something like this tho'. I thought you were faithful to Darnell."

"I guess I was just lonely Mark."

"You coulda come to me. You know how I feel about you and I wouldn't ask you to have no abortion."

"I didn't go to anybody. He was just there at the right place at the right time and I just went with the flow."

"Well, whatever you do Bae, I'll be here for you if you need me."

"Mark?"

"Yeah Bae."

"Do you think God will forgive me if I have an abortion?"

Deborah Marbury

dark january

It takes a fool to learn,
That love don't love nobody.

A few weeks later, I was preparing to go to an abortion clinic. I cried to Mark about it almost every night. Finally, I came to the realization that this was the only thing I was courageous enough to do. I just didn't have the guts to be a single mother and face all the consequences that came with the circumstances upon which I had become pregnant.

Besides, I believed I could get God to forgive me for aborting my child. I had often heard that God forgives all sins if we just ask Him. Darnell would never forgive me for having another man's baby and my mother would never be able to hide the disgust in her eyes at my sleeping with Robert while I was engaged to Darnell. I couldn't bear for my mother to be disgusted with me or to be a disappointment to my father's memory. I wondered if he even knew what was going on, and if so, how did he feel about it? Most of all, I didn't want to lose Darnell. I didn't want to be alone. I wanted to get married.

I contacted Robert to inform him that I was willing to go along with his suggestion if he would agree to take me to the clinic and pay for the abortion—that was Michelle's suggestion.

what you do in the dark . . .

"If he wants it done, let him pay for it! Ain't nothin' to it, but for him to do it!"

He seemed more than happy to do it. He picked me up on a cold, but dreary Saturday morning in January and drove me to the clinic. We were silent in the car. When we arrived at the clinic, he ushered me past a mob of angry protesters. He huddled me close to his body and covered my eyes with his coat so I couldn't see their signs. He rushed me inside the building so I couldn't hear them shouting things like, "Murderer!" and "Baby killer!" But their shouts rang out much too loudly to go unnoticed.

Robert pulled me closer to him and squeezed me tightly. He whispered to me, "Just ignore them. We're doing the right thing."

I felt as if he'd done this before and he wanted to make sure that nothing happened that would make me change my mind.

The corridor leading to the office was dimly lit. It felt dark and cold, but I was safe and hidden from the mob outside. I let the receptionist know that I had arrived for my scheduled appointment. I looked around again to see if I knew anyone. There was no one in the waiting area, but there were about twelve names ahead of mine on the sign-in sheet No one I knew.

I took a seat with my accomplice who fell asleep after about ten minutes while I sat nervously waiting to be called. I thought that his sleeping was another ploy to keep me from changing my mind. It prevented me from being able to discuss the situation with him anymore. I wanted to talk to him and I needed him to help me. I didn't really want to do this and he was the only one who could stop me. A half-hour passed. I sat there scared stiff, but I couldn't bring myself to wake him just to hear him say again that we had nothing to offer our child that it was better off dead.

Finally, my name was called. I left Robert asleep to accompany the woman who led me to another dimly lit room. Everything seemed blurry. The woman was talking to me in a soothing voice, asking if I was sure I wanted to go forward with the procedure. I answered mechanically, "yes," to all of her questions. I kept hearing Michelle's voice from the night before saying,

"Girl, it's a piece of cake. I had to get one before. Ain't nothin' to it, but to do it!" So I let Michelle's voice soothe, comfort and reassure me.

"Ain't nothin' to it, but to do it!"

"Ain't nothin' to it, but to do it!"

Then, Mark's voice would interrupt, "You don't have to do it. I'll take care of you. You don't have to do it."

"Ain't nothin' to it, but to do it!"

"You don't have to do it."

"Ain't nothin' to it, but to do it!"

"You don't have to do it."

I was escorted into what appeared to me in my disillusioned state to be an even darker room with an examining table and those stirrups. I got undressed as I was instructed and mounted the table.

"Ain't nothin' to it, but to do it!"

"You don't have to do it."

"Ain't nothin' to it, but to do it!"

"You don't have to do it!"

"I don't want to do it! Robert, please! Don't let me do it!"

Everything went dark.

When the light returned, the woman was holding my hand, smiling and talking to me. It seemed that she was telling me things about herself to comfort me. She told me that concentrating on my career might help ease the pain. She was starting a new job on Monday. Working always helped her chase away the blues.

Eventually, I started to realize what happened and I began to cry. I had sacrificed a child for something, but what? I knew she was a girl. I already missed putting ponytails and barrettes in her hair, taking her to kindergarten, talking to her about boys, men. Men like her father who could make you feel like you were the most important person in the world in the dark and the most insignificant speck of dust in the light.

I wanted to hold her and share my pain with her. I wanted her to know how to deal with men better than I could, better than my mother had prepared me. I wanted her to know how to make men desire her, but still respect and honor her. I didn't know how to do that and that's why my brief acquaintance with her came to be, but it was also why it never came to be. Good-bye, my precious daughter. I won't forget you. I'm sorry.

I was helped into my clothes and escorted into a recovery area with a group of other women who did not seem as distraught as I was by their visit to this place. I began to feel ridiculous as I sat there crying hysterically. The women didn't even look twice at me, but I could feel their annoyance with me at the absurdity of my audacity to be upset about the decision we'd all made. The women who came here had no

what you do in the dark...

regrets about it. I imagined that they had not come in cowering and hiding like I did, but they had marched right past those protesters and mentally gave them the 'finger.'

Weak women who have second thoughts never make it this far. I was out of place and I knew I had to get in line quick. At least that was the impression their solemn, unemotional faces gave me. Or maybe, they just chose to express their pain in more private ways instead of openly crying in a room full of unexpectant mothers. Maybe they were annoyed with me because I didn't have enough pride to compose myself until I was alone, like a dignified woman. I imagined it would have looked rather ridiculous for all of the eight or ten women in the room to be sitting around crying like the babies we never had.

After I had recovered sufficiently to make the trip home, I rejoined my accomplice in the waiting area and we left. Back out into the cold sunlight, I squinted my eyes trying to make the adjustment. The drive back to my apartment was as silent as the earlier ride to the clinic. Once we reached my apartment complex, Robert and I sat in his car for a long while still in complete silence. Then, he gently took my hand into his and squeezed it.

"It's going to be okay," he whispered.

His words, as well as his touch gave freedom to tears that streamed down my face and I sobbed quietly.

"I know."

He escorted me to my apartment and asked if I needed him to get me anything. I told him that I just wanted to be alone and he agreed to leave.

"If I had known that this was going to upset you so much, I would have . . . ." He stopped himself in mid-sentence. "Call me if you need anything," he decided to say instead and he left. I hung onto his last words, "I would have . . . ." I would have *what?* I wondered. I would have done something to make you more comfortable. I would have agreed to marry you so that you could keep the baby. I would have never slept with you in the first place!

Once alone in my apartment, I closed all the shades. After I was satisfied that the daylight was completely shut out from my apartment, I undressed and climbed into bed. I waited for God to say something, but everything was silent. The apartment felt as empty as I did. I slept for the rest of the day and the entire night.

The next day was Sunday. I moped around my dark apartment trying to convince myself that I had done the right thing. Determined to shake off my depression and get back into the world again, I decided that if I just didn't think about God, then I didn't have to worry about going to hell. Besides, death, for me I had to believe, was a long way off. There was no need to worry about that now.

I got up bright and early on Monday morning and prepared to go to work. Maybe, I thought, a full day of divulging other people's secrets would help me to forget my own. I had resolved to put this dark secret behind me, marry my fiancé and get on with my life.

I walked into the office pool of reporters and went straight to my desk to begin working on my latest story. No one looked as if they knew I had an abortion on Saturday, so I began to feel secure that my secret was safe. My life was back intact as if it had all been a bad dream.

I took a sip of hot chocolate and peered into my computer screen. My editor, Margaret Daniels or Marge as we call her, walked up to my desk. She had a woman with her who looked vaguely familiar to me.

"Caren, I'd like for you to meet Jessie Bassett. She's starting today as the new political columnist."

"Hello Ms. Bassett. I'm pleased to meet you. Welcome aboard." I extended my hand to shake hers.

"Nice to *meet* you too." She winked at me and shook my hand. Her bright brown eyes sparkled and smiled at me knowingly.

"Jessie is going to get all the dirt on our local politicians." Marge beamed. "Because we all know that what you do in the dark must come to the light!"

It was the woman! The woman from the abortion clinic! How in the world does a counselor at an abortion clinic end up as a newspaper columnist? How could this be happening to me? Why was this happening to me? I tried to remain calm. After all, it would be unethical for her to tell people about our previous encounter. She wouldn't dare tell anyone and if she did, then maybe I could sue or just go upside her head with a baseball bat!

The day continued without any indication that Jessie Bassett planned to reveal my secret. She didn't even mention it to me. My feeling of security was starting to return. So, when the day finally came to an end, I confidently descended the stairs that led to the exit and stepped out into the dark moonlit evening.

what you do in the dark . . .

I opened my car door and sat behind the wheel. I started the car and turned on the dome light that illuminated my reflection in the rearview mirror. I combed my hair into place with my fingers and touched up my lipstick. I took one last look at myself before turning off the dome light realizing that there was nothing I could do cosmetically that would make me like who I saw in the mirror.

When I pulled into the parking lot at the restaurant where I planned to meet Darnell for dinner, I noticed that there were only a few cars around. I guessed that Monday was not a very popular night for eating out. Football season had just ended with Sunday night's super bowl game so Monday night football was not the reason for the low attendance. Besides, it was only 6:30. Darnell should have already arrived. I didn't see his car anywhere.

"I know he's not going to stand me up." I fussed as I marched hurriedly inside the restaurant.

I asked the hostess for our favorite table, which of course, was available as were most of the tables. She escorted me to the seat immediately and in a very chipper voice, informed me that my server would attend to me shortly.

I hadn't felt good all day and I was sure it was due to extreme hunger. The new addition to the **AA Times** staff had caused me to forget about eating. I worked through the entire day without taking lunch. I watched Jessie's every move, waiting for my life to explode in my face.

I sat at the table and perused the menu intently, hoping to be interrupted soon by Darnell. I considered some buffalo wings as an appetizer, but I ordered a strawberry daiquiri. I decided to wait for Darnell before I got anything to eat.

As I sipped the last of my daiquiri, Darnell approached the table, smiling. I had never been very impressed with his facial features. He was always well groomed and that made him seem more handsome than he actually was. He went to the barber and dentist religiously. His fade was always tight and his teeth almost unnaturally white which contrasted nicely with his smooth, dark skin.

I didn't think I would date him for long when we met on those walks to school. I had always been more attracted to the light-skinned pretty boys. It wasn't until the new Black movement of the mid-eighties by filmmakers like Spike Lee and his movie, **School Daze** that I began to really appreciate the dark-skinned brothers. Darnell, on the other hand, took to me right away probably for the very reason I initially didn't think very much of him.

"Hey Red," he said when he reached our table while kissing me softly on the cheek with full, pillow soft lips.

He took his seat across from me and began to rattle on about his day.

"It was rough on my route today. Next week is going to be even worse. First of the month. Welfare checks. Those project chicks really drive me crazy. Ricky Baldwin, the guy that usually runs my route on the first of the month, is on vacation. I really miss him too."

"I can imagine," I said absently.

"It seems like we should be able to make those women get abortions if they can't take care of their kids. Some of them have five and six kids and collectin' checks that compete quite closely with my own paycheck. All they do is sit at home on their butts, getting high, sleepin' with drug dealers and watchin' soaps. Then, I look at my paycheck and see the big hunk taken out every two weeks for them to just kick it! I guess it's a moral issue." He reasoned to himself more than to me.

Then he explained, "You know, the reason why the state won't pay for them to have abortions. Did you hear that they're tryin' to get a law passed that will allow the state to fund abortions for women who are on welfare? The Ohio state senate could have a lot to do with whether it gets passed or not and there's a seat up for election this year."

I started to feel faint and then everything went dark.

I woke up in a hospital emergency examination room. The light was so bright that it hurt my eyes. It was the second time I had awakened. The first time, I spoke with a nurse who asked me some questions about my last period and the pregnancy. This time, I looked around and Darnell was sitting beside me, holding my hand.

"Hey Red."

"Hey."

"You're gonna be fine. I don't know what happened, but you passed out at the restaurant. I told the nurse you were my wife. I had already added you on my health insurance. I didn't know whether you were covered working for that small time newspaper."

I ignored Darnell's jibe at my job. He'd done it so much; I didn't even believe he meant to be insulting. Neither of us had ever really taken much interest in each other's career. In his opinion, a job just wasn't a real job unless it was sanctioned with government security. The **AA**

what you do in the dark...

Times had only been in existence for a little less than a decade and was marketed only to Blacks, which indicated to Darnell, no security! The fact that he had to pay my rent and car note didn't do much for my argument.

"Do you have any idea what's wrong with you, Red?" he asked with sincere concern. Before I could answer, the doctor, a young goofy-looking white man with a contagious smile, walked in.

"Hi, Mrs. Jennings. How you feelin'?" he asked in a hearty, friendly voice. He stared at me intently for an answer, still grinning.

"I'm okay." I examined him quickly, noticing his ragged blue jeans and tennis shoes. I never understood why young doctors always dressed like that. Dr. Steve Kiley, who was on that old TV show, Marcus Welby, MD., never wore jeans.

"Good. You're gonna be alright," he continued. "I'm just going to let you rest here for another hour or so, then you can go home. I've instructed the nurse to give you some iron pills. You just lost too much blood from the pregnancy you had terminated a couple of days ago."

Complete silence.

"Take care now. The nurse will schedule you for a follow-up visit." And he was gone, taking a part of me with him, my life as I had known it with Darnell.

Darnell didn't ask any questions about the abortion after the doctor left the room or during the ride back to my car. I guess he was too stunned, too hurt and too afraid to face what it all meant. I pretended I was tired and half asleep and therefore not able to talk much. He followed me in his car so that he could see me safely home, then he just beeped his horn after I was inside my apartment building as he drove off.

I was glad for the time alone because I needed to think. I started to undress when my phone started ringing. First, Mark.

"Hey Bae. I have to come check up on you to see how everything went. I'll be over in a few minutes. Okay?"

"Alright."

Next, Jackie.

"Hey Caren, you okay? You didn't look very good at work today. Is everything alright?"

"Yeah, everything's fine Jackie. I've been feeling a little sick lately, upset stomach. I'll be okay."

"You're not pregnant, are you? You haven't looked like yourself in weeks."

"No."

"Pastor Peoples agreed months ago to marry you and Darnell, but he's concerned that you and Darnell have made no arrangements for counseling. He'd like very much for you to join the church too, but it's not a requirement."

I'm sure a baby killer wouldn't be welcome anyway, I thought.

"So when do you think you can start the counseling?"

I thought about what had just happened between Darnell and me, and I realized how pointless this conversation could be.

"There's no rush. I'll get back to you."

"Caren! You're getting married in less than six months! I'd say there's a rush."

"Jackie, I have to go. I'll get back to you as soon as possible. I promise."

"Okay," she agreed reluctantly.

We both hung up and I put on a big cotton flannel nightgown in preparation for Mark's visit. I started to look forward to his visits. If it weren't for him, I'd be all alone in my pain and I was in pain. I longed for my baby. I felt sorry for my fiancé who I knew felt betrayed. I ached for Robert who I wanted to win.

The phone rang again. It was Michelle this time.

"Okay Girlfriend. How did it go?"

"It went alright. Darnell knows."

"Darnell! Why'd you tell him? The whole point of having the abortion is so that no one would know that you were pregnant!"

"I passed out at dinner tonight because I lost too much blood from the abortion. When the doctor came to explain things to me, he mentioned the abortion right in front of Darnell. He thought Darnell was my husband."

"Well, Duh!" Michelle exploded. "Has that doctor lost his ever-loving mind? Doesn't he know that wives cheat on their husbands? Seems like a bell would have went off in his stupid head that a wife wouldn't abort her own husband's child! Girl, you should sue that hospital! Get paid! He has ruined your life! What did Darnell say?"

"Nothing. He just dropped me off at home and went on his merry way. I think he's mad."

"I know he ain't got no attitude! All the screwin' around he's done!"

what you do in the dark . . .

"I don't know Michelle. I'm tired. I need some time to think. I don't know what to do."

"Okay. I'll let you go, but don't worry, we'll figure something out. Alright?"

"Alright Michelle. I'll talk to you later."

I lay quietly in my bed just waiting and wondering if this was all God's punishment. Jessie Bassett showing up on my job from the abortion clinic and Darnell finding out about the abortion. Was God out to get me? I pushed the thought from my mind when I heard my door buzzer. I hurried to let Mark in.

"Hey Bae." He kissed me on the cheek as he entered the apartment. "How'd it go?"

"It went okay," I said heading to the living room sofa as Mark followed. "Except, I passed out when I was with Darnell this evening. I had to be rushed to emergency and the doctor mentioned that I'd passed out because of losing too much blood from the abortion right in front of Darnell. He thought he was my husband. Also, the counselor from the abortion clinic showed up on my job today as our new political columnist."

"Man! You have the worst luck." He took a seat beside me on the sofa, opened a beer he took from his coat pocket, then searched his jean pockets until he pulled out a cigarette.

"Tell me about it," I murmured moving away from him so as not to smell his cigarette smoke as much. I curled my feet underneath my thighs under the cotton nightie.

Mark looked at me in silence for a few uncomfortable moments, then turned away. He took a long swig of his beer and lit his cigarette.

"What's the matter?" I asked.

"You even look sexy in flannel."

I smiled. I think it was the first time I had smiled in days, maybe weeks. Mark was indeed my comforter. He motioned for me to come closer. I didn't really want to because of the cigarette and beer smell that I knew would be on his breath and in his clothes, but I did. He held me close to him with one arm around me while he used the other hand to drink beer and smoke cigarettes. I nestled my face close to his jacket to protect my nose from the smoke. We watched old love stories on TV and eventually I fell asleep. He put me to bed and went home. The phone awakened me for the second time at about 11:45 the next morning. I had been awake earlier at 9 to call off sick from work. The call was from my mother.

"What you doin' at home? What's wrong with you? I called yo' job, and they said you was home sick."

I wanted to say, "Yes mother, I had an abortion Saturday and now I'm a little depressed."

"I think I have a stomach flu," I lied.

"Stomach flu? You've been throwin' up? Carla said you was throwin' up before Christmas! You pregnant?"

"No, Ma. I'm not pregnant."

"Well, yo' sister is about to have a nervous breakdown, you know."

"What you talkin' 'bout Ma?"

"'Cause that damn John don' left her! She act like she can't live without no man!"

I wanted to say, "Could that be because you've always made us feel like we had not completed our lives as women unless we got married, had children and lived happily ever after."

She continued talking, not wanting any feedback from me anyway.

"I wouldn't want no ol' whorish man like John no way! I wouldn't care how much money he had."

I wanted to say, "Whorish, like Daddy?"

"I couldn't stand when your father did his dirt!" She kept spouting off. "God rest his soul, but I didn't put up with that mess. Carla's just willin' to let him do anything! 'Long as he stay and help her with them kids. That's all she's worried about."

I wanted to ask, "What were you worried about?"

"Why don't you call her sometime, Caren? Spend some time with her. She needs somebody to talk to. Lord knows I've tried, but maybe she needs to talk to someone closer to her own age. You got sense. Help your sister. She needs a friend."

"Carla's got plenty of friends. I got my own problems to worry about."

"You got a lot of sense, but I ain't never seen nobody as selfish as you. Now, what problems you got?"

"Just work and the wedding," I responded quickly realizing I was about to give myself away.

"Oh yeah. Just work and the wedding, huh?"

what you do in the dark . . .

"Yeah. That's all. I gotta go right now Ma. I'm not feeling good at all. I'll try to give Carla a call later or maybe tomorrow if I'm feelin' better."

"You know John don' moved in with some woman," my mother shared purposely ignoring my attempt to end the conversation.

"Really." I tried to sound interested even though I hoped she wouldn't elaborate.

"Yeah, and your sister just keeps callin' over there usin' them kids as an excuse. Little John is sick. Jimmy needs some shoes. Little John won't sleep all night since you left. It's just pathetic. If the man don't want her, she need to just let him go. Why would anybody want somebody that don't want them?"

"I don't know," I answered quietly, thinking of Robert. "I guess she's hoping things will change."

"Well, I wouldn't want nobody that didn't want me. Me and your father may not have always gotten along, but he was right where he wanted to be, with me!"

"Yeah," I answered absently.

"Well Girl, let me get off this phone. My stories'll be on in a minute and I wanna see what's gonna happen today on **Loving** and **All My Children**. Besides, you ain't talkin' 'bout nothin'. Bye!"

"Okay," I said happily picking up my remote to turn on the soaps as I hung up the phone.

I kept the room dark and I stayed in the bed under the covers all day only getting up to get something to munch on or to go to the bathroom. Before long the day was over and it was evening. I dozed off for about an hour when I was awakened again by the telephone. This time it was Robert.

"I came to the paper to take you out to lunch. Are you okay? Why didn't you go to work today?"

"Just a little down I guess."

"I wanted to let you know that something very important has come up and I'm going to be out of town for a couple of weeks. I'll need to talk to you when I get back. Are we okay?"

"Depends on what you mean by okay?"

"Are you angry with me?"

"No."

"Good. I'll call you when I get back. You take care of yourself."

"I will."

"Do you need anything?"
"No. I'm fine."
"Great. I'll talk to you soon."
"Alright. Good-bye."
"Bye."

I didn't know what it was, but it felt like Robert was up to something. I guess he still intended to keep seeing me. I suppose our relationship didn't have to end because he wasn't ready to be a father yet. Maybe in time, I would get over the abortion and we could become closer. I wasn't sure of what I wanted anymore. A part of me was angry with him for not supporting my desire to keep our baby. A part of me understood that the whole thing was a bit premature. A part of me just didn't know whether I was really ready to say good-bye to him.

I needed answers, but from whom? I couldn't talk to anyone except Michelle or Mark. Michelle didn't understand how I felt and Mark's judgment was colored by his feelings for me. He wouldn't want me to be with Darnell, Robert or anyone else. I couldn't go to my family, and I didn't think I could go to God either.

I was yet alone.

what you do in the dark . . .

february, no valentine

They smile in your face,
All the time, they wanna take your place.

It had been two weeks since I had heard from Darnell and Valentine's Day was coming up. I was afraid to call him. I didn't know what to say. How could I possibly explain that I had secretly aborted another man's child and still keep him in my life.

"Lie!" Michelle's voice kept telling me. "You think he tells you the truth all the time! Lie! Girl, lie! Ain't nothin' to it, but to do it!" So I opened the Valentine's Day card that I purchased for him and I began to write:

Darnell,

I'm so sorry I didn't tell you about the abortion. I was just too ashamed. I didn't want anyone to know about it, ever. Not you, not anyone. It's not what you think, Darnell. I didn't intend to be unfaithful to you. It's true that I behaved irresponsibly. I admit that. I went to a house party with Michelle one night in November and I had too many drinks. I passed out. I woke up in one of the bedrooms the next morning partially dressed.

I learned later that there was a guy at the party who had helped me to bed after I passed out. I guess he must have helped himself to me as well, but I don't remember any of it. Michelle said she thinks he put something in my drink. She said she had a lot to drink too so she fell asleep on the living room sofa.

I know I should have told you about this when it first happened, but I was just too embarrassed. I've never been involved in anything so crazy. I thought it would be best to just to put it behind me, like it never happened. I hope you can understand and forgive me. I promise I'll never do anything like that again.

All my love,

Caren

I called Michelle to read the note to her. I wanted her to corroborate my story if necessary.

"It's worth a try, Caren," she responded. "Anything is better than the truth. Besides, he'd rather believe that ridiculous story you made up than to know the truth anyway. A man's ego can't take a woman's infidelity. He can't *handle* the truth!" she teased. "Don't worry, he'll go for it," she assured me.

"I hope you're right, Michelle, because I don't know what else I could possibly say."

"Ain't nothin' to it, but to do it" was her familiar reply.

I sent the card in time for Darnell to receive it by Valentine's Day. I was hoping he would read it, forgive me and be back in my life in time to celebrate, that is, if he was home to receive it. He mentioned that he might be leaving town for a while to visit his dying grandmother.

We were doing all kinds of Black History Month and Valentine's Day stories and layouts for the week's edition of the newspaper. I sat at my desk on that Tuesday morning in a daze, staring at my computer screen and worrying about what Darnell's response to my note would be. Soon my thoughts turned to Robert, which awakened a longing in me to hear from him.

"Didn't you do a series of interviews on Councilman Robert Turner?" a perky high-pitched voice asked me.

what you do in the dark...

    I looked up. It was Jessie Bassett, famed abortion counselor turned political columnist. She was a short, petite woman, about 28 years old. Everybody in the office thought she was cute and sweet, but she didn't fool me. She was a viper if ever I saw one. Her neck even seemed abnormally long and she always jerked it from side to side, cracking it I guess. She looked like she was doing that dance called "The Snake" to me.

    Her name even hissed, Jessssie Basssssett and I could swear she sucked air every time she got ready to speak making that hissing sound that contradicted her mousy, squeaky, high-pitched voice. She seemed to have the voice of an innocent little girl who could never harm anyone. I regarded it as the voice of a true serpent that had devoured a rodent and was either mimicking it or using its voice from within her to invoke trust from her next unsuspecting victim.

    I used the utmost caution when dealing with her. I knew that she was readily poised and prepared to strike, spitting a deadly venom of lies, insinuations, speculations, and interrogations that would release poison into the very veins of my existence and suck out everything I was working so hard to keep inside me where it belonged, where no one could see.

    I grew to deplore her bubbly smile and dancing eyes that marked her demeanor every morning for the past two weeks as she took her seat at the desk across from mine. She was positioned so that she faced me, which allowed her to look up from her computer screen periodically and flash that phony smile at me that always seemed to accompany a sparkle in her eyes and a glimpse at the tip of her tongue.

    Everyone at the **AA Times Weekly** took to Jessie almost immediately and for some reason she was a favorite pet of my editor's. I refused to be taken in by her. I knew she was trouble. I looked up at her with obvious contempt as she stood over me waiting for a reply.

    "I'm ssso sorry. I didn't mean to disturb you, but as you know I'm doing a profile on some of Cleveland's single councilmen for my Valentine's Day column. I thought I could get some information from you to help me get started. Marge tells me that you've been working with Robert Turner for over a year covering his community center project. Who's he dating?"

    "I'm sorry, Jessie," I snapped as I got up from my desk and started for the restroom, "but I can't help you." She stayed right on my heels.

"But you worked with him almost exclusively for months, you must have gotten some information about his personal life. There must be something you can tell me."

I charged into the restroom, and marched up to the sink. I turned on the cold water and started to splash my face rapidly.

"I'll see what I have in my notes, but I'm busy with my own stories. Besides, my fiancé and I are going through a rough time right now and I'm just too upset to think about *your* column. Now will you please leave me alone?"

"Oh," I thought I felt her loosening her python grip slightly, "Didn't he approve of the abortion?"

I was breathless. She had me pinned. She had said it! Finally, she'd said what I had anticipated she would one day. Her tongue had finally struck with the first dose of deadly venom.

I could feel myself dying a little inside. And even though she and I were the only people in the bathroom, it felt like she had made the announcement with a bullhorn the way it kept ringing and echoing in my ears. "Didn't he approve of the **abortion? abortion? abortion?**" I struggled to regain my composure.

"Jessie," I said as calmly and as quietly as I could, speaking with slow certainty and intense conservation of each precious breath I took. "My fiancé and I are fine with it, not that it's any of your business. And, I'd appreciate it if you never mentioned our prior acquaintance to me again. I know you're a reporter now, but then you were a counselor sworn to the confidentiality of the patients you advised."

"Caren," her tone sounding like the wicked Witch of the West, "of course you must know that I would *never* tell anyone about our previous encounter. I'm just concerned about you. I know how upset you were about the **abortion**. Remember, I was there. You were regretful, crying hysterically. I haven't mentioned it because I *am* aware of the ethics involved, but it's just you and me here. You can talk to me, you know. Even though I'm working here as a political columnist, I'm still a licensed counselor."

"Jessie, please just leave it alone. I really don't need to talk. That's the last thing I need!"

I stormed out of the bathroom and marched determinedly to my desk grabbing and slamming down everything I touched imagining that it was Jessie I was hurting and not mere inanimate objects. Out of the corner of my eye, I caught disturbed glances of the other reporters in the

what you do in the dark . . .

City Room, all peeping around their computer screens with torn up faces. I plopped into my seat and tried to work on a story, but I couldn't concentrate.

Jessie was driving me crazy. Soon, she would figure out that it was Robert's baby that I had aborted if she kept snooping. Then, it occurred to me that maybe I could convince Marge to get rid of her. Maybe if I complained a little, she would consider letting Jessie go. After all, I had become one of Marge's top reporters in the three years I'd been with the paper, and in the eight years the paper had been in existence, I interned for three summers. Jessie had just joined the staff with prior experience as an abortion counselor I reasoned. Surely, if she represented a problem for one of Marge's most promising reporters, she would be expendable.

Marge sat at her desk staring puzzled at her computer screen. Her half-rimmed spectacles were riding the bridge of her nose as if one swift motion would send them flying across the room. I stood at her door for a few minutes, unnoticed. She was an older woman, in her fifties I guess, sort of attractive. She had style. She wore expensive dark suits and finely manufactured pumps that she'd rush to our desks in with our daily assignments.

She was always in 'work' mode as if the newspaper was her whole life. I suppose if she ever let loose, a man might find her quite appealing. Jackie and I often speculated comically about a suspected involvement between Marge and Mr. Caldwell. As his secretary, Jackie was privy to the comings and goings of Mr. Caldwell and his visitors. She often gave me the 411 on Marge's visits to his office and their closed-door meetings, which aroused my suspicions more.

Mr. Caldwell never spoke with anyone who worked for him except Jackie and Marge, which gave him an air of mystery that inevitably led to office gossip and speculation about his personal life. I think Jackie just engaged me sometimes for her own amusement. She got a kick out of people trying to get information from her. She teased me with comments like, "Marge was in Mr. Caldwell's office this morning when I came in, Girl. Her hair looked a little out of place too. And you know, Marge *never* has a hair out of place."

I would respond, "Girl, shut up! You think they spent the night in there? Why didn't they just go to his place or her place?"

"I don't know, Girl. Maybe they were just tryin' to get a quickie before starting the workday."

I was certain she knew the truth, whatever that was. She was loyal though. I never expected her to tell me if anything were really going on and I knew that she only joked with me about it because she knew I wouldn't gossip with other employees about her comments.

On the other hand, if Michelle had been Mr. Caldwell's secretary, *then* I could get some dirt. Michelle would have told me stories about any and every woman Mr. Caldwell even thought about, plus, she would have a few stories of her own to tell. Mr. Caldwell was a distinguished older gentleman in his late fifties, widowed and serious, very serious. It was really quite hard to imagine him and Marge getting it on, but I'm sure they both had desires just like me. It sure would be nice to know something for sure about those two I thought as I stood in the door preparing to say something, then I could use it to get Marge to fire Jessie.

"Hi, Marge," I said finally. "Can I talk to you for a minute?"

"Sure. What's up?" She looked up from her work, smiling.

Her smile was caring. She was always so nice to me, like a mother almost and here I was entertaining the thought of blackmailing her. I was getting desperate. I had no idea why I had come to Marge's office or more specifically what I had planned to say in order to accomplish what I wanted. I took a seat in the 'chair' where all the reporters sat to discuss and resolve issues with Marge.

I sat in the 'chair' when I assured her that she would not be disappointed if she gave me a chance to work with the paper as an intern. I sat in the 'chair' when I wanted to become a full-time reporter. I sat in the 'chair' when I couldn't figure out what angle to take on the missing teenager. I sat in the 'chair' when I wanted to cover the big meeting at the Board of Education. I sat in the 'chair' when I had to explain why I couldn't get to work on time for a whole month. I sat in the 'chair' when I was tired of being a general assignment reporter, and I sat in the 'chair' when I wanted more time to work on Robert's community center project. Other reporters sat in the 'chair' with similar concerns. We all left with issues thoroughly discussed, problems solved and reprimands deeply understood.

"I'd like to know more about Jessie," I started.

"Oh, Jessie Bassett?" She regarded her fondly as usual. She couldn't contain her smile whenever her name was mentioned.

"Yes," I replied trying to sound firm, worried, unimpressed, but not as annoyed as I really was.

what you do in the dark . . .

"Jessie hasn't been giving you any trouble, has she?"

"Well, no, not really. I just wondered where she came from and how she ended up here?"

"Oh, I'm glad you asked. It's a great story, actually. We're really fortunate to have her. She's a highly regarded women's counselor and freelance writer. I'm surprised you haven't heard of her. She's written articles for magazines like Essence, Ebony, Redbook and a lot of the top women's and African American magazines. Right now she's working on a nice abortion piece. It's real emotional, but she's also exploring political aspects to the issue as well. It details some real life experiences from women who have terminated their pregnancies *and* it exposes politicians' real views on the issue. This girl is so up close and personal that she does abortion counseling for research. She's got the right background for the job too. Her bachelor's is in Journalism with a minor in Political Science and she also has a master's in Psychology, all from Case Western. She'll make a couple thousand dollars easily with this piece, especially with state legislation pending on that abortion issue and a new state senator to be elected in November."

"So why is she here?" I asked, still too concerned with the threat she was to me to be impressed by her resume and even more so now that I knew that the very reason she was even privy to my secret was for the very purpose of exposing it to the world.

"I'm hoping she can tie in some local politics on the abortion issue for us. She could certainly make people sit up and take notice of the **AA Times**. Besides, she needs a full-time position that can sustain her during the times she's working on freelance projects and waiting for checks to come in. She's ready to devote more time to writing and less to counseling. Also, she says she likes it here in Cleveland and we're the only reputable paper in town that could make room for her right now."

"Lucky us," I mumbled.

"What was that?" Marge inquired.

"I'm glad to have her with us," I lied. "I have to get back to work now. I'll do what I can to make her feel welcome."

I got up from the 'chair' where none of my problems had been resolved and turned to leave the office. Marge surveyed me with quizzical eyes over the top of her spectacles as if she knew there was something more to my visit than I had shared, but she was the type that never pushed for information. She had this unmoving belief that it just wasn't necessary. It seemed a very unlikely trait in a person working for a newspaper, but whenever asked why she didn't encourage us to goad people for information for our stories, she'd always say, "What you do in the dark is sure to come to the light! Don't worry, you'll get your story. There's more than one way to skin a cat. Just keep your eyes and ears open." She often used age-old lines like that, but she would also advise us to find creative ways to get our stories. "Watch for clues in a person's character, lifestyle, friends, associates and things like that. Patience is a virtue."

I imagined that for Marge to be so enamored with Jessie, she must be astute in methodical and ingenious ways of uncovering secrets that Marge so rigorously tried to instill in her writers. It caused my stomach to flip-flop and my heart to dip, but I knew if Marge liked Jessie's research style, then Jessie always got her story with or without the cooperation of her subject.

"Oh," I remarked as I was leaving Marge's office, "I just hope that all of Jessie's responsibilities to other editors doesn't interfere with her commitment to us."

God is a jealous God, but Marge Daniels was a jealous editor. She had let go many a reporter who had faltered in meeting deadlines for her while pursuing other writing interests over the years. She demanded the best and the most from all of us, no exceptions! I was sure my comment had planted a nice seed of concern that would grow into animosity between the two of them in the months to come. Hopefully, it would come into full bloom before Jessie uncovered all the details of my secret. That was the best I could do to control Jessie for the moment.

****

The day after Valentine's Day was Friday and I dragged into the office pool of reporters that morning discouraged because I still had not heard from Darnell, Robert or even Mark. As I approached my work area, I saw Jessie putting flowers on my desk.

"Ssso!" she hissed and squeaked, as I got closer. "You got flowers for Valentine's Day!" She had the card in her hand. "I'm ssso sorry." She faked an apologetic look. "The card fell on the floor. It says that the flowers are from your favorite councilman, Robert."

I was gasping for breath again and I snatched the card from her hand.

what you do in the dark...

"It also says that he's sorry he couldn't see you on Valentine's Day. He's in Columbus on business. Robert Turner's not your fiancé, is he?" Her eyes flamed with intrigue.

I just rolled my eyes at her and plopped into my chair.

"If you don't mind, Jessie. I have a story to finish. Marge hates for us to waste time socializing when we have deadlines to meet."

"I *am* working on my story, Caren. Remember, Cleveland's Most Eligible Bachelors, Our Councilmen."

"I thought that was for the Valentine's Day issue. Valentine's Day is over. Besides, I don't see how you're working on your story when you're standing here questioning me about my personal life."

"Ssso, there *is* something personal going on between you and Councilman Turner?" She was tightening that python grip again, and there was little room for escape.

"Jessie, there's nothing going on between Robert Turner and me. I'm engaged to be married, and Robert's just a good friend and business associate. We made plans to work on Valentine's Day because my fiancé is out of town and the plans for the community center are needing more and more attention the closer it gets to completion. He probably just sent the flowers to show his appreciation for my efforts on his behalf. Everybody knows how smooth Robert is. He gives women flowers all the time."

"I guess that was a bit presumptuous of me. I suppose if you were engaged to Robert, there would have been an announcement or something in the paper. After all, that would be society news, especially since he's about to announce his candidacy in the race for the vacant state senate seat. It would really help his campaign if he were getting married soon."

****

It was good to be home. I had a lot to think about after Jessie's announcement. So, that was why Robert was out of town. He was about to run for a seat in the state senate. I wondered why he didn't tell me. Did this have anything to do with his decision not to keep our baby? I guess it would not have looked right to have an illegitimate child on the way if you're about to launch an election campaign. Like Jessie said, it would have helped his image if he were to marry. He could have married me and the baby would not have been born out of wedlock. No one had to know that we conceived prior to the marriage. Although, something told me that Robert didn't know he was going to run for office when I had the abortion.

Something happened to cause him to take this course of action. He always seemed totally engrossed in working with Ward One as a councilman. He seemed dedicated to the position and he gave me the impression that he planned to hold on to the position indefinitely. Things just weren't adding up.

After I thought about it for a long time and couldn't come up with any feasible answers, I decided to forget about it. I was sure Robert would explain when he came home. It was time for me to give my sister a call to see what was going on with her before my mother lit another fire under me. I'd wallowed in the muddy mess of my own problems long enough. I needed a distraction.

"Carla, what's up?" I said softly when I heard her voice.

"Nothin' Sis. Just got finished givin' the kids their dinner."

"Oh yeah. What y'all eatin'?"

"Steak and rice with gravy. You ate yet? Wanna come over for dinner?"

"Okay," I responded enthusiastically. "I'll be over in a few minutes."

It was good to get out for a while. I had spent too much time in my apartment sulking over Robert, the abortion and Darnell. Mark was busy most nights doing what he does. He couldn't comfort me every night. I put on some old jeans and a T-shirt and headed to my sister's house. She lived in Shaker Heights, another eastern suburb of Cleveland about ten minutes from my mother's house and about fifteen minutes from my own apartment.

I whizzed down Lee Road after exiting I-480, drove past Miles and Harvard until I came to Scottsdale. I made a left, then a right on my sister's street, Menlo. She had a beautiful brick home, her dream home. John purchased it for them shortly after their wedding. She met him when she was a legal assistant at Regal and Dorsey Law Firm where he practiced law.

As I pulled into the driveway, I began to wonder why John was cheating on Carla and why he would leave this beautiful home and his two boys to go live with some other woman. I wondered if I should tell Carla that Mama had told me all of her business. She had to know by now that there were no secrets among us. If you tell one of us, it's as if you told all three.

what you do in the dark . . .

My niece, Sheila, came running out to my car as I turned off the engine. It was pretty chilly out and she wasn't wearing a coat. She was a teenager now and starting to blossom. I began to worry about how she would deal with the male gender. I hoped she'd do a better job than the rest of the Boogerton women. My worries dissipated when she gave me her usual childish greeting.

"Hi Aunt Carrie!"

I hated that name. It sounded like she was talking to somebody's Big Mama from down South. Sheila was my favorite niece so I let her get away with it even though it made me cringe each time she said it.

"Hey Knucklehead!" I said hugging her tightly and kissing her on the cheek. "Where's your mom?"

"In the house. She's fixin' you a plate. John's gone." She added the last bit of information emphatically.

"She's preparing a plate," I corrected her. "You know your mother doesn't want you to talk like that."

She never called John, Daddy, like her brothers. She was probably already eight or nine when John came on the scene. All the family she needed was my mother and father, Carla and me. John wasn't necessary for Sheila, although she seemed willing to allow her mother to have him around if that was what *she* wanted. I thought I detected a note of relief in her voice when she made the announcement about John's departure.

We entered the house through the back door. Carla didn't allow anyone to come through her front door. Her living room was a showcase for **Better Homes & Gardens**; or at least she acted like it was, so no one was allowed to enter it.

I was glad to get a good, home-cooked meal. I didn't really like to cook and I was tired of eating out.

"What's up, Sis?" Carla greeted me.

Sheila and I walked into her huge kitchen, which also looked like a **Better Homes & Garden** showcase. It had a country theme with lots of doo-dads, print-coordinated towels, plaques on the walls and fancy cookware hanging from ceiling rafters that I knew she never used.

"Nothin' much," I responded as I sat down at her sturdy oak wood dinette table, which had decorative checkered blue, white and yellow placemats with matching seat cushions in oak wood chairs.

The floor was tiled with an expensive brick marble. She placed a beautiful pastel blue stoneware plate with white and yellow daisies peeking through steaming white rice and a juicy steak both covered with brown gravy and cooked onions. The aroma was intoxicating. I grabbed my fork and dug in. Then, she placed a tall, cold glass of lemonade in front of me along with some hot buttered dinner rolls on a saucer. I was in heaven. Thank God for sisters that know how to throw down in the kitchen, I thought.

I glanced at her occasionally as I ate. She was tidying up, as usual, wiping counters and making sure everything was in its proper place. There was a part of me that admired her. She had a certain style and class about her that I didn't know anything about. She always looked perfect. She even had beautiful nighttime apparel and wraps for her hair when she went to bed. She was a real lady.

I knew Carla thoroughly enjoyed being the wife of a successful lawyer. It afforded her to live the way she had always dreamed. She always wanted to be a wife and a mother like our mother. I wanted a career and a husband. Maybe I didn't necessarily want to be a wife. I just wanted a man around to do the things that men do, but I wanted him to be committed to doing those things for me and only me!

I looked at Carla again. Being a wife was who she was. It was her identity. The license plate on her BMW read MRS JNZ. Mine read, CAREN 1.

"How are the wedding plans coming?" She asked as she took a seat across from me at the table. Sheila leaned against her.

"Where are the boys?"

"Upstairs. They're playing in their room."

"Oh." I took a long, loud swig of the lemonade.

"Wanna listen to some music?"

"Yeah."

"Girl, I got the Whispers. You know, **In The Mood**."

"Oh yeah. I like that. Put that on."

She had a small stereo on the island in the center of her kitchen. She put in the cassette and pressed play, and the Whispers were crooning, *Let me put you in the mood*, softly in the background.

I tried to think of some clever or appropriate answers to Carla's impending questions as I watched her prepare to sit down again. I knew she wasn't going to let me get away with avoiding her question about my wedding plans. Sheila sat in the chair next to me.

"Have you worked on any interesting stories lately, Aunt Carrie?"

"No, not really, Sheila."

"What about Mama's councilman?" Carla interjected.

what you do in the dark . . .

"Well, yeah. I'm still working on that, but there's really nothing new to tell."

"He sure is fine. I bet you wish you were available, huh?"

"How's John?"

"How's your wedding plans coming?"

"Mama said he left to go live with some other woman."

"Sheila, go see what your brothers are doing."

"Oh, I'm sorry," I said biting my lip.

Sheila dragged with quiet stomps upstairs. She knew better than to protest too loudly.

"It's alright. She probably knows anyway."

I turned my attention back to my meal.

"So I guess you didn't do anything for Valentine's Day either?" I asked after a long silence.

"Nope," she admitted.

"Did you and Darnell do anything?"

Oops. I did it again. I walked right into that one. I remembered Darnell had told me he'd probably go with his family soon to visit his grandmother just before the hospital incident. He told me that his father hadn't seen her in about twenty years.

"He went to visit his grandmother in Florida. She's dying."

"Really," Carla sympathized. "I'm sorry to hear that. You should have gone with him."

"I couldn't really get off from work. There's a new political columnist that may be out for my job. I have to be on my best behavior. It's not a good time to take off."

"Really. Who is she? Where'd she come from?"

"She's some hot shot national freelance writer and women's counselor. My editor worships the ground she walks on."

"Why do you think she's out for your job?"

"Just a feeling."

"Well, Caren, you know you can be paranoid at times. I'm sure there's enough room for both of you."

"There *is* enough room, but some people just feel threatened by other people with talent that's all."

"You sure it's not you."

"Positive. Can we change the subject?"

"No problem. How's your wedding plans coming?"

The phone rang. "Thank you Jesus!" I said to myself.

"Hello." She answered it immediately. I could tell she was hoping it was John. Her face frowned with disappointment.

"Hey Ma."

"Sittin' here talkin' to Caren."

"Yeah. She came over to have dinner with us."

Carla pointed to the phone to signal that Mama wanted to talk to me. I furiously shook my head and mouthed, "No!"

"She just went to the bathroom. You want me to have her call you back?"

"No, I haven't heard from John."

"Okay. I'll call you later."

Just then, I heard keys turning in Carla's back door. John walked in as Carla hung up the phone.

"Yeah. What's goin' on?" he asked in a deep, angry voice. He was a tall man with a loud voice, and an intimidating physique. If I had been Carla, I would have been afraid to marry him.

"Hey John," I said timidly.

"Hey. How are you, Caren?" His eyes were still intent on Carla so I knew he wasn't really waiting for a reply to his question. "Why do you keep calling my woman's house?" he bellowed.

I knew it was time for me to leave.

"I am your wife!" Carla declared.

"I'll tell you what. You better not call there again!"

"I'll do whatever I damn well please!"

I got up to leave.

"You don't have to leave Caren!" she yelled.

"I have to get home and go to bed. I have an early day tomorrow," I pleaded.

"Okay. Call me."

I quickly slipped out the back door. Carla and John were yelling back and forth as I seated myself behind the steering wheel. I wondered why the men in both of our lives could not be faithful to us. It had to be something we inherited from our mother.

After all, she had married the first adulterer, but at least *they* had made it to the altar. My chances for that were growing slimmer all the time. Then, suddenly it hit me as I was driving home that my mother had been alone on Valentine's Day too. Her fourth one without my father, and I hadn't even called her. Maybe we should have thrown a great big No Valentine Pity Party.

what you do in the dark . . .

march in, march out

Make up to break up that's all we do.
First you love me, then you hate me, it's a game for fools.

"Look what the wind blew in," I said as Robert marched past my threshold, dressed impeccably as usual in a designer suit.
"Hey Sweetheart." He kissed me gently, but quickly on the lips.
"What brings you here?" I asked.
"You, of course." He smiled slyly and sauntered with assured steps to my living room. He took a seat on my sofa and motioned for me to join him. I did.
"I'm sorry I've been out of touch for so long. I went home to Florida. I had a death in the family. Also, I'm running for a seat in the Ohio state senate, you know. I've been in Columbus for the past few weeks taking care of business."
"Yes, I heard. Although, I was a little upset that I didn't hear it from you."
"I've been busy with the details. That's why I haven't called. You understand, don't you?"
"Sure."
"Did you get my flowers?"
"Yes. They were nice, but you shouldn't have sent them to the paper. We have a new political columnist now, Jessie Bassett. She just

happens to be the same woman who counseled me at the abortion clinic and she's hot after news about your personal life. She read your card and she's suspicious about our involvement."

"Yeah. I heard about her. She's definitely trouble. She has contacts in Columbus and she's been in touch with them about me for some reason. I can't believe our luck to have the very counselor that handled your abortion be in the business of exposing politicians' views on abortion. I've been told about the expose she's working on. It's definitely bad news for my campaign especially with her working so closely with you."

"Robert, what's goin' on? Why am I the last to know about everything?"

"It's complicated. Hey, I sure have missed you."

"What?"

"I've been thinking about you everyday. I know you're probably still upset about the baby. I'm still unsure about this two-timing thing you're doing with your fiancé, but I'm still very attracted to you Caren."

"What are you saying, Robert? You want us to keep seeing each other?"

"Well, we'll have to be more careful with Jessie Bassett snooping around and we may have to see each other only during business hours. I've got a nice sofa in my office."

"Robert." I blushed.

"We can sort out the details of this mess later. Right now, I just want to be with you sometimes. Is that okay?"

"I suppose so."

"Good."

"So when are you going to fill me in on what's going on?"

"There's not a whole lot to tell. Some friends of mine from Columbus encouraged me to take this opportunity to broaden my political base, so I agreed. They had some connections that could open a lot of doors for me and I think I can do more for Ward One as a state senator."

"I guess you could. I just never knew you had any interest in climbing the political ladder."

"I've got some good people behind me. I didn't want to let them down."

"Who are these people?"

what you do in the dark...

"Don't worry about that Sweetheart. I just want you to keep quiet about the abortion, keep helping me with the community center project and keep on loving me like you did the night of the fundraiser. Everything will be okay. You'll see."

"Keep quiet about the abortion?"

"I'm sure you know how it could hurt my chances to get elected if people knew I had paid to have my own child aborted. There's some legislation being proposed to allow the state to pay for abortions for women on ADC, and, of course, the Ohio state senate will be voting on it next year. I could be one of those state senators. My advisers think I should remain neutral on the abortion issue to keep from splitting the vote."

"Splitting the vote?"

"Between pro-choice taxpayers who feel they're paying too much for welfare recipients already and those who think that this could bring long-term relief from paying for women who are having too many children on welfare."

"And if you had to vote on this issue?"

"I'd vote for the legislation to pass. If a woman wants to have an abortion, she shouldn't be denied because she can't pay for it."

"Oh, I see."

"You disagree."

"I don't know what I feel. How can I disagree when *I* had an abortion?"

"We both know you didn't want to."

"This isn't really about whether it's right or not, but whose going to pay for it?"

"It would seem that way, but with abortion it always boils down to whether it's right or not, no matter what particular issue is on the table."

"Do you think it's right to hide your real stand on the issue just so you can get elected?"

"I'm just doing what my advisers said would be best. I'm playing the game, Caren."

"Is that what people's lives and feelings amount to with you, playing a game?"

"Sweetheart. Please don't do this. I'm doing the best I can. Look, we won't be able to see a lot of each other during this campaign. Do we have to spend this precious time debating political issues? You haven't even kissed me."

He pulled me close and kissed my lips gently at first, then more passionately.

"I've missed you so much. Did you miss me?"

"Yeah, I did," I admitted.

He started to kiss me again, then stopped suddenly.

"Do you think Jessie saw me at the clinic?"

"No."

"Do you think any of the protesters recognized me?"

"No."

"How can you be so sure?"

"Jessie would have mentioned it. It would have been in the news as soon as she got wind you were running for office."

"I guess you're right."

"Why are you doing this to yourself? I don't think this is a good time for you to run."

"I'm glad I didn't marry you."

"What?"

"Sweetheart. You're supposed to support your man, not discourage him. I'm in the race now, Caren. Please don't bring me down."

"I just don't think I can take all this lying and sneaking around."

Robert raised his eyebrows in disbelief.

"You're the only person I ever cheated on my fiancé with!"

"Listen, I think the whole situation is overwhelming, but nothing's gone wrong yet. Let's worry about problems when they come. For now, can we just get back to being together? You've got me saying things to you that I shouldn't say and I certainly don't mean. I think you're a very loyal and trustworthy person. I know you're not used to any of these things I'm asking you to do. I'm not used to it either. I'm sorry, okay?"

"Okay."

"You are so beautiful," he whispered as he kissed my earlobe. "I don't want to fight. I just want to make love to one of the most beautiful women I've ever met. Is that okay?"

I knew just like the first time we were together that it wasn't the right thing to do, but his presence was powerful and his touch was gentle and tender. His cologne was intoxicating and his kiss was mesmerizing. He sensed my apprehension as he continued to kiss me slowly and deliberately so he reached into his pocket to pull out a condom. He showed it to me and waited for a look of resolve in my eyes to answer his questioning gaze. I nodded and he began to kiss me again,

what you do in the dark . . .

this time undressing me. We made love on my living room floor, the kitchen floor, and the bathroom floor where afterwards we showered.

I sat on the bed in my terrycloth robe watching him dress, hoping that our lovemaking had somehow secured a commitment from him, but I knew that it hadn't. Each time we came, he had held up a new condom full of sperm to illustrate the impossibility of conception. He whispered that I had nothing to worry about, but meaning *he* had nothing to worry about and I had nothing, nothing of him to call my own.

I sat there wishing I could say something deep or moving, something so profound that he'd be so touched by it that he would never want to leave me. Instead, I sat there silently as he finished dressing, hoping God would intervene on my behalf. Then, I remembered that I wasn't on very good terms with God right now, being a baby killer and all. God probably wasn't very pleased with this kind of behavior anyway. Surely, He had to know that people didn't reserve sex for marriage anymore. Robert kissed me lightly on the cheek and promised he'd call me as soon as he got the chance.

It was about 8:00 in the evening on Saturday, a cool, windy March evening and I was wondering what to do with the rest of the evening. Robert had only been gone ten minutes when my telephone rang.

"I got your card and I miss the hell out of you."

"Darnell?"

"Yes, Red it's me."

"I wasn't sure if I'd ever hear from you again."

"We've been together for ten years. I'm not going anywhere. I just needed time to think. We all make mistakes. We both know that I've made my share. I just don't like to think about you being with someone else no matter how it happened. I hope you'll be more careful about who you keep company with in the future. You could have been seriously hurt. You could have gotten some kind of disease or something. Do you realize that you were raped?"

"I wouldn't call it that."

"That's what it was."

"I guess I'd just like to forget about it. The doctor said I didn't contract any diseases and the baby is gone. I don't want to keep reliving it."

"Okay. I understand. Listen, Craig and Tyrone have dates with a couple of girls and they want to go bowling. You wanna go?"

"Yeah, sure. What time do you want me to be ready?"
"Can you be ready in an hour?"
"Sure."
"Okay. I'll see you soon. Love you."
"Now you know how I feel about that."
"*I* love you."
"I love you too."

I did love Darnell. He was like an old pair of jeans. He was worn out, but he was comfortable, easy and mine. I hurried through my dresser drawers collecting underwear: panties, bra, and socks. From my closet, I got my favorite pair of jeans and a sorority T-shirt from my Central State days. I pulled out my ironing board and set it up in the kitchen. I pressed my jeans and T-shirt, and then I sat on my bed to put lotion on my body, remembering how Robert had just caressed each and every part of me. I forced myself to forget about Robert and concentrate on Darnell, my future husband. I got dressed and bumped curls into my hair with my curling iron. My hair had gone limp from the lovemaking and shower with Robert. The phone rang just as I finished applying my make-up.

"What's up, Girl?" Michelle greeted me.

"Hey, Girl. Everything's great. Robert just left, and Darnell is back in my life. We're going bowling with Craig and Tyrone in a few minutes."

"I see I've taught you well. You got'em marchin' in and out right on schedule like toy soldiers. My Girl! So how'd you accomplish all this in one day?"

"Robert is running for state senator. He came over to make sure I wouldn't tell anyone about the abortion. He says he misses me. We made love again."

"I hope you protected yourself this time."

"Yeah, he took care of it."

"Good. So how'd you end up with plans to go out with Darnell and his loser friends?"

"He just called. He got the card and the note. He believed me, but he's worried. He said I was raped."

"Well, that's what they call it when a man has sex with a woman without her permission. I'm surprised he's not trying to get you to find the guy and press charges."

what you do in the dark . . .

"Thank God. I tell you, Michelle, I don't think I can take all this lying and sneaking around much longer. What happened to the simple life?"

"Robert Turner is what happened to the simple life. I can't believe you slept with him again after the way he treated you."

"I don't know Michelle. He just does something to me. He is so fine and he makes me feel so good. He has to be the greatest lover in the world! And, I conceived a child with him. I never conceived a child with anyone before. I never felt the way he makes me feel."

"That's because you ain't never been with nobody else, but Darnell. I told you that you need to get more experience before you get married. You don't want to buy nothin' until you've shopped around a little bit. You might find that Darnell is lacking some things that you need."

"You may be right, but I feel secure with Darnell. Darnell takes good care of me. He provides for me. He'd make a better husband. I want to be married and have children and Robert isn't interested in that right now. Although Jessie did say it would be better for his campaign if he were married. Maybe he'll change his mind. I wish he would change his mind and save me from the boredom of being with Darnell."

"I know that's right. Who's Jessie?"

"Girl, you won't believe it. She's the woman who counseled me at the abortion clinic. Now, she's working at the **AA Times** as a political columnist. She's nosing around about Robert's personal life too and she came straight to me."

"That doesn't sound good. So, are you going to continue to see Robert after the way he treated you *and* with this Jessie snooping around?"

"Robert says we can handle her. Besides, I don't think he meant to hurt me."

"Men mean everything they do. I hope you're not sleeping with him for free. Darnell's spending cash and he's not even getting it. You better make Mr. Councilman put out when you put out."

"Michelle, I can't just ask him for money."

"He don't mind asking for what he wants. Look Girl. Don't play. It ain't nothin' to it, but to do it. When is the next time you guys plan to hook up?"

"He wants to have some kind of rendez-vous in his office when he gets a chance."

"Oh, he likes adventure. Well, you make sure you get dinner or lunch and a new outfit. When he calls just tell him you want something special or sexy to wear when you see him. I'm telling you. Don't give it up for free. That's just not cool."

"Okay, Michelle. I'll give it a try."

"Don't try. Do it. You know, it ain't nothin'"

"To it, but to do it! I know. I'll catch you later Girl. Darnell will be here in a minute."

"Alright. Peace out."

****

Craig and Tyrone worked at the Post Office with Darnell. They were letter carriers too. Craig and Tyrone were always with different women. I felt sorry for their women because they were getting played. They were totally in the dark, deceived. They each thought that they were Craig or Tyrone's only woman and Darnell forbade me to tell them anything different. I kept their secrets because I thought it made me special, a part of their little club, for men only. It never occurred to me that their women kept secrets from me as well.

Craig and Tyrone were nice looking guys, but their jobs made them look better than they actually were, at least to the kind of women they dated. They drove stylish sports cars, owned nice homes and wore fashionable clothes, as did Darnell. Craig was tall, slim and light-skinned. He kept his head shaved to hide the premature 'hole in his natural.' His lips were big and pink and his teeth were slightly stained from all the cigarettes he smoked. Tyrone was short, stocky and muscular. His skin was dark brown and his hair was dark and wavy. He had a gold tooth that he constantly sucked when he looked at women as his eyes groped their bodies as if they were hands. Tyrone made me feel uncomfortable at times. He always looked at me like I was a pork chop and he was a hungry ex-Muslim. He would often greet me with a very tight hug that made me feel like I had just been frisked for a Louis Farrakhan appearance.

Craig just regarded me with puppy dog eyes and acted like everything I said was ingenious. He was impressed that Darnell had a woman who was a college graduate and wrote for a newspaper. I failed to see why Darnell liked hanging out with Craig and Tyrone so much. They were intellectually inferior to him in my opinion. I just put up with

what you do in the dark . . .

them so that I could be with my man. Craig and Tyrone's girlfriends were classless and stupid too. Not only did I feel sorry for them because they were getting played, but I abhorred socializing with them because they were so 'ghetto.' I tried not to let on how I really felt to Darnell because I knew he would use it as an excuse not to include me when they did things together. So tonight, it was Shalonda and Laquita. You could tell they were some typical project tramps.

"Did I knock'em all down 'Rone?" Laquita asked after she'd lunged a house ball down the gutter that bounced back out and knocked all the pins down.

"Naw, that don't count Baby," Tyrone replied palming her butt. "Better luck next time."

"My turn! My turn!" Shalonda shouted as she ran up to the lanes, grabbed a ball and threw it down the alley, all in one movement, which exasperated the serious bowler in the adjacent lane.

"Strike!" she yelled. "Put my strike down, Nigga!"

I slid down in my seat thinking it was going to be a long night. Darnell sat next to me.

"They're a trip, ain't they?" he whispered in my ear. I smiled weakly without answering.

"You look great tonight. I missed you."

"I missed you too." I nestled closer to him.

"You know we're going to have to talk about this business with Michelle and that scandalous party."

My body tensed. I hoped that I had gotten past this issue.

"Darnell, I told you I don't want to talk about it anymore."

"We don't have to talk about what happened, but maybe you need to rethink your relationship with Michelle. She put you in a very dangerous situation. Doesn't that make you mad? Maybe you shouldn't hang out with her anymore."

Darnell and Michelle had never liked each other. Darnell said she had too much influence over me. Michelle said I let him control me too much. I felt that if I could put up with derelicts like Craig and Tyrone, he could damn well put up with Michelle.

"And maybe you shouldn't hang out with these 'ghetto' people you hang out with!" I yelled.

Tyrone, Craig, Laquita, and Shalonda looked up in astonishment. Darnell looked at me as if he wanted to strangle me. Everyone was silent. Embarrassed and infuriated, I marched out of the bowling alley. I could hear Laquita and Shalonda yelling.

"I know that tramp ain't talkin' 'bout me!"

I used my set of keys to drive Darnell's car home. I knew that Craig or Tyrone would drive him to my apartment to pick up his car. We'd had blow-ups like this before. I didn't want to be there when he came to pick up the car so I ran into the apartment and made a quick call to Mark. Mark agreed to meet me halfway between his house and my apartment so that we could take a walk. I changed into some heavy sweats and tennis shoes. I put on a heavy jacket and went to meet my friend.

It was almost ten. I noticed him approaching me as I walked down Bartlett Avenue toward Rockside Road. The sky was dark and clear. The air was chilly, but not uncomfortable. The wind was crisp. There was an occasional gust that hit my face. The light from the street lamps and the residential lampposts that lined the street made Mark easy to recognize. He was dressed in jeans, a heavy jacket, and a skullcap. The tips of his cornrows were dangling from the back of his cap. As he got closer, I could see those sparkling hazel eyes, and his warm, inviting smile. He gave me a big hug.

"Hi Bae."

"Hey Mark."

"How you feelin'?" he asked as we started to walk toward Rockside Road.

"I'm okay I guess."

"Are you okay about the abortion?"

"Sometimes I think I am. Other times I'm not sure. I think I really wanted the baby."

"I know you did, but you wouldn't listen to me when I tried to tell you that you didn't have to go through with it."

"Hmmh," I responded not wanting to reveal what I was thinking, which was that he didn't have anything to offer us if I had decided to keep the baby.

"You just don't think I'm good enough for you. Right?"

"Mark, I didn't say that."

"You don't have to."

"Let's not do this Mark. I need you. I don't want to fight."

what you do in the dark...

"Caren, it's just hard to listen to you talkin' 'bout how much you need me, but you don't want me for the things that really count. How long am I supposed to let you use me?"

"So now I'm using you?"

"What would you call it?"

"I thought we were friends."

"You know I want more than that."

"Mark, I don't want to have this conversation, not while I'm trying to deal with so much right now. Please, just be my friend."

Mark was quiet for a long while, then he took my hand in his as we walked. We turned right on Rockside Road going in the opposite direction of the bowling alley where I had left Darnell at the corner of Rockside and Northfield. We headed toward the houses in the neighborhood where Mark lived.

"So what's goin' on now?" he asked finally.

"Robert's running for state senator. I told you before that Darnell knows about the abortion. I made up a story about how I got pregnant. So we're back together, but everything's a mess."

"Hmmh," Mark responded. He looked at the ground.

"You don't want to talk about this?"

"Did you ever think that maybe *I* have some problems I need to talk about with a friend sometimes?"

"Mark, you don't have to take this attitude with me. If you want to tell me something, just tell me."

"My mom is sick."

"I'm sorry to hear that. Can I do anything?"

"Caren, my mother is the only person in this world who loves me. All I want to know is that if for some reason she has to leave me that somebody else in this world cares about me."

"Mark, you know I care about you. You're one of my closest friends."

"I don't know Caren. Sometimes I think that I don't mean nothin' to you. I'm always here for you, Caren. Whenever you need me, I'm here, but what I need to know is, will you be there for me when I need you?"

"I'll be here for you, Mark. I promise."

"Good. Well, let's talk about you. What's goin' on with you and Robert?"

I laughed. "Let's just talk about us. Remember when I was on the drill team for Kennedy High School? You used to hang out at our practices. You remember the drills we used to do?"

"Yeah. I'd follow you anywhere."

"I'm starting to get cold. Let's do some of those drills to warm up."

"You're crazy. I'm not marchin' down these streets like no fool Bae."

"Come on! It'll be fun. We can march back to my apartment. Maybe Darnell has picked up his car by now."

"Okay," he agreed reluctantly. "Your left, your left, your left, right, left!" He shouted the drill instructions.

We marched around the block and back to my apartment. Darnell's car was gone. We went up to my apartment and watched some movies until I fell asleep. As usual, Mark put me to bed, and went home. That night I had a dream that I kept hearing little feet marching away from me and I was trying desperately to keep up with them.

When I went to work the next day, Jackie greeted me with an insistent, "We're going to lunch together today," as I signed in on the reporter's log.

Her signature extension braids were framing her Hershey chocolate face in a pageboy style instead of being pulled back into a ponytail.

"Okay," I said looking at her questioningly.

"Wedding plans?" she responded.

"Oh yeah. I guess we do need to talk."

"What's the matter Girlfriend? You are getting married, aren't you?"

"As far as I know."

"Then, you're going to have to start getting some of the details together. You and Darnell need to set up your counseling with Pastor Peoples too if you still want him to perform the ceremony."

"Counseling?"

"Yes Caren. Remember? Pastor Peoples likes to be sure that the couples that he marries know what they're getting into. His father counseled Bernard and me before we married and I have to tell you, it was great preparation for our married life."

"Jackie," I responded looking into her beaming face and realizing it was time to come clean, a little anyway. "Darnell and I are going through some problems right now. I don't know where we stand for sure. I'll come to church on Easter. Maybe by then, I'll be more certain of where

what you do in the dark . . .

Darnell and I stand. That's only a couple of weeks away. Would that be okay?"

"What happened?" she asked looking very concerned. Before I could answer, Mr. Caldwell stepped out of his office and into Jackie's reception area. He gave me a stern look that asked why wasn't I in the City Room working.

"Jackie," he said as if I weren't there. "Could you type this for me?" He handed her a sheet of paper with some handwriting on it.

"I'll talk to you later Jackie," I said as I turned to enter the City Room.

"Okay Caren," she replied. "I'll tell Pastor Peoples to expect to talk to you around Easter."

"Thanks. That will be fine."

I closed the door behind me and headed for my desk. Jessie was already poised to strike as I sat down and logged in on my computer.

"Ssso, Robert's back in town," she started.

"Yes, he is," I stated absently.

"Ssso, you've seen him?"

"Yes I have."

"You doin' another story about the community center project?"

"No."

"Then, why'd he come to see you?"

"We're friends."

"You make friends with everyone you interview for the paper? How can you keep any kind of objectivity?"

"Is there some point to this line of questioning?"

"I need your help."

"With what?"

"There are some political heavyweights in Columbus who I believe Councilman Turner has aligned himself. Something related to the abortion legislation. Has the councilman mentioned anything to you?"

"Mentioned anything like what?"

"Names for one. Has he told you who he talked to when he was in Columbus?"

"No. Is there some reason why he should? Whose name are you looking to hear him mention?"

"Kirkland perhaps."

"No. I haven't heard him mention any Kirklands."

Jessie leaned back in her chair. Her soft spiral curls framed her face as usual. The length dropped gently at the nape of her neck. Several co-workers had commented that they thought her head of curls made her look like a cute, petite, sophisticated and womanly Shirley Temple. She reminded *me* of Medusa. She was twirling her pencil in between her thumb and index finger which revealed a short, chubby, French-manicured hand adorned with a couple of tasteful diamond rings and a modest diamond tennis bracelet on her wrist. It was about one carat. She wore a finely tailored red, two-piece suit and a white silk blouse. I had to admit to myself that I did envy her style. She seemed so together. Sharp!

"The Kirklands are a family of prominent African-American lawyers, doctors, and politicians. They wield a lot of power in Ohio. They're everywhere and they usually get whatever they want. What they want now is to control the state senate."

"Why?" I was drawn in now.

"Abortion and welfare."

"What about abortion and welfare?"

"They want that law to pass that will allow women on welfare to use their healthcare benefits to pay for their abortions."

"What is it to them?"

"They have doctors in their family who perform abortions. They want in on that money."

"Oh," I responded quietly.

"Ssso, will you help me find out if Councilman Turner is connected with them?"

"Why don't you just ask him?" I was annoyed with her again.

"Why won't you cooperate with me on this? Do you have something to hide other than what I already know?" She raised her voice. She was exasperated with me. It felt good to get under her skin for a change. I smiled.

"No. I have nothing to hide," I responded coolly.

"Well, we'll just see about that!" she threatened as she marched off fiercely in her exquisite red leather pumps and a matching red leather designer briefcase swinging on its strap from her shoulder.

Her curls bounced as she made her exit from the City Room. I had to cover my mouth to keep from laughing out loud. Then suddenly, I remembered that I *did* have a whole lot to hide and antagonizing Jessie was probably not the smartest thing to do. She was furious with me and she was on to something about Robert. Maybe Robert and I needed to put our heads together, I thought. I picked up the phone and called Robert to invite him to lunch. He told me that he couldn't get away for lunch, but he would call me later that evening when I was at home.

It was about six-thirty when I got home, and I quickly changed from my skirt and blazer into some sweats and a T-shirt. I wanted to be relaxed and comfortable when Robert called to discuss our problem. I put on some Maze featuring Frankie Beverly. I found their music relaxing, good for soul searching and thinking. I propped myself up in my bed on a couple of pillows and pulled my journal from under my bed to write out my thoughts. **Lovely Inspiration** played softly as I tried to sort out my feelings on paper about Darnell, Robert, the abortion, the wedding and Jessie. All I could write was,

I'm worried about a lot of things today. I don't know what to do. I don't know where to turn.

I closed the entry with my usual,

"Miss you Daddy!"

As I slid the journal back under the bed, my phone rang.

"What's up Sweetheart? What was so urgent you needed to speak to me about?"

"I can't get a hello. How was your day?"

"Look Caren. I'm a little annoyed with you, alright? I told you we had to be more careful. Then, what do you do? You call me and want to go out to lunch. Do you realize how serious this is? We're talking about my career Caren! My livelihood! This isn't about Caren is lonely. Caren needs attention!"

"You know I called because I wanted to help you, but I can see that you ain't worth helping!"

"Caren wait! Don't hang up! I'm sorry. I'm just under a lot of pressure. Please, tell me what's goin' on?"

I took a deep breath. I realized that I needed Robert's help as much as he needed mine.

"It's Jessie Bassett. She's asking a lot of questions about people you know in Columbus. She mentioned something about you being tied to the Kirkland family. They're supposed to be influential. Who are they Robert? What do you know about them?"

"I wonder who her sources are?" Robert asked, whispering to himself.

"I thought you would know. Robert, what is going on with you? Do you know these Kirklands? What is Jessie talking about?"

"Nothing for you to worry about. Jessie sounds like she's just grasping at straws, trying to make a name for herself. Be careful around her Caren. Don't tell her anything about us. Hey, when can I see you?"

"I don't know. What do you have in mind?"

"I've got to work late tomorrow night. Why don't you stop by my office around midnight? Make sure no one sees you."

"Robert! Don't you think that's a bit late?"

"I'm sorry Sweetheart. It won't be like this for long. See you tomorrow night?"

"Okay. Tomorrow night it is."

"Bye Sweetheart."

"Bye."

what you do in the dark . . .

april showers

*If loving you is wrong,
I don't wanna be right.*

It was Easter Sunday and I had promised Jackie that I would attend worship services to make arrangements with Reverend Peoples for Darnell and me to start marital counseling. I looked out of my window at the pouring rain and I tried to think of a reason I could use to get out of keeping my promise. I didn't want to disappoint Jackie or mess up my wedding plans so reluctantly I began to assemble my new Easter outfit.

In making the short commute to the church in my mother's neighborhood, I managed to splash muddy water on my white pantyhose while hurrying from my apartment to the car. I lost all the curl from my hair and the skirt of my two-piece white suit got wrinkled. By the time I made it into the church, I had a few dirt spots on my skirt and my black trench coat was soaking wet.

It was about five minutes to eleven when I arrived. The church was already packed. It was an average-sized building, but there seemed to be hundreds of people filing into the pews. It had been at least five years since I had even visited Matthias. It was totally remodeled. I had forgotten a lot of the rituals that the church practiced. I rarely looked back at life in the church when I decided to leave not long after I lost my virginity to Darnell. It had come down to a choice between the man

I loved and the God I had never really known. We weren't ready to get married then and if I didn't have sex with him, someone else would. I just couldn't keep going to church knowing that I would continue to fornicate. I didn't want to be a hypocrite. I remember how Jackie used to criticize me for coming to church and sleeping with Darnell. She said I was straddling the fence and I needed to make a choice. Maybe now I could come back. Maybe after Darnell and I got married, I would be welcome again.

Who was I trying to fool? My future with Darnell was growing dimmer by the minute and my affair with Robert wasn't helping. I spotted Jackie as I headed up to about the fourth row of pews in the middle section. There were about twelve rows of pews, three sections and a balcony with about four rows and two sections. The choir stand looked like it seated about 100 people. There was an older man sitting at a big piano and a younger woman sitting at an organ. I noticed drums too. Maybe the music and singing will be good I thought as I took a seat next to Jackie, Bernard and their two children. Jackie's husband still looked as handsome as he did in high school and their kids, an eight year old daughter, Bernadette and a six year old son, Bernard Jr. were cute and well behaved.

"I'm glad you made it in spite of the weather." Jackie said hugging me gently. Her smile was full of encouragement.

"I'm a woman of my word. You know that Girlfriend."

Bernard smiled at me and nodded hello. I smiled and waved at him and to the kids.

I sat quietly trying to make some sense of my life as the worship service began. A group of deacons stood in front of the congregation and started what according to the church program was called the devotional period. They read a verse or two from the Bible, led a prayer and sang a church hymn, maybe not in that order. Then, they asked for testimonies. I remembered that part of the service from when I was a member. I used to get up every year on my birthday and thank the Lord for allowing me to see another year. That was the only testimony I ever gave.

These people were standing up telling all their personal business, about how the Lord had brought them through alcohol and drug addictions, problems with their wives and husbands and even financial problems. The congregation was shouting "Amen!" and praising the

what you do in the dark . . .

Lord. I sat quietly, glancing at my watch occasionally and checking to see how much further we had to go on the church program.

They passed the collection plate around a couple of times and the choir sang a few songs. Then, it was finally time for the sermon, which meant that once I made it through that, it would be just a few formalities before it was time to go.

Reverend Peoples stepped up to the podium in the pulpit and greeted the congregation with a hearty, "Happy Resurrection Day Saints!" They returned the greeting in chorus. Reverend Peoples was a very handsome, young preacher. He wasn't the old Reverend Peoples I remembered from when I was a teenager. Jackie said this Reverend Peoples, the son, was about eight to ten years older than we were, about thirty-five.

He was tall and thick with a light brown complexion, well-groomed sandy brown hair and big brown eyes. His lips were full and he had a few gaps between his teeth. He was indeed handsome. I knew if I ever became a church member again, I would definitely come back to this church. I hadn't heard him preach yet though. I hoped he would be interesting to listen to. I remembered sleeping through a lot of his father's sermons. I hoped he would lift my spirits because after all I'd been through, I needed some spiritual uplifting.

"Did you notice Mark Townsend's mother's name on the sick and shut-in list?" Jackie whispered to me pointing to a Mrs. Gladys Townsend on the church bulletin.

"Mark Townsend?" I asked in bewilderment.

"Yeah, you remember Mark Townsend. We grew up with Mark and I believe you told me you'd seen him at your apartment complex. He was the maintenance man or something?"

"Yeah, I did. His mother still goes to this church?"

"Yeah. She never left."

"My mother told me when I was in college that she still came here even though she'd moved to Bedford Heights."

"Matthias is the kind of church you grow old in. You should have stayed. You should come back."

"I'm not living right Jackie. You know that."

"The Lord says come as you are."

"That's not what you said when I left."

"I've grown."

"What's wrong with Mark's mother?"

"They announced a couple of weeks ago that she had a heart attack. I don't think they expect her to make it. We need to send some flowers, a card or something. We should call Mark, see how he's holding up."

"Yeah. I'll call him when I get home."

Jackie turned her attention to Reverend Peoples and I wondered how Mark was doing for a few minutes, but before long I was thinking about Robert and our midnight rendezvous. He had really rocked my world that night! Suddenly, I heard Reverend Peoples bellow, "The dirt of our lives is sin!" I was jolted and I started to focus in on what he was saying.

"My brothers and sisters, the dirt of our lives, the sin of our lives leaves a stain that no human detergent can get clean. The dirt of our lives leaves scars. So we need to be careful when we fool around with sin. I know a lot of you think that you can participate in some sin and no one will ever find out, but my brothers and sisters, God knows, and be sure that your sin . . ."

The Reverend paused, and the congregation answered in chorus, "will find you out!"

"Cause what you do in the dark . . ." he led again.

Everyone answered, "will come to the light!"

I thought about the many times I had heard Marge say that as Reverend Peoples went into this story about how this king called David in first Samuel or somewhere around there in the Bible. He had slept with a woman named, Bathsheba, the wife of one of his best soldiers, Uriah. He tried to cover up the fact that he had gotten her pregnant by calling Uriah home from the war to sleep with her. Her husband was a loyal man. He slept at the doorstep of King David's palace in order to protect him instead of going home to be with his wife.

So, according to Reverend Peoples, when that plan didn't work, King David gave one of his men instructions to put Uriah on the front line of the war so that he would be killed. After Uriah was killed, King David gave the woman enough time to mourn her husband. Then, he took her for his wife. King David thought he had gotten away with what he had done until God sent a prophet, Nathan, who told King David that the Lord knew what he had done, but had already forgiven him.

Then, Reverend Peoples started listing all the ways God punished this King David for his sins. First, God did not allow the child that King David and Bathsheba conceived in adultery to live. Next, one of his sons raped his own sister. Another son caused him to have to flee from his

what you do in the dark . . .

palace and this son slept with King David's wives on the rooftop of the palace for everyone to see.

Reverend Peoples reiterated that even though you may do your dirt in the dark, when God catches up to you, all your sins will be in the light for everyone to see. I started to imagine Jessie telling the world in a newspaper article about my affair with Robert and the subsequent abortion of our child. It couldn't really happen I reasoned. Things like that only happen in the movies or on soap operas.

"The dirt of our lives, my brothers and sisters, are often times perpetuated in the things we watch on TV, the soap operas, the night-time dramas. Be careful what you are entertained by."

I was tired of Reverend Peoples now. He didn't know what he was talking about. I hated when people insisted that our actions are the result of the media, what we watch on TV or the music we listen to. I am perfectly capable of making my own decisions. It doesn't matter what I watch on TV or what kind of music I listen to. What *I* did in the dark was going to stay in the dark! No one could prove anything! I would take this secret to my grave. Besides, if God could forgive this King David for adultery and murder, He could certainly forgive me for fornication and abortion. I fought back tears as I begged God in my mind to please forgive me and not to punish me like he'd punished King David.

"My brothers and sisters, God does forgive our sins, but he doesn't always release us from the consequences of our sins. But thanks be to God that he does release us from the ultimate consequence of sin. It says in His word that the wages of sin is death! But the gift of God is eternal life! It's only through the blood of Jesus that we can truly be cleansed from the dirt of our lives, which is sin. He shed his blood for us when He died on the cross on Friday evening. But this great Resurrection Day we celebrate because early on Sunday morning, He got up with all power conquering death and sin for each and every one of us who will believe. It's time to come and accept His gift of love, which is our salvation. The doors of the church are open."

Jackie gave me a questioning look, but I bowed my head. I thought about my wedding. I'd be worthy soon maybe. I thought about the abortion. Had God forgiven me for that? I thought about Robert and how good it felt to be with him. I couldn't give Robert up now, not yet. What if Darnell and I didn't make it? I had to have someone on standby and Robert didn't want to get married. I still wasn't welcome.

"Are you going to talk to Pastor Peoples?"

"Yeah. I'll talk to him after service to set up a counseling session. I hope Darnell can make it."

"He'd better make it."

After I got home from worship service, Darnell called to invite me over for dinner at his parents' home. Darnell's grandmother had died in February and he had been going on about how her death had ended a twenty-year feud between his father and his aunt.

Darnell's Aunt Elsie had moved away twenty years earlier with her mother, her husband, Lou, and their son. According to Darnell, he believed the feud stemmed over differences about the care of their mother who had suffered a serious stroke and needed special 'around-the-clock' care.

Darnell's father, Arthur Jennings, wanted to put her in a nursing home, but his sister Elsie insisted on hiring a nurse and caring for her at home. She had cursed Darnell's father out thoroughly for even suggesting they put their mother in a home. She packed her mother and family up and moved back to their hometown in Pensacola, Florida to get support from their mother's sisters and brothers. Grandmother Jennings eventually recovered from the stroke, but died from heart failure at age 79. Aunt Elsie had never called or spoken with her brother since their fallout until she called to tell him that their mother was dying.

Darnell had explained all of this to me when he told me why it took him so long to respond to my Valentine's Day card. He had gone to Florida as I had guessed. The family patched things up while they were there and now Mr. Jennings' sister and her family were coming to visit for Easter. Darnell's family always made a big fuss over holiday dinners especially his mother and she expected me to help with the preparations. So Darnell picked me up at about 4:00 p.m. Dinner was going to be at six.

It was still raining heavily as we drove to his parents' home, which was midway between his Warrensville Heights condo and my Bedford Heights apartment in another southeastern suburb, Maple Heights. The ten-minute drive seemed longer as the sound of the windshield wipers quickly whipped back and forth almost drowning out the sounds of a love ballad playing softly on the radio.

"I talked to Reverend Peoples today after church about our wedding ceremony. I made an appointment for our first counseling session," I mentioned to gauge where we stood.

what you do in the dark . . .

"You know my mother wants us to get married at her church," he responded sarcastically knowing how I abhorred 'holiness' churches.

"Well, she ain't too old for her wants to hurt," I quipped.

"Now, what's wrong with my mother's church? It was good enough for me," he said still teasing because he knew that I knew he couldn't wait to leave when he became an adult.

"I heard about'em. You can't wear make-up. You can't wear pants. You have to speak in tongues. I guess I shouldn't criticize. Jackie says that we shouldn't put down a church's particular practices just because we don't understand them. She says the important thing is that they teach the truth about Jesus Christ."

"She's right, but wherever you want to get married is fine with me. You know that."

"You still believe in Jesus Christ, Darnell?"

"You can't be a child of Mattie Jennings if you don't!" He laughed. "What about you?"

"I don't know. You know some religions say that Jesus was just a prophet. How do you know which one is right?"

"You don't *know* Caren. You *believe*. Like the saying goes, you have to stand for something or you'll fall for anything."

"So why don't you go to church anymore?"

"Too many hypocrites in the church."

"What about your mother's church?"

"They're the biggest."

"And your mother?"

"She's the only saint."

"You sound a bit biased."

"I'm supposed to be."

"You're crazy."

"Crazy 'bout you Red."

My mind and heart were more at ease now with Darnell's assurance that he still wanted to get married and the fall of the heavy rains on the car were starting to feel more soothing as we turned into his parents' driveway. I dreaded getting showered again for about the fourth or fifth time that day. As soon as we came into the house, Darnell's mother put me to work in the kitchen where she felt a woman belonged.

Mattie Jennings was a short woman with long black hair that she wore in a bun. She looked as if she were quite attractive as a young woman, but now in her fifties, it seemed that her big holiday dinners had taken their toll on her figure as well as her tired, worn face.

I helped Mrs. Jennings set the table and put the finishing touches on some of the dishes. They always had big, buffet-style dinners complete with all my favorite soul food dishes like macaroni and cheese, roast beef, ham, turkey, dressing, turnip and mustard greens and a variety of cakes and pies.

From where I was standing in the dining room, I could see Uncle Joe, Mrs. Jennings' brother, coming in the front door. He greeted everyone with a loud, hearty, down South, country laugh.

"Hey there now, everybody. What's goin' on! Big Daddy's in the house!" he bellowed.

I heard Darnell's father greet him.

"What's up there now, brother-in-law? And you know, I'm the only Big Daddy in this house!"

They laughed heartily as Darnell took Uncle Joe's coat, his Aunt Elsie came in behind Uncle Joe with her husband, Lou.

"Caren! Come in here," Darnell called from the living room. "I want you to meet my aunt and uncle from Florida."

I joined them in the living room gladly leaving Mrs. Jennings to the remaining dinner preparations.

"Aunt Elsie," Darnell said, pulling me to his side, "this is my fiancée, Caren. Caren, this is my Aunt Elsie Turner and her husband, Lou Turner. Of course, you already know Uncle Joe."

"Pleased to meet you," I said to the couple extending a handshake to them both.

"She's a fine little thing Darnie. You done gone an' got yo'self a redbone. You know them redbones is mean, but they sho' is fine," Uncle Lou said grabbing me and hugging me tightly.

"Yeah. She is a pretty little thing Darnie," Aunt Elsie agreed. "Mattie tells me she smart too, work for a newspaper. If I'd 'a been here in Cleveland and saw her first, I'd 'a fixed her up with our boy, Robbie."

What a coincidence. Another Robert Turner, I thought.

"Yeah, Caren. My cousin Robert's the councilman in your mother's ward," Darnell interjected. "I just met him for the first time since we were kids when I went to my grandmother's funeral. Do you know him? You interview local politicians sometimes, don't you?"

My mouth just about dropped to the floor as I stood there surveying Aunt Elsie, comparing her tall, slim frame, chocolate complexion, dark

what you do in the dark . . .

wavy hair and full brown lips to my memory of Robert's features. Then, I looked at Uncle Lou. They did look like older versions of Robert or rather, he looked like them. I fell into a nearby chair in the midst of the crowd of relatives who were steadily converging upon the living room and I tried to digest what I had just learned.

"Boy, Robbie sho' would be jealous of you Darnie. You know he like redbones too. He'll be here in a minute," Uncle Lou continued.

I was beside myself with fear. I wanted to leave. I sat at the table quietly when it was time to eat. I was glad when everyone began eating so no one would be interested in talking for a while, especially asking me more questions about whether I'd ever worked with Robert.

The doorbell rang. Darnell answered it.

"What's up Cousin?" I heard Robert's voice approaching the dining room.

"Hey everybody! It's my cousin, Councilman Robert Turner, one of Ohio's next state senators," Darnell announced.

David, Darnell's younger brother, came downstairs to join the family. He was eighteen and almost an exact replica of Darnell, only he was taller. His girlfriend, Linda, was right behind him. She must have gone to the bathroom or something. No way Mattie Jennings allowed them to spend time together upstairs alone.

"Hey Cuz." David greeted and hugged Robert. "This is my girl, Linda." Linda spoke gently. She was a skinny, brown-skinned girl with a stylish short haircut, big eyes and a shy grin. She constantly made goo-goo eyes at Darnell and Robert looked at her a little too long for my tastes.

"Robbie, I want you to meet my fiancée, Caren."

Robert looked at me. It was obvious that he was not the least bit shaken by my presence.

"Hello Caren," Robert said smoothly. "I've already had the pleasure of meeting *this* lovely young lady. She interviews me for the paper all the time. Haven't you ever read any of her articles?"

"In the **AA Times**?" Darnell responded. "Man, I don't read that paper."

"The **African American Times Weekly** is the most progressive voice in Ohio's Black community," Robert defended. "You don't know what you're missing. Besides, if a beautiful sister like Caren was doing the writing, I'd read the Bible from beginning to end in one night just to see what she had to say."

"Looks like you got a fan, Red."

I tried to hide my blush by looking down at my plate.

Robert sat directly across from me at the table and he played footsie with me all through dinner. I thought I would faint from anxiety. I noticed Linda smiling at Darnell. She had a crush on Darnell. It was obvious to just about everyone in the family, but no one regarded it seriously.

The two of them played flirting games all the time. I never felt threatened by it, but David did. He would playfully punch Darnell as hard as he could every time he passed him. Darnell would laugh and say, "Alright man, keep on playin'! Don't let me have to break off in yo' behind in front of yo' little girlfriend."

"Man, you ain't gon' do nothin' but get you butt kicked!" David retorted.

"Okay now! It ain't gonna be none of that mess in here today!" Mrs. Jennings shouted.

"You better tell him something then," Darnell shot back.

"Tell *him* something!" David yelled.

"Both of you, stop it now. Still act like kids," Mr. Jennings broke in.

So when David couldn't punch Darnell anymore, he turned to flirting with me.

"You look very pretty today Caren."

"Doesn't she?" Robert agreed.

"Yeah, you know them redbones are the prettiest thangs you ever wanted to see," Uncle Lou chimed in.

"Finish eatin' Lou," Aunt Elsie demanded.

I ate my dinner slowly, leaving quite a bit on my plate, which always infuriated Mrs. Jennings, but I was too unsettled to worry about pleasing her. I wanted to get away from everyone. Finally, I remembered some boxes of household things Mrs. Jennings had promised me that were stored in the basement.

"Mrs. Jennings, do you mind if I go look through those things in the basement we talked about before?"

"Sure Honey. You go on down there and pick out what you need. You know where everything is."

Grateful for the chance to get away from everyone, I rushed to the basement, closed myself up in the laundry room, sat in the middle of the floor, broke down and cried. My life was coming apart faster than I could put it back together. Once I thought I had a handle on one

what you do in the dark . . .

situation, another would come and threaten everything I wanted again. I was going to lose Darnell for sure if he found out I had been sleeping with his first cousin.

After a while as I wiped my eyes, I saw a pair of black and white Stacy Adams pointed at my feet where I sat on the floor with my knees in my chest and my head resting on them. Then, a hand reached down to me like Billy Dee did to Diana Ross in **Lady Sings the Blues**. I looked up into Robert's smiling face. He helped me to my feet, and locked the laundry room door.

"Why are you crying Sweetheart? Isn't this the funniest thing you ever experienced in your life?"

"What's so funny about finding out you've been sleeping with your fiancé's first cousin?" I pouted.

"It's not such a big deal. Darnell and I barely know each other. An affair can't get any more adventurous than this! Political intrigue, family ties, scandals and lies. I think it's exciting."

"You're sick. Don't you care about your cousin?"

"Care about my cousin? Like I said before, I don't even *know* him. Besides, he doesn't care about you. So why should you or I care about him? I know his type. You're just his faithful standby. You're his main woman, but not his *only* woman. You think he's faithful to you? He doesn't even believe in fidelity. None of the men in this family do. Wake up Caren. Get in the game. If you're gonna play, play to win, or else get played."

I had no idea what Robert was talking about, but I didn't want him to know it. He was five years older and I didn't want to appear naïve. I remained silent.

"He doesn't love you Sweetheart. If he did, then you wouldn't need me. You do need me, don't you Sweetheart? When you're home alone nights, where do you think he is? If he really loved you, then you wouldn't have time for me. He'd be the one keeping you satisfied. But that's my job now, isn't it Sweetheart? Don't I keep you satisfied?"

I stood frozen.

"You do want me, don't you Sweetheart? You can have me right now if you want. He won't even miss you. I missed you the moment you left the room. He *still* hasn't come looking for you. He's probably still flirting with Linda. Come on Sweetheart. This might be my only chance to be with you for weeks. The campaign is about to kick into high gear. The primary election is next month."

"Right here?"

"Right here."

I could feel his presence in my space before he even touched me. My body was already heating up to his despicable proposal. He touched my face and my body responded. It turned into liquid butter running down the painted white brick walls of that basement as if it was a hot cob of corn.

He kissed my neck and his lips felt soft, his breath was sweet.

"What if somebody catches us?"

"They won't."

"But they're right upstairs."

"Ssh."

He kept kissing me and undressing me. It was exciting. What a great story it would make to tell Michelle. She always engaged in exciting, adventurous lovemaking. She told me about elevators, business offices, beaches and parks. I felt like Erica Kane in one of her love scenes and the only words that came to my mind were the lyrics from that old song that said *If loving you is wrong, I don't wanna be right.*

"Ain't nothin' to it, but to do it." Michelle's voice told me.

"I need you Sweetheart. Just relax. It'll be okay. It'll be fun. No one will catch us."

"You're sure."

"Positive."

"I don't know Robert."

"I need you Sweetheart. I *love* you."

Suddenly, I couldn't remember any of my desperate requests to keep our child, any of his broken promises or any of the lonely nights I hoped he would call. He was with me now and he needed me. He *loved* me. His hands were everywhere, caressing me, waking up senses I didn't even know were asleep. His lips were so close to my breasts that they perked up in anticipation.

I didn't care about anything he'd done in the past or any of the people upstairs. All I cared about was this man giving me more pleasure than I could stand without moaning over and over again until I felt his naked chest against mine. His shirt was in my mouth to muffle my moans and groans. I could hear him calling my name.

"Caren! Caren! Where are you? Caren, are you down there?"

"Yes! Yes!" I tried to respond through the shirt wedged in my mouth. Then, he started moving faster than I wanted him to.

what you do in the dark . . .

"Caren!" he called again. I wished he would stop calling me like that. He was ruining the mood. Suddenly, he shuddered and stopped.

"Darnell is down here," he whispered. He got up quickly, grabbed his shirt from my mouth and ducked behind the washer. I picked up a dirty shirt from a laundry basket and wet it in the basement sink, letting the water run at just a trickle so Darnell couldn't hear it. I cleaned myself up quickly, fixed my clothes and hair and then I unlocked the laundry room door. Darnell busted through.

"What are you doing in here?"

"Looking for the boxes your mother had stored for me."

"Why'd you have the door locked?"

"I guess I've just been down here thinking."

"Thinking about what Red?" he said pulling me close to him. "Me, I hope. You need to take care of your man. It's been a long time."

I felt squeamish. I wasn't sure if Darnell noticed the smell of Robert's cologne or the scent of our sex. Instinctively, I stepped away from his intended embrace, trembling.

"What's the matter Red?"

"I really like this washer." I turned to inspect it more closely. I played with the buttons. "Can we get one like this when we get married?"

"Whatever you want Red. Now come here. I've missed you." He tried to kiss me on the neck. "Why are you shaking?"

"It's cold down here."

"I can warm you up," he said trying to kiss my neck again.

"Stop Darnell. I'm not in the mood."

"You should be in the mood. We haven't been together in months. Or maybe you'd rather be with the father of your aborted child?"

"Darnell, now that comment was unnecessary. I'm just worried about some things. I'm stressed out, okay? I'm ready to go. I'll wait for you in the car."

"Just use your keys and drive yourself. I can't leave with a house full of family members. I'll have David bring me to pick up the car later."

"You can at least see me out!" I demanded trying to make sure Robert would have a chance to come out of his hiding place. Darnell went to get my coat and met me at the back door. We walked out into the pouring rain, which made me feel a little more confident about any scent I might have been wearing when Darnell kissed me on the cheek and said he was sorry.

I felt a bit cleansed on the outside by God's shower from heaven, but inside I felt cheap and dirty. I felt used and discarded by Robert. This was all fun and games to him. It wasn't fun anymore for me.

What Robert and I had just shared was not the passionate lovemaking that I had expected. It was just sex. He had heard Darnell coming downstairs, but he was willing to risk my reputation for his orgasm. I was finally starting to see that Robert was using me. He needed me to help him with his community center project and keep quiet about the abortion until he got elected.

Darnell told me that he would see me later when he came to pick up his car. It started to rain harder as Darnell opened the car door for me. I was a mess driving home. I was confused, hurt and angry. The rain was pouring profusely and it was difficult to think straight or see through my tears and the rain.

Why couldn't I just leave Robert alone? Why was I letting Robert use me? I had done things that I never thought I would do. I couldn't believe that I had just had sex with Robert, Darnell's cousin, in his mother's very own house with the whole family just footsteps away. How did I go from being almost virginal to becoming just short of a common whore?

When I got home, the phone was ringing. I was afraid to answer it. It might have been Robert. Maybe he would want for us to wait in the backseat of Darnell's car and have sex quietly while Darnell was driving back home just for the excitement, the adventure, the intrigue and hope that he wouldn't take just one glance back.

I would probably do it too, because he knew how to push my buttons. The phone continued to ring. He didn't want me. He wanted sex and silence. The phone was still ringing. It couldn't be Robert yet. He'd wait at least another week or so before he put me on his sex schedule again. It was probably Darnell calling to see if I made it home safely. I picked up the phone.

"Yes!" I answered out of breath.

"My mother died today," Mark sobbed.

what you do in the dark . . .

may flowers

When you needed roses, I should have been the one
To send you a sweet bouquet.

My mother always did hate flowers as gifts. "Just give me the money!" She'd often say when Carla and I were in a quandary as to what to get her for any special occasion. I went to a flower shop in Randall Park Mall anyway to get flowers for Mother's Day.

I rationalized that a nice silk floral arrangement for her cocktail table would look nice with her new living room décor. I knew she would eventually appreciate them especially if I slipped a fifty in with the card.

I rushed through the mall early that Sunday afternoon with plans to stop at the card shop on the way out and be at my mother's within the hour for dinner.

Carla and I planned to cook dinner and spend the day with my mother, which would not be easy because Mary Boogerton didn't always have an agreeable temperament.

I walked swiftly until I reached my destination. I paused for a moment before entering the shop to catch my breath. I wanted to look composed and attractive. I hated to look unkempt in public. I knew my hair had probably blown out of place from the windy breeze outside.

I ran my fingers through my hair to put it back into place using the shop's glass as a highly inadequate mirror. I noticed a man at the counter paying for flowers. His back was turned to me, but I could tell he was quite attractive. His hair was well groomed and his designer suit had a nice fit.

It only took a couple seconds more for me to recognize that it was Robert. He was buying flowers for his mother I guessed. Darnell told me she was still in town. I hadn't spoken with Robert since Easter.

He had become increasingly busy with the campaign especially after having won one of the top spots in the primary election the week before. He delegated most of the final details for the community center to its intended director who I was assigned to interview instead of Robert. Robert had now become Jessie's territory.

My attraction to Robert was beginning to feel like an addiction. I dreamed and fantasized about him constantly. The midnight rendezvous, the first night together that started on the elevator, the way we had made love in every room of my apartment. He was so exciting. Even the episode on Easter didn't seem so bad anymore.

Yet sometimes I still felt dirty, whorish and used. I tried to convince myself that there was no point in continuing a relationship with Robert, but I just couldn't erase the past few months with Robert from my life. I just couldn't stop wanting him. Besides, if I stopped seeing him, that wouldn't make me feel any better about myself. My virtue was gone. I couldn't have Robert the way I wanted him because he just wasn't willing to commit. So, I often tried to convince myself that Darnell was the better choice because *he* took care of me and he really *loved* me, but he didn't seem to have any time for me. I just wanted to be loved by somebody, anybody.

"Hello Robert." I approached him casually.

"Caren." He turned to greet me. He didn't look pleased to see me, which irritated me.

"Buying flowers for your mother?"

"I haven't heard from you. How've you been?"

"You always say that."

"Say what?"

"I haven't heard from you. You always try to act like the only reason we haven't spoken is because *I* haven't called *you*."

"Well, you know I like to take things at your pace since you're involved with Darnell."

It infuriated me how he always used my relationship with Darnell to escape fault.

what you do in the dark...

"Like you really give a damn about Darnell and me!"

He wasn't going to get away with it this time.

"Caren, if this is going to be an argument, I don't think we should have it here in public. I *am* a state senatorial candidate, you know."

"Oh yes I know, your most honorable councilman and future state senator, I know."

Noticing the cashier looking at us, he grabbed my arm and pulled me out of the shop leaving the flowers on the counter. The card dropped to the floor as we exited the shop.

Instinctively, I picked it up. It read, "To Veronica, my beautiful wife-to-be. All my love, Robert."

"Who the hell is Veronica?"

"*My* fiancée!" he replied sarcastically.

"You're engaged?"

"Caren, I don't have time to discuss this with you, especially not in public. I'll just say this: You can't have it both ways."

"You never wanted me Robert. You never asked me to leave Darnell for you."

"Now why in God's name would I ask you to do that?"

"Because you said you loved me."

"And what the hell does love have to do with anything?"

"I thought that when you love somebody you try to find a way to be with them. I thought *we* were trying to be together."

"We were together, and it was great. Now it's time for us to move on."

"Just like that."

"Just like that."

He turned and headed back into the shop, picked up the flowers and walked past me as if I weren't even standing there. I stood there, speechless, watching the man who was supposed to *save* me from drowning in a sea of boredom and loneliness with Darnell drift away to seek another mission. He had merely thrown me a life preserver and left me to get to safety on my own.

Suddenly, he turned and walked back toward me.

"Caren," he said taking my hand in his while holding the flowers in his other hand, "I didn't mean to hurt you or disappoint you. I've never been exactly sure of what you wanted or expected from this relationship, especially after I asked you to have the abortion. I wasn't even sure of what I was willing to give until now."

He paused and looked at me for a moment, trying to gauge my emotions, I supposed.

"Listen," he continued, "Veronica came back into my life just recently. We were pretty deeply involved some years ago and I don't think either of us had ever gotten over the other. I ran into her when I was in Columbus a couple of months ago and we discovered we still cared for each other very much. Now, that doesn't mean that you never meant anything to me, but Caren, you have to admit, we were over before we began."

He reached for my other hand letting the flowers drop to the floor. He searched my eyes for some kind of reaction. I stood there silently, holding back tears.

"You couldn't possibly have expected me to give you my heart while you were engaged to another man," he started again. "It became even more obvious to me that you still love him when I overheard you talking to him in the basement on Easter. You told him about the abortion. You told me you didn't want anybody to know about it."

"I didn't tell him. He found out."

"Do you love him?"

"I don't know."

"I know. I've always known. That's why it would never work for us. You see, it doesn't matter how he feels about you. I know he doesn't love you the way you deserve to be loved. What matters is how you feel about him and you love him more than he deserves. We could never be as long as he has even the smallest part of your heart. You just wanted me because he wasn't enough. I deserve better than that!"

I was silent. I just stood there, silent. I wanted to say something, but there was nothing to say. I felt a strong powerful connection to this man with whom I had conceived my first child, but he didn't feel the same. I wasn't worthy of him. He was going to start a new life with another woman and I had to accept it.

So I stood there silent, knowing that the slightest word would betray me as I stood there trying to appear unaffected. I nodded in agreement and I waited in that same spot until he picked up his flowers, kissed me on the cheek, told me he'd call me and disappeared into the crowd of last minute Mother's Day shoppers.

****

what you do in the dark . . .

My mother's kitchen was filled with the smell of collard greens, macaroni and cheese and baked chicken with dressing. Carla had cooked the dinner without me. She was a great cook. My mother had taught her well. I spent more time with my father growing up. While Carla was with my mother in the kitchen, I would follow my father around helping him 'fix' things. Once at age four when he was adding another room onto our house, I took his drill and made a big hole in a newly constructed wall while his back was turned.

"Look Daddy, I helping you!" I exclaimed.

I remember the frustrated look on his face as he snatched the drill from me and said, "Oh boy! Give me that thang, Gal!" Then, he yelled to my mother, "Mary! Come get this gal! She don' put a hole in the wall!"

I realized over the years that he wasn't very happy with my assistance after hearing the story told several times to friends and relatives, but I could tell he was slightly amused with the memory. I started ending my journal entries, "Miss you Daddy!" in 1988 after he died. A drunk driver ran a red light and smashed into his car. My father suffered serious internal injuries. He died a few days later.

After his death, my mother was almost impossible to please. She acted as if she were the only one who had suffered a loss. I think my father was her best friend. They argued a lot. He cheated sometimes. She lied about money, but they seemed comfortable with their arrangement. My mother played on Carla's and my sympathy for months. We were jumping through hoops trying to make her happy, but all she did was complain.

"Y'all don't care nothin' 'bout me. If your father was here, he'd see to it that these bills got paid. He'd run my errands for me. I don' took care of y'all all these years and now I can't get you to do nothin' for me."

We did everything for her. We shopped for her groceries, cleaned her house, cooked her meals and took care of her business. Nothing was enough. We hardly had time to attend to our own lives. Finally, we resolved to do what we could and leave her to take care of her own responsibilities from time to time.

Then, she resorted to what had caused a lifelong sibling rivalry between my sister and me, comparing.

"Carla is the only one that ever does anything for me."

"Caren is the only daughter I can depend on."

"Carla would never let me go without anything I needed."

"Caren does everything I tell her to do."
"Carla is the only one who talks to me."
"Caren is the only one who gets good grades."
"Carla is the only one who gets along with her teachers."

I tried not to let my mother's taunting get to me, but Carla would get highly upset when she came down on the wrong side of one of my mother's comparisons. I got upset with my mother for causing Carla and me to fight, but I felt helpless to stop it. Knowledge or ignorance of the cause of the war never seemed to make a difference. War was just going to happen. We both fought desperately, Carla, to gain my mother's approval and me, to prove that her approval didn't matter. It angered me that my mother was able to wield so much control over us, but she had set a familial pattern that no one seemed able to break.

She was closer to Carla, but I think she was most proud of me because I had graduated from college and worked for a newspaper. Carla graduated from high school, trained to be a legal secretary, met and married John and had two children. My father would always say he loved both Carla and me the same, but I think we all knew he was more proud of me. He always praised me for how well I did in school. He bragged to friends and family about me all the time. He was especially proud, too, that I had gone to college. He wanted Carla to go, but she just wasn't interested in anymore school.

As I walked through the kitchen in from the side door taking in the tantalizing aroma of Carla's dishes simmering on the stove and baking in the oven, I heard my mother's voice on the telephone over the screams and yells of Carla's children playing with neighborhood kids in the yard.

"No, Girl. That's Carla cookin'. Caren don't cook. She's Miss Career Woman, you know. She supposed to be helpin', but I just heard her come through the door. Yeah, Girl. Cookin' me Mother's Day dinner."

I ran into Carla who came out of the bathroom into the hallway, which was only two or three steps from the entrance to the living room where I was headed.

"What's up Sis?" she greeted me. "You can make the cornbread. Everything else is almost ready."

I nodded, went into the living room and headed toward the sofa. My mother had a small newly decorated living room thanks to Carla's decorating. The light pastel multi-colored sofa was a bit large for the room, but it went well with the light wood tables and multi-colored lamp bases that matched the sofa's fabric. I placed the silk floral arrangement

what you do in the dark . . .

in the center of the cocktail table and placed my mother's card in front of it. There were two pastel blue rocker recliners that brought out one of the colors on the sofa and matched the mini blinds and matching sheers that covered the front window. A large screen color TV sat in direct view from the sofa encased in a light wood entertainment center that also housed a stereo.

My sister had done a great job redecorating after my father died and it helped my mother start her new life without him. I plopped on the sofa with its large comfortable pillow seats and let the cushions engulf and caress me.

"Are you gonna make the cornbread?" Carla pressed.

"Yeah!" I snapped. "Do you mind if I sit down for a minute!"

"Everything is almost done! You haven't done anything else!"

"Well hello, Miss Caren," my mother greeted me as she walked in from her bedroom to join us. "So, you finally decided to make an appearance."

Mary Boogerton's presence was jolting, yet comforting. Her stride was slow and steady. She was probably one of the most self-assured women I'd ever known. She always seemed to be in control. She had wide searching brown eyes that could quickly change from hot to warm to cold right along with her moods.

"Hello Mother," I responded. I always called her Mother whenever I wanted to make her feel important or when she was getting on my nerves. Since I had just arrived and it was Mother's Day, I believed I was trying to make her feel important.

"Carla has really outdone herself today. Do you smell all that good food cookin' in there? I thought you were supposed to be helpin'."

I huffed, rolled my eyes as I walked past her so she couldn't see me do it and went into the kitchen to make the cornbread realizing that maybe I wasn't trying to make her feel important.

"Whew!" she teased. "Looks like somebody's got 'dey habits on today! Where's my Mother's Day gift? And you haven't even told me Happy Mother's Day yet!"

"It's on the table!" I shouted from the kitchen, "Happy Mother's Day!"

I looked through the cupboards now in an attempt to find a baking pan. I was determined to ignore her now. The kitchen had a very homey feel to it. Carla had installed new cabinets that were a light-colored wood. The newly tiled floor was beige, adorned with multi-colored throw rugs. The refrigerator and stove were fairly new and they were almond with brown trim.

I found a baking pan. It was old and blackened from hundreds of uses. My mother still had a lot of old dishes, pots and pans that didn't quite fit in with her newly remodeled kitchen. Carla had a hard time getting Mama to throw away anything. The living room still had several old-fashioned knick-knacks, which looked severely out of place in their new, contemporary environment.

"Oh this is nice," my mother called to me, "especially the money. Thanks Daughter dear!"

Carla sat at the kitchen table watching me. My mother sat in one of the living room recliners, which was in direct view of Carla.

"So, where's Darnell?" Carla went first.

"Spending Mother's Day with *his* mother," I answered to imply that it was a logical deduction.

"Are y'all still getting married next month? You haven't said much about it lately."

"Don't seem like you been makin' any plans either." It was my mother's turn now.

"I guess so," I answered Carla's question and ignored my mother's comment.

"You guess!" Mama shouted. "You don't guess about getting married. Either you are or you ain't!"

I didn't respond.

"Well, when you find out for sho', let me know."

"How come you say, you guess?" Carla asked. "Y'all ain't getting along?"

"We're getting along fine. I just haven't been doing much planning."

"Well, how do you expect to have a wedding with no planning? Do you have a caterer? Have you sent out the invitations? Have you decided where you're going to have the ceremony? You should have asked me if you needed help," Carla went on.

"Jackie's been taking care of the details for the wedding ceremony. Darnell's mother is making the food. Michelle is coordinating everything else. I went with Jackie to church just last month to meet Reverend Peoples in order to set up counseling and arrange for him to officiate the wedding ceremony."

"How come you didn't ask your sister to be in the wedding?"

"I don't know."

what you do in the dark . . .

"That's okay. I don't need to be in her wedding."

"You're gonna learn one day to stop putting your friends before your family. Carla ain't never been like that. She had you in her wedding."

"She can be in the wedding."

"I don't want to be in the wedding now!"

"I don't blame her. I wouldn't want to be no afterthought either!"

"Well, why bother to bring it up then?"

"I just wanted to know why you treat yo' sister so bad."

"I didn't think she wanted to be in it."

"You just didn't want me to be in it. You've never liked me Caren!"

"I don't think she's crazy about either one of us," my mother added.

I didn't respond.

"You don't seem too excited 'bout getting married either if you ask me," she continued.

"Do we have to talk about this?"

Carla and Mama looked at each other and were silent.

After a few moments my mother started to hum one of her favorite Sam Cooke songs, Carla started setting the table. I mixed some Jiffy cornbread mix and put it in the oven.

"Tell you the truth," Mama started again, "I don't know what I'm gonna do about either one of my daughters. One don't know if she's getting married and the other one don't know if she's staying married."

Carla huffed and sat down again, but Mama kept right on talking as if she didn't notice Carla's mood although we were both sure she had.

"I stayed married to your father for 30 years before he died. Couples just ain't like they used to be. In my day, couples stayed together through thick and thin. These lowdown men just leavin' their wives left and right. And now, these women don't wanna take responsibility for these babies they don' laid up and got. Did you know that Johnnie Mae's 18-year-old daughter had an abortion? I just don't know what the world is comin' to. And Johnnie Mae said she was glad she did it. 'Said she didn't wanna be stuck raisin' no grandchildren. I ain't raise my kids like that. I don't care when y'all have kids and who you have'em with. If you get pregnant, just have the baby. We'll just have to make a way somehow. Matter-of-fact, the Lord will make a way! Johnnie Mae need to read her Bible!"

I wanted to crawl into Mama's lap and hug her tightly, confess my sin and beg her for forgiveness. Most of all, I wanted her to hold me and tell me that even though I had done something terribly wrong, she still loved me. I never thought Mama was capable of that kind of love. It seemed like love and approval went together with her. Yet, if she loved me like I realized that I loved the daughter that I aborted, then maybe I had my mother all wrong.

I realized that if I had just allowed my baby to live, I could have forgiven her anything. Mama would have forgiven me for getting pregnant the way I did. I knew that now. I could have kept my daughter, but she wouldn't forgive me for the abortion and God probably wouldn't either.

It was too late now. My daughter was gone. There was no use disappointing my mother by telling her the truth now. I wanted to tell her. I knew she'd be able to tell me if God could ever forgive me for what I did, but from the way she was going on about Johnnie Mae and her daughter, I knew the answer without asking the question.

After the cornbread was done, we all ate. Carla packed up the kids and left shortly after dinner. I stayed a little while with my mother. We played some Sam Cooke and Al Green. I sat quietly on the floor by the stereo while my mother rocked in one of the recliners singing and reminiscing about Daddy.

I was as lonely as she was. I felt more pathetic though. At least she had experienced the love of a good man for thirty years. A man who thought enough of her to marry her and father two children with her. Robert was marrying someone else and had refused to father our child. I didn't even know if I still wanted to marry Darnell and even if I did, I often felt like he didn't really want to marry me.

After a few hours of commiserating with Mama, I decided to go home. The day had been draining. I just wanted to crawl into bed and forget this painful Mother's Day that I had spent with my mother and not the mother-to-be that I should have been. I would have been about six months along by now.

The door buzzer was ringing as I entered my apartment. I reached inside and hit the intercom, "Yes!"

"It's me. Mark. Buzz me up!"

I hit the buzzer to unlock the door and I left the door to my apartment open for him to enter. I was glad Mark had come to visit. I needed him. I hadn't talked to him since Easter when he told me that his mother had died. I didn't know what to say to him. He seemed so upset that day he had called crying.

what you do in the dark . . .

Frankly, I didn't like talking to him when he was like that. I hoped he was okay now. He appeared in my living room after a few moments holding a bouquet of carnations.

"Happy Mother's Day, Caren!" He shoved the flowers into my face and took a seat on my sofa.

"What's your problem? And what's with the Happy Mother's Day. That's a terrible thing to joke about. You know I'm not a mother."

"Oh, you're a mother alright!"

"Mark, what's going on? Why are talking to me like this?"

"Somebody needs to remind you what it feels like to lose someone you love to death!"

"What are you talking about?"

"I just wanted you to remember that when a life is lost, people hurt. But maybe you don't understand that because the life you lost, you took. So why would you care about anybody else dying!"

"You're talking crazy! Is this about your mother?"

"Yeah, you damn right it's about my mother. Caren, I've been good to you. I held you when you were pregnant. I even offered to help you with the baby if you wanted to keep it. I comforted you when you were lonely for yo' fiance. I was there for you through it all. I've been a true friend or at least I've tried to be. But when I needed you, you wasn't there for me. You didn't even come to my mama's funeral. You didn't even ask me if there was anything you could do. You didn't even send a damn sympathy card! And you promised if I ever needed you that you'd be there for me. No wonder Darnell or Robert don't want to spend no time with you. You ain't got no room in yo' life for nobody but you!"

He sat there staring at me, waiting for a response. I was stunned. Mark had never spoken so harshly to me before. He stood up, shook his head in contempt, then he stormed out.

I stood there for a moment, ashamed of how I had let Mark down, hurt by some of his cutting words, but to my surprise, I started to smile. For the first time I realized that I really meant something to Mark. It was important to him that I share this burden with him. I was touched. It felt good to be needed by someone, to matter to someone. He was angry because I was not there for him. I mattered to Mark and I vowed to myself that from now on he was going to matter to me. I put his flowers in a vase and placed them on the nightstand next to my bed. When I went to sleep, I dreamed I heard the footsteps again. Tiny footsteps. I still couldn't catch them.

That next day, Monday morning, it was back to work again and more than likely another sparring match with Jessie. I reluctantly sat down at my computer, looked up to meet her face and realized that there was no hissing Jessie poised to strike. I logged onto my computer, and began to read my e-mail. I had one, from whom else, Jessie:

I'll be in Columbus this week. I know you'll miss me. When I return, I should have some dirt on your boy, Turner. He's about to take a fall, Girlfriend. Hope you don't hit the ground with him. 'Fess up before it's too late. See you next week!

What in the world was Jessie talking about? What could she possibly find out in Columbus that would affect me? What did my affair with Robert and the abortion have to do with it? Why did I have to confess?

Okay, I reasoned. If Jessie could confirm that Robert had a child aborted, that would reveal his stand on the abortion issue as pro-choice. This could cost him the election. That much was clear. But why was Jessie in Columbus? Why was she concerned about this family, the Kirklands and their political connections? What did they have to do with Robert? Why had Robert left me in the dark about everything? Why didn't he ever mention his interest in running for state senator during any of our interviews? Why would he suddenly abandon his position as councilman that he once seemed so dedicated to? What did I have to do with it? Why was Jessie threatening me about telling the truth? It seemed that she was after something much bigger than just uncovering the affair between Robert and me and the abortion of our child. I'd talk to Marge, I decided, but as I got up from my desk, I noticed Marge approaching me.

"Good morning Caren."

"Hi Marge. I was just about to come talk with you."

"What about?"

I hesitated. I hadn't decided how I wanted to approach the subject without revealing what I didn't want Marge to know.

"Uh, Councilman Turner's bid for state senator."

"That's Jessie's story," she answered matter-of-factly.

"I know, but she asks me a lot of questions about Councilman Turner and we've become pretty good friends. Actually, he's my fiancé's first cousin. I'm worried about him. It looks like she's out to get him."

"That's her job, Caren. If there's something the public needs to know before he's elected, I hired her to uncover it. Caren, you have to

what you do in the dark . . .

learn how to remain objective if you're going to make it in this business. You can't make friends with all the people you interview. And as far as his relationship to your fiancé, you can't let that interfere with your objectivity either. Come on now, I may need you to watch our backs on this one. Jessie may decide to go off on her own. I need you to keep a clear head. You implied yourself that we may not be able to trust Jessie. Now check yourself and keep your eyes and ears open. I'll fill you in more when the time is right."

"Marge. I'm scared!" I blurted out, "I need to know what's going on!"

"Scared?" Marge looked bewildered. She stepped back from me obviously surprised by my outburst.

I quickly took my seat and tried to compose myself. "I'm overreacting I guess."

"Yes, maybe you are." She gave me a concerned look. "Do you need some time off?"

"No. I'll be alright."

"Good. I won't send you on any assignments today. Just rewrite the stack of news releases that are in the bin. It's a slow day; the other reporters can handle the outside assignments. It'll be good to have you here in the office in case we hear something from Jessie that needs to be checked out here in Cleveland. So relax. Get a cup of coffee or something. Then, get started on those news releases. Alright."

"No problem Marge. I'll take care of them."

Deborah Marbury

no bride in june

Congratulations! I thought it would have been me.

Darnell's whole family was all abuzz about Robert's upcoming wedding to Veronica who, I learned through Jessie's column, was a prominent lawyer from a wealthy family with strong political ties. The Kirklands. All the pictures that featured Robert and Veronica made them appear to be a very attractive, happy couple.

Robert's parents were staying with the Jennings family in order to help with preparations for the wedding scheduled for the third Saturday in June. Darnell and I were supposed to have our wedding on the second Saturday in June. That is, until he came to me with a request that we postpone in light of Robert's impending nuptials.

"I have some bad news," he started as we were driving to the movies on the first Sunday in June. It was a very dark evening as I recall. A thundershower threatened all of Cuyahoga County and there we were driving around like we had nothing to fear. It gave me an uneasy feeling, though, like God was angry about something. It reminded me of when He made it rain for forty days and forty nights after telling Noah to build the ark. I'd been told about that story many times in Sunday school as a child.

"What is it?" I asked alarmed.

"My family thinks we should postpone our wedding. Robert is getting married, you know. It's supposed to be a big society thing. Might

what you do in the dark...

help his chances of getting elected too. We all want to help. I know you're probably disappointed, but we can get married anytime. Besides, I've been thinking about some of the things Reverend Peoples has been telling us to consider in our counseling sessions and I think maybe we need a little more time anyway."

Reverend Peoples had been talking to us about loving each other the way God loves us. Agape love. That's what he called it. Said we needed to make sure God was first, and Darnell should come right after God for me. I should come right after God for Darnell. He told us to read I Corinthians 13 and from that try to understand what love really means. He also told us that we should be two whole and complete people in and of ourselves. We should not try to complete one another or feel a need to be completed by the other, but rather we should complement each other.

Darnell looked worried at a lot of our sessions, doubtful. I really didn't pay much attention to Reverend Peoples. His advice was for people that planned on going to church all the time. I just wanted him to marry us. I could handle any problems that came up in the marriage on my own if we ever made it to the altar.

Except, my secret always seemed to be standing between us like a big brick wall, so high we couldn't get over it, so low we couldn't get under it, and so wide we couldn't get around it. He still hadn't forgiven me for conceiving someone else's child and deep inside I knew he didn't really believe that I had conceived the way I described in that note.

Our conversations had become strained. I didn't want to make love with him anymore. I told him that since it had been so long already we should just wait until we got married, so that our first night as man and wife would be special. He had started to come around for visits less and less. Our relationship was unraveling slowly, but surely. I was afraid we were never going to marry and I wasn't even sure if I wanted to marry him anymore. My heart was so broken over Robert's upcoming wedding, I was sure that I was in love with Robert.

"I'll send out notices tomorrow. There's still time." I responded, relaxing from my tensed state.

Darnell seemed surprised by my lack of protest. He didn't question it though. I guess he thought he shouldn't look a gift horse in the mouth. I was getting tired of pretending, trying to save something that just wasn't salvageable. I was hurt that both these men had so easily dismissed me. I was prone to delusions of self-indulgence and I wanted to believe that I was the star of everyone's story, at least those lives I had touched significantly.

Trying to be honest with myself now, I remained silent as Darnell drove. I didn't want my epiphany to be disturbed by meaningless dialogue with him about issues that had most certainly outgrown our sincere concern.

We went through the motions of the evening's events silently. Only saying what we needed to say. Darnell's uneasiness, I'm sure, came from his assumption that I was unhappy about his announcement that he wanted to postpone our wedding. He had probably resolved to let me suffer in silence.

I contemplated and evaluated my feelings about Robert's wedding, as well as my own cancelled wedding. What surprised me most was that I kept wondering what Mark was doing. I felt so unsettled. I didn't know where I stood with him now. I hoped he would forgive me for being so insensitive about his mother's death. I hoped he would give me the chance to prove to him that I really valued our friendship.

I was so lost in thought that the evening seemed to pass without my being quite sure what happened. The storm never broke. The thunder just rumbled every now and then, as if God, though still angry, had decided to give us another chance. We saw a movie. We got something to eat as usual, but what happened in between seemed a blur.

Finally, Darnell pulled into my parking lot. He told me that he needed to get home so he could get up early for work in the morning. I thanked him for taking me out. Something I did from time to time to assure him that he wasn't being taken for granted.

I'd read in Essence or Ebony that thanking a man for a date was a good way to keep a relationship together. I was programmed on 'keep your man' mode. I had become so accustomed to working to keep him that I didn't even bother to check to see if I still wanted him.

****

I was still reflective the next day at work. I didn't want to be there. It was hard to think about interviewing people, researching stories and writing articles when I felt so misdirected and so without a purpose. Was I supposed to try to win Robert's love? Was I supposed to try to rebuild my relationship with Darnell? I began to lose interest in both those

what you do in the dark...

goals, mostly because I knew I couldn't attain them. I thought about calling Mark, but I didn't think he wanted to hear from me right now.

"Sssoo, there's a ribbon-cutting ceremony for Robert Turner's community center today. Marge thought you should cover it with me. She acts like I can't do anything without you. Like she doesn't trust me or something."

Jessie's eyes pierced through me for a response. I knew that Marge was only trying to be fair to me after seeing how upset I seemed to be about Jessie's investigation. I also knew that the seed I'd planted about Jessie's probable disloyalty was starting to take root.

I needed something to break where Jessie was concerned. I was sick of her! She watched me like a hawk and dropped hints that she still suspected a relationship between Robert and me even though he was marrying Veronica.

At times I felt that I didn't have a whole lot of motivation for keeping my affair with Robert a secret anymore other than my reputation with my mother. Who wanted to hear her rant and rave for months on end about how whorishly I had behaved and how I was going to hell for having an abortion? I could care less about Robert's career. Robert didn't care about hurting me and my days with Darnell were numbered anyway. The writing was on the wall. Yet, I didn't want a break up with Darnell to be my fault.

So, I decided that I was not going to let Jessie uncover my secret. She could suspect all she wanted. She couldn't prove a thing. I needed to make sure that she never could. I decided to follow another one of Michelle's theories, although not her invention, but one she swore by. Keep your friends close and your enemies closer. If Jessie was getting closer to uncovering my secret, I needed to get the news first hand so that I could try to head her off.

I was on pretty decent terms with Jessie now. I learned to tolerate her. I had even become intrigued with what I thought she might know about Robert and these Kirklands. I wanted to know too.

"Sure Jessie. What time?" I responded to her request about the assignment.

"Great! We need to leave in an hour. You can ride with me."

"No problem. I'll be ready."

I joined Jessie in her fire engine red 1990 Corvette an hour later and we were off to cover the opening of Robert's community center. I was impressed with Jessie's car. Her freelance projects must certainly pay well, I thought. I knew she couldn't afford this car on any **AA Times** salary.

As we rode along with Jessie blaring 93FM WZAK, I thought about the impassioned and dedicated man that sat down to lunch with me almost a year ago to discuss his plans to open a community center and what it would mean for his constituents.

He spoke so enthusiastically about how this center was going to give the young people in the neighborhood something to do after school, keep them off the streets. It would provide an opportunity for senior citizens to fellowship with one another during the day. Local businesses could hold seminars, forums and recreational activities there to help strengthen, educate and rebuild families in the community. It would also house a daycare center.

He described how local businesses, city, state and federal government as well as the constituents could contribute to this venture and help it come to fruition. Then, he talked about the dinner dance that was planned to help raise funds with the help of the people. That was the dinner dance that gave birth to our illicit relationship.

I took notes hurriedly while he spoke passionately and took the most distinguished looking bites out of his burger. Every now and then, he would stop talking and eating, his eyes focusing on me as if he had just discovered I was there. He looked at me as if my presence distracted him and then he would refocus and continue. I was flattered.

"Ssso, I heard that you attended a fund raiser for this center with Councilman Turner this past November. What was it? A dinner dance?" Jessie yelled over the wind and the radio.

"What?" I responded trying to dismiss my reminiscing momentarily. Jessie turned down the radio.

"You and Robert attended a dinner dance together, right?"

"Yeah, we did. I wanted to talk to the guests and find out what their thoughts were on the project. Publicity. You know."

"Ssso, who'd you talk to?"

"Wow! That was back in November. I don't remember."

"Person I talked to said you guys never left each other's side."

"Okay, Jessie. What are you getting at?"

"You and Robert were involved. It was his baby you aborted and that's why you and your fiancé are always having problems."

what you do in the dark . . .

"You have a great imagination. That might be good for fiction, but not real life. You might get sued if don't get your facts straight before you try to print any of that crap in a newspaper article."

"Caren, you were seen kissing him in his car that night in the parking lot. You guys were dancing so close at the fundraiser that you couldn't get a breath of fresh air between you, according to my sources."

"Well your sources are wrong. We're friends. He's my fiancé's cousin."

"Yeah. That's really going to make this story juicy. State Senatorial Candidate Aborts Baby With Cousin's Fiancée. Sounds like a man you can trust. You know if you count the weeks between the night the fundraiser was held and the day you appeared at the clinic, it adds up to just about how far along you were when you aborted."

"Where do you come up with these ideas?"

"I don't come up with them. I just uncover them."

"Why would you want to hurt me or Robert like that? What have we ever done to you?"

"I just want you to confirm that the jerk fathered the child you aborted and I'll keep your name out of it. It's him I want, not you. But if I have to use other people to get to the story, then I can't protect you. The whole truth is going to come out. Maybe if we can break the story with the emphasis on him, we can just downplay your role. The people need to know what this slime ball is really like before they elect him in November. And I'm going to be the journalist who gives the people the truth, with or without your help. I'm just trying to look out for you. It would be a lot easier for you if you helped."

"Robert would make a great state senator. He deserves to be elected."

"Still hooked on 'em even after he dumped you. He must have really put it on you, Girlfriend. Maybe I oughta try it out."

"That's disgusting."

"Jealous, huh?"

"Robert and I are just friends. There's no reason for me to be jealous."

"Stick to the lie. I like that in you. Stick to your story, Girl. It's going to bring you down, but you gotta do what you gotta do."

"I'm telling the truth Jessie."

"So if you're telling the truth. Whose baby did you abort?"

I was speechless. I wasn't prepared to answer that question. I knew she wouldn't believe that story I gave Darnell. She also wouldn't believe that I would abort my fiancé's child. She knew I had been too upset about the abortion to do it unless I was trying to hide my pregnancy and why would I want to hide being pregnant by the man I was about to marry?

"That's none of your business, Jessie."

"That's because it was Robert's," she smiled teasingly trying to lighten the mood between us, but working slyly to gain my confidence. I smiled too, then turned to look out of the window. I stared at the houses and buildings we passed until we arrived at the community center.

"Your fiancé works at the post office downtown right?"

"Yeah, why?"

"Ask him if he knows my sister, Janice Bassett. She's a clerk there."

"I'll be sure to mention it to him." I paused, then said, "There is one thing I'd like to know, Jessie."

"What's that?"

"If you could prove that I slept with Robert, just how do you plan to reveal that I aborted his baby without breaking patient confidentiality. I wouldn't mind driving this Corvette you know."

"*You'll* admit it when I'm done with you. I won't have to risk anything." She smiled and pointed toward the building. "There's Veronica Kirkland going up the steps. She looks great doesn't she? She has a lot of style."

"Yeah, she's got it goin' on," I sighed blandly. "What's the story on her? You mentioned trying to find out if Robert had some connection to the Kirkland family and she's a Kirkland. What's goin' on?"

"Ssso, now you want some information from me. I give as good as I get, Girlfriend."

"For the last time, I don't have anything to give you Jessie."

"Then, I guess you can't get anything from me, now can you?"

"Fine." I got out of the car and slammed the door.

"Easssy on my 'vette, Girlfriend."

She got out of the car and followed me to the modest-sized, newly constructed white building with the words, "Ward One Community Center" protruding from the building's wall next to its glass doors that were held closed by a big red ribbon.

what you do in the dark . . .

Robert, Veronica, the center's newly appointed director and a representative from the mayor's office were standing in front of the door. A couple of cameramen, three photographers, one I recognized as our own and two other newspaper reporters were standing on the steps in front of Robert. A couple more TV cameras were approaching.

I felt queasy as I walked with Jessie to join the other reporters. I tried to look interested, but not too interested as I came within Robert's view of me. He looked as if he tensed somewhat at my presence, and that relaxed me a little.

I got a closer look at Veronica and tensed again. She was wearing an expensive pastel blue linen two-piece suit with a light gray silk blouse and pastel blue pumps. She wore her hair in a very elegantly styled French roll with a long piece of hair coming down on the right side of her face.

She had smooth, banana-colored skin and beautiful, extremely straight white teeth that sparkled when she smiled. She smiled a lot, too, especially for the cameras as she clung elegantly to Robert's side. She looked exquisite standing next to Robert and it infuriated me.

They looked like the picture perfect couple, the kind of couple that a handsome, young politician was expected to belong to. I felt inadequate, like all those looks Robert gave me during our first lunch were a lie. He couldn't have possibly been distracted by my presence if he could date women like Veronica.

"Ssso, get a grip Girlfriend. Your cat claws are showing." Jessie said interrupting my inspection.

"What do you need me to do here?" I asked flippantly.

"I'm going to tell our photographer to get some shots of the ceremony and the building. You talk to Robert and Veronica and I'll talk to the mayor's office and the center's director after the ceremony. They've agreed to give us interviews first."

"I don't want to talk to Robert and Veronica!" I protested almost loud enough for everyone to hear.

"A little touchy, aren't we? You've been talking to Robert about the planning of this center for a year. It makes perfect sense that you should talk to him about its completion and grand opening. Marge insisted on it."

"Damn!" I whispered.

"Now, I wonder, just why you wouldn't want to talk to your favorite councilman who sent you flowers for Valentine's Day, who slow danced with you and kissed you at his last fundraiser and whose career and projects you've covered for a year? Could it be Veronica that's got your panties in a bunch?"

"*You've* got my panties in a bunch. I'm tired of your constant insinuations. You think I don't see what you're trying to do by insisting that I interview those two. It's not going to work. There's nothing for you to see. I'll talk to them, okay! No problem."

"Good! I'll be watching, I mean, I'll talk to the others."

We stood there quietly on the steps while the mayor's office gave commendations to Robert for his work in the community. Then, the director voiced his vision for the center. Next, Robert and Veronica talked about their hopes for the center and ended with a statement of their desire for the center to still be around for their children to enjoy.

Finally, the ribbon was cut and the media and other distinguished guests were given a tour of the facility. I made it through the interview with Robert and Veronica. Jessie didn't get the rise out of me she intended. I managed to control my envy by concentrating on Veronica's big nose. She was pretty in spite of it, but it definitely lost her a few points on the beauty rating scale.

She had stubby fingernails too. They weren't nicely manicured like mine. You would think a woman with that much style, class and money would keep her hands manicured. Her feet were big too. I kept kicking them under the table throughout the interview, accidentally, of course. I could tell by the way she grimaced whenever my foot hit hers that she must have had corns, which really made me happy because I knew Robert loved to kiss toes and fondle feet.

Of course, I did almost fall apart when after I asked her, "How do you think your career plans will change after you're married?" she replied, "I'm sorry. Are you asking me or Robert?"

"You," I said.

"Oh, I thought you were looking at him."

****

A couple of weeks later, it was Robert and Veronica's wedding day and I declined Darnell's invitation to attend as his guest. Cramps, I told him. I decided it was time to reconcile with Mark. I couldn't wait for the festivities to be underway so I could be assured of being left alone. It was around 8 p.m. when I finally called Mark. I had rehearsed apologies,

what you do in the dark . . .

made mental agendas for our evening together and petitioned God all day for Mark to forgive me. I was ready to be with my friend again.

Mark must have missed me too because he didn't hesitate to accept my apology and my invitation to come over. We watched the end of a NBA championship playoff game. We snacked on chips, dip and pop. We talked about what had been going on in our lives since we last spoke.

"My mom left the house to me. It's all paid for. I just have to pay taxes on it twice a year. I got a job doing janitorial work for Metro Hospital. It pays great. I can afford to take care of the utilities, keep groceries in the house and have a little something for myself," Mark announced to me proudly.

"That's great Mark."

"I stopped selling weed too. I'm ready to make some changes in my life, Bae. I want my life to have more meaning."

"How so?"

"I don't know. I think I want to get closer to God."

"That's good."

"You think so?"

"Yeah." It touched me that Mark still wanted my approval and my encouragement.

"I've really missed you, Bae, but I've realized some things about you too."

"Yeah. Like what?"

"You ain't all that."

"What?"

"You ain't all that. You know you be tryin' to act like you so much better than me. Like I ain't good enough for you or somethin'. And I was gon' give you that because you educated, independent, classy and all that, but yo' head is messed up."

"What?"

"You messed up in the head, Bae." He took my hand in his. "Look, I'm just tryin' to be real with you. You know how much I care about you. I ain't tryin' to hurt yo' feelings or nothin' like that, but you livin' in some kinda fantasy world. You killin' babies 'cause you think havin' a baby without bein' married is gonna hurt yo' image. You got yo' man thinkin' that you ain't never slept with nobody but him and you sleepin' with his first cousin 'cause he's a politician and you tryin' to make a come up. That's messed up Bae. I've lost a lot of respect for you. You need to check yo'self."

"If that's what you think about me Mark, then why are you here? I don't need to hear this. My fiancé has cancelled our wedding and the man I cheated on him with is marrying another woman. I've lost out and I'm hurting. I don't need you to throw it all up in my face."

"I'm here because I am yo' friend, Bae. I always have been. Life is short. I don't want to see you treat yo'self like a loser. I want you to be happy. You're a treasure, don't treat yo'self like a tramp."

"How am I treating myself like a tramp?"

"By letting men use you. Darnell has used you since you were in high school and Robert used you to get his career off the ground and to set him up for a woman with money and connections. Without all the press you gave him in those newspaper articles you wrote, that woman he's marrying probably wouldn't have given him the time of day."

"Robert said they were involved before."

"Yeah well, if she had wanted him for what he was, they woulda never split up. She wants what you made him."

Mark and I talked for hours. At eleven, we decided to watch the news. They showed clips of Robert and Veronica's wedding in the upcoming highlights and announced they would give an update on the sit-in at Cleveland State for the former Vice President of Minority Affairs. Mark put his arm around me and we snuggled close on my sofa.

"Are you okay?" he asked when the clips of Robert and Veronica aired.

"Sure. I'm fine."

"When you realize how special you are, you'll get married too Bae. You'll see."

When the news came back on, the first thing they started to talk about was Robert and Veronica's wedding. They showed quick clips of the community center announcing some of Robert's accomplishments as city councilman of Ward One. They talked about some high profile cases that Veronica had won in Columbus, none of which meant anything to me. They said she was the daughter of State Auditor, Vincent Kirkland and his brother George Kirkland was a close friend of the Governor's as well as a high-ranking official of his staff.

"I wish I knew what was behind Robert's marrying her." I said more to myself than to Mark.

what you do in the dark . . .

"Are you still hung up on him? He married her because that's who he wants to be with, Bae."

"No Mark. It's more than that. Something's not right about them."

"Let it go, Bae. He's with her now."

"No, really Mark. Jessie Bassett is on to something that has to do with the Kirkland family, Robert's election and this impending legislation on abortion. There's a connection, but nobody's talking."

"That's deep, but why do you care? Robert's not your problem anymore."

"I wish I didn't have to care, but because of my abortion of Robert's child, Jessie's targeted me in her investigation. She's out to make a name for herself and exposing Robert's stand on the abortion issue is going to be the hottest news in Cleveland and in Ohio if she can pull it off."

"Do you think she will?"

"She knows I had an abortion. She suspects Robert and I had something going on. She can also guess that the child I aborted was not Darnell's. She knows the truth. She just can't prove it."

"So what you gonna do?"

"I don't know. What can I do?"

"Can she prove it was Robert's baby?"

"I don't think so. How could she?"

"He went to the clinic with you. Did she see him?"

"No. If she had, she would have said so by now."

"Did anybody see him?"

"Protesters."

"Do you think they were close enough to recognize him?"

"No. We were huddled close together and he was hiding me from them. I think he even held his coat up to shield us from their view."

"I don't know Bae. That may be where you messed up. Have you ever been to his house?"

"No."

"So y'all made the baby here or at a hotel?"

"Here."

"Well, you know Mrs. Bagley across the hall is nosy as hell. You think she ever saw him over here."

"I don't know. I never paid it any attention."

"You guys wasn't thinkin' at all."

"Well, just because he visited me in my apartment doesn't mean we had sex."

"That's true, but people are gonna wonder what he needed to discuss with you at your apartment that you couldn't talk about at his office during regular business hours."

"Okay Mark that's enough. I can't worry over this anymore. What's done is done. Let's just hope that Jessie won't find out anything else."

"Fine. Look, I hope you don't mind, but I need a joint. Can I fire one up? My nerves are just shot between missin' my mama and worryin' 'bout you."

"I thought you were giving up weed."

"I said I wasn't gonna sell it. I didn't say nothin' 'bout smokin' it. Maybe I'll stop eventually."

"Well, if you must," I conceded. I moved away from him as he rolled his joint and lit it.

I watched him from the sofa as he sat on the living room floor smoking the joint as if I weren't even there. He had never smoked around me before and I didn't really want to be around him anymore. I laid my head on the arm of the sofa and closed my eyes and wished he would leave.

The next morning was Sunday. I didn't wake up until 11. I was still cuddled up on the living room sofa. Mark was sprawled out on the floor surrounded by about five empty bottles of beer. I rubbed the sleep from my eyes and sat up on the sofa. Why hadn't he gone home last night? He was a pitiful sight. He was so ghetto, I thought.

There was no way he could ever be my man. He seemed so smart sometimes, but other times he seemed so dumb. It was daytime and I didn't want Mark around anymore. I didn't want anyone to see him leaving my apartment in the daytime. I didn't need him to comfort me anymore. I got up from the sofa and nudged his arm with my foot.

"Mark! Get up!"

He rolled over slowly and rubbed his eyes. "Yeah. What's up?"

"It's 11:00 in the morning. You better get up and go home."

"Why? Ain't nobody waitin' for me there."

"I'm about to go out," I lied.

"Oh. Where you goin' on a Sunday mornin'? Church? Let's go together. I'd like to spend the day with you."

"Mark. I can't spend the day with you. I have things to do. Come on. Get up. I'll call you later, okay."

He sat up on the floor and fumbled around for his E-Z widers. He put them in his pocket and started picking up the beer bottles.

what you do in the dark . . .

"A brother can't get no breakfast 'fore he go home?" he teased.

"Mark. I don't have time to cook. I have to go. Now, come on. Get up and go home."

"Alright. Chill. I'm goin'."

He got up slowly and tried to brush himself off and straighten himself up, but he still had that 'ready rose' look, as my mother would say. He stumbled a few steps and then headed for the door. I followed him.

"Can a brother get a good-bye hug or kiss or somethin'?" He stretched his arms out to me while struggling to keep from falling. I gave him a quick hug accompanied by a peck on the cheek.

"Come on. Get out of here," I urged, "I'll call you once I'm in for the evening."

"How come you only call me at night?" he asked as I backed him into the hallway.

"I don't only call you at night Mark. Come on now. We'll spend the day together another time. Alright?"

"Alright. Call me."

"Okay I will."

"Oh, and Bae?"

"Yes Mark."

"I love you."

"Love you too."

Deborah Marbury

julies

Using lies as alibis, just a devil in disguise.

We planned a big cookout at my mother's house for the fourth of July. Darnell and I made plans to each spend the day with our own families, and get together later that evening to see fireworks at the Garfield Heights Metropark.

I invited Jackie and Michelle over my mother's house and Carla invited a couple of her friends. I wanted to invite Mark, but I still wasn't ready to bring Mark around my friends and family. Besides, he was just a friend and I didn't want anyone to get the wrong idea about our relationship.

I decided that I would call Mark the next day. A couple of my mother's friends, her sister and brother and my father's two sisters and two brothers were coming as well. My mother was excited about the annual Ward One parade that was scheduled to come through our neighborhood sometime that day. She and Carla were decorating the front porch in preparation. They put up a big banner that said, "Congratulations on your Wedding State Senator Turner!" My mother had several 'Elect Robert Turner for State Senator' signs planted in her front yard.

They set up the porch furniture, brought out the stereo speakers and put a pitcher of lemonade and other refreshments on the table in order to make everything just right for them to sit and watch the parade go by.

what you do in the dark . . .

I was a bit less excited about the event. I did nothing to prepare for it. I sat on the hood of my car in the driveway where I could see my paternal uncle, CJ, who lived just a couple of streets over, firing up the grill.

WZAK 93FM blared from my car radio as I alternated watching my uncle in the backyard and my sister's boys in the front yard jumping over the signs. My niece, Sheila was on the porch with my mother and sister, waiting for His Highness to ride by in the royal parade. Jackie and Michelle pulled up one behind the other into my mother's driveway and parked behind my sister's car, which was parked behind mine.

"What's up, Girls?" I hollered to my lifelong friends.

"Heeey!" They sang to greet me in unison, sounding like Wanda, Jamie Foxx's **In Living Color** character.

They joined me on the hood of my car. It sank a little under the weight. Michelle was wearing sunglasses and hot orange jean shorts with a yellow cut off shirt that revealed her flat belly while hiding its button beneath the top snap of her shorts. Her high-heeled orange and yellow sandals showed off pedicured feet and orange nail polish with yellow nail art that matched her fingernails and outfit.

Jackie was wearing a long, multi-colored sundress with African print, which favored yellow over the other colors. The three of us had been accustomed since high school to getting our fair share of attention from men, but somehow it didn't seem to stop each of us from feeling inadequate in one area or another. Inadequacies that seemed to direct the paths we followed in life. Michelle to money and sex, Jackie to God and church and me to education and self-determination.

"Jessie was looking for you Friday," Jackie told me teasingly. She knew I didn't like Jessie, but she wasn't sure why. She made comments like that to see if I would share something with her.

"Jessie can kiss my behind," I pouted and pulled my legs up on top of the car's hood and wrapped my arms around my knees.

"What's up with Jessie?" Michelle inquired. "She still causin' problems?"

"What problems has she been causin'?" Jackie asked.

"She's been trying to uncover some dirt on Councilman Turner," I told her.

"Oh, no wonder you don't like her," Jackie replied. "I know you don't like nobody sayin' nothin' bad 'bout Councilman Turner!" She mimicked a Kim Wayans' character from **In Living Color**.

"He ain't all that!" Michelle retorted.

"How do you know?" Jackie asked.

I gave Michelle a look to let her know that I didn't want Jackie to know about my affair with Robert.

"I just know," she responded finally. She gave me a look of her own, which let me know that she didn't approve of me hiding secrets from Jackie.

"He has a good public record," Jackie defended.

"He may have a good *public* record, but it's his *private* record I'm worried about."

"What are you talking about Michelle?"

"Are you gonna tell her?"

"Michelle!"

"Girl, you grown! Why you so afraid of what she's gonna say? She ain't yo' mama!"

I put my head on top of my knees as I embraced them tighter.

"I had an affair with Robert and he dumped me for Veronica," I admitted more to my knees than to Jackie.

"I told you he was a player! I told you he just wanted to make you another notch on his belt! How could you sleep with him when you're supposed to be marrying Darnell?"

"I don't know," I sulked. I let go of my knees and allowed my legs to stretch full length while sliding my bottom off the car until my feet hit the concrete driveway and brought my body to an abrupt stop. I leaned against the car and looked down at my black biker shorts from which healthy thighs and legs emerged toward athletic-socked ankles and Nike tennis-shoed feet.

"Look," Michelle jumped in, "Darnell's been steppin' out on her, leavin' her all alone and Robert's been after her for a year. He's been tellin' her all that good romantic stuff Darnell ain't been tellin' her. He's been sendin' her flowers and takin' her to lunch and dinner. Darnell's been neglectin' her. She's been lonely and hell, Robert's fine! Who wouldn't give in?"

"I wouldn't," Jackie answered immediately.

"You don't know what you would do. You've never walked in her shoes. You ain't that damn holy. You get lonely sometimes too. You get on my nerves wit' yo' holier than thou self!"

"Don't get mad at me 'cause I got morals!"

what you do in the dark . . .

"Well if you so godly, then why don't you show a little compassion sometimes? Ain't y'all church people supposed to show some love and understanding sometimes? What y'all call it, Christian charity? Damn!"

"It's okay Michelle. Jackie is just trying to help."

"Well, she needs to try a little harder, so what's up with this Jessie Bassett at work? What's the deal with her?"

They rolled their eyes at each other, but they weren't mad at each other. They never agreed on anything and they were used to it.

"Yeah, I wanna know why y'all can't get along either. Is it because she took over your story on Robert Turner?"

"No Jackie. It's because she's also an abortion counselor. She counseled me. I had an abortion. She believes it was Robert's child."

"Shut up!" Jackie exclaimed like Little Richard.

Michelle followed. "Ain't that deep?"

"You ain't lying," Jackie gasped. "No wonder she asks so many questions about your whereabouts. She checks the reporters' log all the time for your weekly comings and goings. One day, she requested logs from a year back. I saw her tapping her pen on the days you went to Councilman Turner's office like she was counting them. So, does she have anything on you?"

"She mentioned something about someone seeing us kissing at the dinner dance in November."

"Oh you ain't tell me y'all went to that dinner dance."

"I don't tell you a lot of things, Jackie."

"Well, I thought we were friends."

"With friends like you who needs enemies?" Michelle jumped in.

Jackie looked perplexed. "I've been a good friend to you. To both of you," she said glaring at Michelle.

"You too damn judgmental! You think you know everything. If it ain't done yo' way, then it ain't right. Everybody don't think the way you do, Miss Thang!"

"Caren?"

"You do judge a lot." I tried not to hurt her feelings.

Jackie folded her arms and started to pace in front of me.

"So why's your abortion so important to Jessie?" she asked.

"Because Robert is running for a state senate seat and there's an important abortion issue coming up for a vote in the state legislature. He's been dodging his stand on the abortion because he knows it could cost him the election. Jessie wants him exposed as a pro-choice advocate. She knows that if she's the one to reveal his stand on the issue it would be a big story for her."

"You gotta admire her ambition," Michelle teased.

"Do you think you or Robert can stop her? Keep this whole thing under wraps?" Jackie questioned with concern.

"I don't know."

"Kick her nosy behind!" Michelle asserted, "I bet she wouldn't be all up in my business like that."

"I can't do that, Michelle. I'm a professional."

"You're a professional from 9 to 5. At 5:01, you can follow that tramp to her house. Then, you'll be two people settlin' a disagreement. I say beat her natural Black behind! I bet you that'll stop her from mindin' other folks business! You want me to do it. I'll stomp her 'til her nose bleeds!"

"Michelle, cut it out! You're trippin'!" I teased her.

"Good afternoon people of the #1 Ward in the City of Cleveland. The ward where fantasies do come true. We made the community center a reality and with your support, we can make my election to the state senate a reality! This is your councilman and future state senator, Robert Turner, wishing you all a Happy Independence Day! And what better way to celebrate the birth of a free country than by exercising your right to vote in the general election in November."

Robert's voice came booming through a megaphone over the sounds of the John F. Kennedy High School's marching band playing, **Fantasy** by Guy.

"Speak of the devil," Jackie murmured moving toward the trunk of my car.

I could see my mother and sister sitting on the porch. My mother was waving excitedly as the parade passed. The participants walked by slowly smiling and waving to us and the other neighbors who were sitting on their porches.

The parade wasn't very long. There were a couple of community groups, Kennedy's drill team and marching band, Robert was bringing up the rear with his campaign staff walking ahead of his old style black and white Cadillac with the drop top let back.

Robert and Veronica were seated on the top of the back seat with their feet resting on the car seat. Veronica waved and smiled at people on the other side of the street. Robert was on our side. I sat on the trunk of my car facing them to get a better view and I watched them intently

what you do in the dark . . .

as they passed. Robert's eyes met mine. He stopped talking on his bullhorn and stared at me, knowing Veronica was too busy showboating to the other side of the street to notice him. He blew a kiss.

My mother shouted, "Back at ya' Councilman Turner! How you?"

"Just fine Mrs. Boogerton." He spoke into the bullhorn again. "Good to see you. You're lookin' good!"

Soon I was staring at the back of Robert and Veronica's heads until Uncle CJ's loud, raspy voice broke my trance. Uncle CJ was about fifty-five years old. He was a medium build with a bent over walk and handsome features. His head was bald showcasing his reddish brown skin. His lips were full and he wore extremely straight, white dentures that were so perfect you knew they weren't real teeth. His eyes were light brown like my father's and he had a narrow nose. Uncle CJ started toward us wearing his usual hunter green work uniform and dirty brogans. He continued to call out to us from where he had been firing up the grill in the backyard.

"Hey Caren, Mary, Carla! Y'all wanna eat? Caren, go tell yo' mama to bring the meat out here! How we gon' have a cookout without no meat! The fire ready! The fire been ready! Don't take all day for me to start no fire! Mary come on wit the meat! Caren got her company here and everythang and y'all ain't even put the meat on the grill! Everybody else'll be here in a minute! Come on now. Bring the meat out!"

"Carla, go take that man the meat I got in that roaster pan in the kitchen fo' I have to kill'em!" I heard my mother fussin' on the front porch.

Jackie, Michelle, and I looked at each other for a few moments, wondering if we should comment on the processional we had just watched or my mother and uncle fussing at each other.

"I haven't said hello to your mother." Jackie finally broke the silence and headed toward the front porch.

"Me neither," Michelle agreed and followed Jackie.

I walked slowly behind them.

****

A couple of weeks later, I decided I was ready to put my life in order. The last few months had been chaotic to say the least. I had gotten through Robert's wedding day thanks to Mark, but now I felt it

Deborah Marbury

was time to seriously consider my future. Mark had told me that I would get married when I got myself together and I felt together.

Robert was married. It was over between us. Although Mark was a good friend, he just wouldn't make a good husband. Too many issues. I had invested all my adult life with my fiancé and I wasn't going to just let all that time go to waste. I could be faithful to him now. I just knew it. I believed we were destined to be together. After all, we'd been through a lot in the past year and even though things had become strained between us, neither of us had said good-bye.

As I relaxed in my bed, listening to the radio, I immersed myself in thoughts about Darnell. I listened to the **Just The Two of Us Show** with Lynn Tolliver and Ralph Poole every Saturday. I had done so since I graduated from high school. They were playing some oldie but goodie love songs that reminded me of the good ol' days with Darnell. We were so in love then. I wanted to recapture what we had.

I knew what Robert said to me that Easter night in Jennings' basement was true. Darnell was not and probably had never been faithful to me. I had often come across women's phone numbers in his pockets, heard from friends that they had seen him out somewhere with someone else. Lord only knows what he was doing when he was away in the service while I was at Central State.

His explanations were always reassuring and he'd always point out how well he took care of me by buying me expensive gifts and giving me money when I needed it. He paid my rent and my car note. He took me to nice restaurants, concerts and trips every now and then. And, of course, he would always reason that because we had been together so long, he must love me. He could have left a long time ago if he didn't.

So I overlooked the infidelities, I believe, because my mother had done so with my father and my father was a good man. He took care of my mother and he was a good father, the best. Darnell was a good man too. He took care of me. Besides, I also believed that if you were committed to a man, you didn't leave him if he's unfaithful. You just accept that men will tend to behave that way. They can't help it.

You stay with them through the good times and the bad. You weather the storms and enjoy the sunny days. You pray for fewer rainy days. Besides, everybody knows that if a man provides for you financially, then that means he really loves you. That's what most women believe. Mark always referred to it as being a 'kept' woman.

what you do in the dark . . .

The way I looked at life then reminds me of an article I read recently in the May 1998 issue of Ebony called, "The Ten Biggest Mistakes Women Make in Relationships." I made all ten.

Two weeks after our 4th of July date was cancelled because Darnell couldn't get out of some family obligation, I decided to go and visit him at his condo one Saturday morning. I figured it was time we put our cards on the table to see if we were really going to try to make our relationship work. I put on some jeans and a T-shirt, jumped in my car and zipped through the intersections of Northfield Road from Bedford Heights to Warrensville Heights until I arrived to make my surprise visit. I used my key to go inside, but Darnell was not there.

"That's what I get for trying to surprise him," I scorned myself.

He didn't have a lot of furniture. There was a white leather sofa and recliner in the living room, a 48" projection screen television, a rack system, but no pictures on the walls, no cocktail or end tables and no lamps. In the middle of the brown-carpeted floor, which contrasted poorly with the white furniture and bare white walls, was an exercise bench with weights sprawled all around it. I decided to wait for him.

I plopped into the recliner with the remote control, switched the power on and started to channel surf. There was absolutely nothing on television on Saturday mornings. The new cartoons were terrible. Cable didn't do much to improve your options. I turned on a movie that was already in progress on HBO. I pushed the recliner into the laying position, knowing I would probably nap instead of watching the movie, as I hated to watch movies that had already started. Unlike Darnell, who loved to try to figure out from the unfolding events what must have happened at the beginning.

I began to daydream about my future with Darnell living in this place. I started to think of ways to make it look and feel more like a home. I turned and looked at the empty dining room behind me. I got up. I walked through it into the kitchen, which had almond-colored appliances. I noticed that Darnell had no throw rugs or decorative dishtowels. There were no plaques on the walls with sayings like 'Caren's Kitchen.' No electric can opener. No blender. No mixer. Just a few pots and pans from a 7-piece collection that he'd probably bought at a discount store along with the dinnerware set for four that was dispersed among the dish pan, the dish rack, the counter top and the cabinet. The dish rack was blue, the dishpan was white and the counter top was brown.

"No coordination!" I grimaced.

On top of all that, he had no canister set. He always retrieved sugar, flour and other food items directly from the package they came in. He'll be much better off when I move in, I thought. I started to feel all warm and tingly about Darnell and I wished that he were with me so that I could hold him, kiss him and renew my commitment to him so that we could put our lives back together. I wanted 'us' back and I wanted it now.

I went into his bedroom where the feelings I was having would feel more appropriate. Darnell's bedroom was huge and showcased a king size waterbed with a hulking dark oak frame that boasted four sturdy posts, which held up a very masculine-looking canopy encasing a mirror. I recalled the reflection in that mirror of Darnell's dark chocolate body hovering over me on lusty nights when we had been more attentive to each other. The dresser and armoire matched the bed and each piece had drawers with gold swinging handles. There was a beautiful black and gold comforter on the bed that matched the sheet set and the curtains. I bought the set for him when he first moved into the condo two years ago.

I threw myself into the unmade bed on my belly and waited for the water to settle under my body. I grabbed one of his huge, fluffy pillows to rest my head on as I rolled over on my back and gazed at my reflection in the mirror. I thought I looked quite attractive lying there and I smiled and posed in ways that I thought would make Darnell want to make love to me if he should walk in and find me there.

I soon grew bored with that game and I sprawled myself across the bed hanging my upper torso over one side and began to run my fingers through the fibers of the carpet. It was plush and soft to feel, but its brown color made me cringe at its ugliness. It abhorred me so much; I instinctively withdrew my hands from its fibers and began to tap the wood base of the bed. A bedding skirt covered it. I lay there for a few minutes just tapping and thinking until I felt the swinging handle on a drawer. I never noticed that the bed had drawers inside its base before. I pulled the drawer open and raised the skirt to inspect what was inside.

A trashy-looking woman in a tight fitting, up to her butt, down to her breasts dress was staring up at me provocatively. I smiled.

"Typical man."

what you do in the dark . . .

    I thought that Darnell must secretly collect sexy pictures of trashy women. I picked it up and noticed that it was a picture from a 35mm camera. I turned it over. It was autographed,

> To Darnell,
> My future husband.
>   All my luv,
>
>   Mercedes Jackson-Jennings

    I looked down into the drawer again, and noticed more pictures of the same trashy tramp, pictures of her alone in trashy outfits, pictures of her with Darnell at different nightclubs and other events. There was even a picture of her with Darnell on a cruise along with Craig, Tyrone, Laquita and Shalonda.

    He had never taken me on a cruise! The dog! There was a Christmas card, a birthday card, a Valentine's Day card, a Sweetest Day card and several letters. All from Mercedes Jackson-Jennings. The pictures, cards, letters and dates indicated that they must have been seeing each other for the past year or two.

    Suddenly, all the years I'd been with Darnell no longer held any weight or significance. His declarations that each year was proof of his undying love for me brought the foundation of our relationship to a crumbling heap of nothingness.

    I picked up a letter dated, March 15, 1990. It read,

> Dear Darnell,
>
> I sorry for getting mad at you last night and putting you out but I jest git so tried of you staying with that heffa. Shalonda and Laquita told me how the stuck up heffa akted when you went boling. When you gone tell her bout us so we can git married like you said. I luv you so much Darnell. I wont us to be together. I luv you and the baby luv you to.
>
>   Mercedes Jackson-Jennings

I must have read that note a hundred times trying to make sense of it. This girl must be out of her mind to think that Darnell was going to marry her. What baby? I kept looking at the pictures. There was just no way in the world Darnell could be seriously interested in a trampy piece of project trash like her. There had to be some explanation, but the reality of those cards, letters and pictures would not let me rationalize anything except Darnell was seriously involved with this woman.

My heart sank and I felt a panicked need to do something to eliminate her from Darnell's life. I quickly opened the drawer to Darnell's nightstand and retrieved his address book. I searched frantically for Mercedes Jackson's phone number. I found it under the M's recorded as just Mercedes and it had four stars by her name.

Before I could dial the number, curiosity spurned me to look up my own name and there I was under the C's with no stars. I was furious. I dialed Mercedes' number and listened to the phone ring while tapping my foot impatiently on the floor as I pictured imaginary steam escaping from my ears.

"Hello!" she shouted into the phone after the third ring.

"May I speak to Mercedes Jackson?" I asked politely.

"'Dis her."

"Is Darnell there?"

"Who the hell is 'dis?"

"This is his fiancée, Caren."

"Heffa, don't call my damn house!"

Before I could say another word, she slammed down the phone. I didn't know what to do. My mind was racing, but getting nowhere fast. I was scared and trembling with rage. I wanted to call the trick back! How dare she hang up on me! The skank! The skeezer! I called her every name, but a child of God as I ranted, raved and paced Darnell's bedroom. I was afraid she meant the end for Darnell and me. I had an acute awareness that if Darnell left me, I would really be ALONE!

The fear, anxiety, pacing and worry thoroughly exhausted me and I fell into a deep sleep. I awakened after several hours to Darnell kissing me on the cheek. I looked into his smiling face. He was wearing his postal uniform.

"You had to work today?" I asked rubbing my eyes.

"Yeah Red. What you doing here?"

"I wanted to surprise you. I've missed you. I wanted to talk. See if we could try to put the past behind us and start over." I sat up on the bed trying to come completely out of my sleep.

"I don't have a problem with that Red." He smiled as if he had nothing to hide. "What do you want to talk about?"

"Things have been so distant between us lately, but I know that I still love you. Do you still love me?"

"You know I do."

"Then, why can't we spend more time together? Why do you have to spend so much time with Craig and Tyrone? And when you do why do you have to exclude me?"

"We both know the answer to that, don't we? Just look at how you acted the last time we went out together. You don't like my friends and that's a problem."

"You don't like mine."

"My friends didn't get me raped and pregnant!"

"I thought we weren't going to talk about that anymore."

"You're the one who wanted to talk things out. That's an issue for me. I don't believe you're telling the truth about how you got pregnant. How can I marry someone I can't trust?"

"Can I trust you?"

"You know me. My loyalty has always been to you, but it's you we're talking about here. You're the one who got pregnant."

"Just because you can't get pregnant doesn't mean you can't be guilty of the same thing. Who is this?" I demanded, holding up Mercedes' picture and letter, "Has she had your child?"

"So now you're going through my things!" he yelled and snatched the picture and note from my hand. He got up from the bed and began to pace the floor.

"Yes, I went through your things! How else would I find out the truth? Were you going to tell me about her? And why does this illiterate tramp call you her future husband? What does she mean by she loves you and the baby loves you? Do you have a baby with her?"

"You're the detective, snooping through people's personal belongings. You tell *me*, since you know so much!"

"Forget it Darnell! You'd only lie anyway. All you do is lie!" I said scooting over the waving waterbed and finding my way to the edge. I went out into the living room where my purse, shoes and car keys were.

I picked up my purse and keys, slipped into my shoes and stormed out the door. Darnell was right on my heels.

"Caren, you're the one who's lying! I never lied about Mercedes. I just never told you about her. You knew I'd been with other women!" he yelled from the front door.

I jumped into my car and blew my horn like a maniac for him to let me out because he had pulled his car into the driveway behind me. He jumped into his car, pulled out and followed me as I sped through the intersections back to my own apartment.

I zipped into my parking space and stomped to the door of the building. I stepped into the lobby and searched through my purse for my door key. Darnell joined me in the lobby as I located the key and opened the door. He followed me in.

"What the hell do you want?" I screamed at him.

"We're not done talking," he said forcefully.

"We are as far as I'm concerned."

I pushed two on the small elevator.

"We'll see about that when we get to your apartment."

Moments after the silent elevator ride, I slammed open my door and stormed into the apartment.

"Now what do you want Darnell?"

He walked passed me furiously and went into my bedroom. I followed him. I stared at him in wonderment as I watched him pull my journal from under my bed where I naively thought no one would ever find it. A brief flash of him playing with the carpet while hanging over the side of my bed the same way I had fallen into his secret world went through my mind as I stood there, frozen.

*Maybe it's because he's boring. Or . . . maybe it's because **he's** been unfaithful. I guess it's because I'm tired of being alone. All I know is that I'm excited about the date I have tonight with my new friend. My new friend is sexy, exciting and handsome. He makes me feel like I got it goin' on! **He** makes me feel like a woman and everybody knows that men are just like jobs. You don't leave the one you have until you find another one.*

As he read my words aloud, they seemed to have more impact than when I was their only audience.

"So what's this all about Caren?" he demanded shaking the journal in my face.

All I could think was that I was glad I hadn't used any names. At least he didn't know that the man I'd went out with was his first cousin, Robert. I was too embarrassed to speak. I stood there, dumbfounded.

"This entry is dated November 7. Isn't that around the time you told me you were raped by some unknown man at a party with Michelle and became pregnant? I know you didn't go to any party with Michelle, but I bet she helped you concoct this trumped up story. Didn't she?"

"I never said I was raped."

"You said somebody had sex with you without your consent. That's rape. I was worried about you. I hurt for you. How can I marry somebody who would lie about something like that?"

"Stop it Darnell. I don't want to talk about it."

"Who was it Caren?"

"None of your business! It's the past. It's over. I have no intention of ever being with him again. You had no right to read my journal."

"Just like you had no right to go through my things. How else was I going to find out the truth as you put it?"

That comment hit me hard like a boomerang.

"I'm sorry," I said, defeated.

"Yes. That you are." His words pierced my heart like darts and his eyes threw daggers. The disgust and contempt in his eyes made me feel like a Lilliputian from Gulliver's Travels. We had lied to each other over and over. We had hurt each other deeply. We had broken sacred trusts. We had wronged each other. We were caught in a cycle of trying to use the other's faults to justify our own. But, we were still here after all these years, trying to hold on to something. We still wanted something that only the other could provide. We still cared for each other. I was sure of it. Didn't that count for something?

"Is the journal the real reason you cancelled our wedding last month?" I asked after several moments of silence. Tears welled up in my eyes.

"I've known since April. Yes. That's why I cancelled the wedding. I was hoping you would tell me the truth."

"Or maybe you were just hoping to trade me in for a Mercedes!"

"Well I guess for men, women are just like cars."

We laughed.

"I shouldn't have lied to you Darnell. I'm sorry. I was ashamed. I didn't want you to think that I wasn't trustworthy. I slept with the guy because I was lonely, not because I can't be trusted. I needed you and you were never there."

I started to cry. He watched me silently for several minutes as I sobbed and sobbed as I whispered repeatedly, "I'm sorry."

He walked toward me slowly, carefully and wrapped his arms around me. We stood there, holding each other, crying.

"I'm sorry too," he said finally. He led me to my bed and we lay there in each other's arms until we fell asleep.

what you do in the dark . . .

hot august

Hot fun in the summertime!

"Mommy! Please help me! Please don't let me die!" A little girl cried out as I lay on a beach towel taking in the sun on a sandy beach in Florida while on vacation with Darnell visiting his family.

I was only half awake, but I sat up when I heard the little girl's cry. I looked around, but I didn't see her mother anywhere. I had been lying there for a while I supposed with my sunglasses covering my sleeping eyes.

I looked around for help, but no one was there. I got up slowly focusing in on the little girl who was drifting farther out into the water and calling for her mother to help her. I started to run to her, but when I got to the edge of the water, I remembered I didn't know how to swim.

"Help! Somebody help!" I yelled frantically.

"Mommy! Please help me! Don't let me die!" The little girl was crying sweetly and pitifully.

There was nothing I could do to save her. To try to swim out to her would be sacrificing my own life. I looked around and around, turning in circles like a dog chasing his tail and stopping periodically to look at the little girl. She looked directly into my eyes. She had light brown almond-shaped eyes like mine. Involuntarily, my attention turned to her lips.

They whispered to me. "Mommy. Please don't kill me. I love you. I'll be good. I won't make you sad. I promise. Please don't kill me." Her lips were like mine.

I started toward her. The water was getting higher and higher against my body, past my knees, thighs and stomach. When it got to my neck, I got scared again. I turned and waded back to the safety of the beach.

"I'm sorry. I can't save you!" I screamed out to the girl as I turned away.

"Mommy! Please! Please don't let me die!" she cried out frantically, then she started to disappear into the water. I could hear her feet kicking against the water, like tiny footsteps.

"I'm sorry!" I kept sobbing.

Tears were dripping into my ears and staining my pillowcase as I awakened from a fretful sleep. I wiped my eyes with my hands as I looked around for the tissue box I kept on my nightstand realizing that I was going to make my eyes turn red and puffy if I kept rubbing them.

My tears mixed with sweat dripped onto parts of my hair causing it to look sort of mangled around the ends. It was hot in my bedroom. It was the last Sunday of August. The temperature had to be in the high 90s. I looked out of my bedroom window where the shade had not been pulled down before I went to bed the previous night through the sheer white curtains that swayed gently to the light breeze that came through the screen and I saw it was daylight.

I heard the birds chirping having their morning conversation against the sounds of passing cars on Interstate 271. I looked at my alarm clock. The red numbers staring back at me said 7:03. I turned to look at Darnell who lay beside me. We had made love for the first time in months, a year actually.

After a two-week hiatus from me, he decided that he wanted to try to work things out. He told me that he would end things with Mercedes so that we could have a fresh start. I promised that I would never cheat on him again, but I still chose to keep the identity of my lover a secret.

I assured him of how very much I loved him by making love with him for hours. He told me that he had loved me for so long that he didn't think he knew how to love anyone else. I wasn't quite convinced in light of his long-term relationship with Mercedes, but I also couldn't believe that he would actually prefer a hootchie to me. I got up to turn on the ceiling fan, then returned to bed where I snuggled close to Darnell and whispered in his ear.

what you do in the dark...

"Let's make a baby."

He turned to me lazily, yawning and stretching. He wrapped me in his arms. I started to kiss him tenderly. I kissed his lips, his cheeks, gently nibbling his ear until he started to respond to me and we made love again. We tried new positions that I had always been too inhibited before Robert to try. We made love in every room and on every piece of furniture in my apartment.

He had some tricks that he'd never tried with me before too. I wondered where he was coming up with all these kinky ideas. Mercedes Jackson came to mind, but I quickly pushed her out where she belonged. I wondered if he wanted to ask if my sexuality had heightened because of my lover as I suspected was the case with him. I tried desperately to keep Robert and Mercedes out of my thoughts and concentrate on Darnell and me. I didn't want anything to mess up our reconciliation. I was ready to marry him and have his children. After our morning lovemaking, we showered and dressed. I hoped that I had conceived his child.

"You're still on the pill, aren't you?" he asked slipping on his jean shorts.

"What difference does it make? We're getting married soon and I'm ready to have a baby."

"You may think you're ready, but trust me Red, we're not ready. I hope you're still on the pill."

I didn't respond. I hadn't been on the pill for a year. I stopped taking them a few months after Darnell and I set our wedding date. They were making me sick and I figured I'd just ask Darnell to use something else when the time came. It never came, until last night.

"I thought I heard you say something about making a baby earlier. Are you on the pill? Are you trying to get pregnant?"

"I'm just trying to love you Darnell."

"What does that mean? Red, we can't have no babies right now."

"Fine."

"So you're on the pill, right?"

"You should have worried about that before now."

Darnell was fully dressed now and preparing to leave. He sat on the edge of the bed, brushing his waves. I felt disconnected from him now. Like he had gotten all he wanted from me and he didn't want anymore.

"So are you on the pill for the hundredth time?"

"Are we getting married?"

Darnell ceased his grooming and moved closer to where I lay on the bed watching him.

"Red, I've loved you since I was old enough to know what love is. I've enjoyed this time we've spent together. It's been the best time I've ever spent with any woman. I know we've both made mistakes that we've decided to try to forgive each other for, but they're not easily forgotten. I think we need more time before we start discussing marriage again."

I sat up and leaned back onto my headboard. I stared down at my biker shorts, letting my eyes stroll down my thighs and legs to my bare feet. I dropped my upper torso sideways onto the bed and sprawled across it. I felt like I could deal with the disappointment of Darnell's words better lying down.

Darnell came over and sat next to my head and stroked my wet, mangled hair softly. The ceiling fan continued to whirl quietly over our heads. The bed was a mess from our morning and afternoon delight. We were both sweating lightly. His touch was soothing where anyone else's would have literally made me feel hot and bothered.

I rolled onto my back and took his hand into mine and kissed it.

"Darnell, please. Can't we get past this? Let's get on with our lives. There's no sense in dwelling on the past. What's done is done. Let's just move on."

"We will. Let's just take our time. I need that. As a man, I need that. Do you understand?"

"I guess I'll have to," I said feeling the conviction of his words. I knew when he had to do something 'as a man' that he was serious about it.

"Come on," he said patting me on my hip to signal he wanted me to get up and see him to the door. "I have to go now. I'll call you later."

I scooted out of the bed and walked with him to the door. As I opened it for him, he turned and pulled me into his arms.

"I do still love you, Red. Very much."

"Yeah, me too."

And he was gone.

It was so stuffy in my apartment. My air conditioner wasn't working and the fans just weren't getting the job done. I threw myself onto my bed and spread myself across it. It was too hot to move. I lay perfectly still under that ceiling fan to keep as cool as I possibly could. It seemed to just blow the hot air around.

what you do in the dark . . .

It was early evening when I decided I just couldn't take the heat anymore.

"Hello."

"Hey Mark. It's me. Caren."

"Hey Bae. How you doin' these days? I haven't seen or heard from you in a while. I miss you. What's up? You ain't mad at me, are you?"

"I'm hot as hell, but I'm not mad at you. I called you after the fourth, but you weren't home."

"So what's up?"

"I'm burning up over here. It's Sunday and there are no maintenance people around. The air conditioner isn't working. Can you come take a look at it?"

"No problem Bae. I'll be right over."

"Thanks Mark. I look forward to seeing you. I've got a lot to tell you."

I hung up the phone and lay still under the ceiling fan waiting for Mark to deliver me from the unbearable heat. I missed him too. I didn't know how he'd feel about it, but I couldn't wait to tell him about my reconciliation with Darnell.

I wanted to let him know that I had finally gotten myself together. It bothered me that I had disappointed Mark because I knew how much he thought of me. It was a real hit in the gut to have him say that he had been disgusted by my actions of late.

He would be proud of me now I hoped, even though he might be a little disappointed that he and I would never be a couple. I turned on some Public Enemy and blared *Fight the Power*.

It took me to scenes of Spike Lee's movie, **Do The Right Thing**. Mark and I had walked to the Southgate Cinema to see one of the late shows last summer. Mark loved rap music and Public Enemy was the only rap music I had. I loved the way Radio Raheem kept playing *Fight the Power* on that big radio in the movie.

I thought Mark might be hungry when he got to my apartment. It was dinnertime, but it was too hot to cook. I ordered a pizza. I got out my ice bucket, filled it with ice and put a bottle of wine in it to chill. I took out two wineglasses and decided I wanted my reunion with Mark to be a little less noisy so I turned off Public Enemy and turned on some Dazz Band. My 'slow jams' tape that I had made from about five or six Dazz Band albums.

The door buzzer rang after about three songs had played and I playfully sang **Knock, Knock** as I opened the door. I greeted Mark with a warm friendly hug.

"Hey What's up?"

"You got it Bae. You sho' look sexy in those biker shorts."

"Behave yourself Mark."

"Why I gotta behave? You shouldn't wear nothin' like that if you don't want me to say nothin' about it."

"Come on in. What you been up to lately?"

I smiled at him and appraised him discreetly. He had on mesh black Nike shorts with a white swoosh in the bottom left corner and a matching tank, white Nike socks with a black swoosh, and black and white Nike tennis shoes. He wore a lightweight Nike jacket that I imagined must have made him hot, but I made no comment about it.

His attire was a little more stylish than his usual jeans or work pants. He took the jacket off and folded it carefully on his arm as he walked toward my sofa. His ensemble complemented his strong, muscular physique quite nicely. His reddish brown skin glistened with a light mist of sweat that made him look delectable. His thuggish demeanor just couldn't overshadow how handsome and sexy he truly was. Those sparkling hazel eyes refused to be ignored. I pushed those thoughts from my head quickly as I sat down with him on the sofa.

"I ain't been doin' much. Tryin' to get right. I've been thinkin' 'bout joinin' my mother's church. She told me she wished I would try to find the Lord before she died."

He laid his jacket carefully over the arm of the sofa near where he sat. I threw some giant pillows on the floor and we slid down from the sofa to sit on them.

"I can't imagine you in church," I kidded him, "but this is the second time you've mentioned wanting to get closer to God. You must be serious."

I remembered that his mother's church was Matthias. I thought about the days, he, Jackie and I had gone to Sunday school there. The church that Jackie still attended. I didn't mention that I knew what church he was talking about for fear that I would remind him of how insensitive I'd been when his mother died.

"I am serious. I think it just may be what I need in my life right now. I've been through a lot Bae."

what you do in the dark . . .

"Tell me about it," I agreed. I thought about the big mess I'd gotten myself into with Robert, Darnell and Jessie Bassett.

There was an awkward silence for a moment when our eyes met. I blushed at the effect those beautiful hazel eyes of his always had on me. I looked down at my bare feet. The next thing I knew his hand was lifting my chin forcing my eyes to meet his alluring gaze. He never made fun of my lazy eye since we'd become teenagers. Although, he'd probably cracked so many jokes about my last name and my eye during elementary and middle school that he'd ran out by high school.

"Why is it so hard for you to look at me Bae?"

"It's not hard for me to look at you. It's just not polite to stare," I responded nervously.

"I don't mind if you stare," he told me softly. I blushed again and looked away. "Can I stare at you then?" he asked.

"If you want to."

"I want to."

"I ordered some pizza for us, but you can drink some wine with me while we wait for them to deliver it."

"Wine? With you?" He laughed.

"Well, it's okay to have a glass of wine every now and then."

"That's what I've been trying to tell you for years," he teased me.

He got up and walked over to the air conditioner as I headed for the kitchen to get the wine and glasses.

"Let me check this thing out now so I can enjoy my pizza when it gets here. I got a lot to tell you Bae."

"Oh?" I called from the kitchen.

"Yeah, a whole lot." His voice quieted, then got loud again. "It looks like the wires are loose in this unit. I used to have to reconnect them all the time when I worked here. It's no big deal. I'll have it workin' in no time. You need to tell them to get you another unit though. It's time for a new one."

I returned to living room to find Mark replacing the facing on the air conditioner. I put the ice bucket with the wine and the glasses on the floor and resumed my seat on the pillow.

"It should be cooling off soon," he told me as he took his seat next to me again.

The Dazz Band was singing, ***Invitation to Love*** which flowed right into the next selection, ***Bad Girl.*** Mark lifted his glass.

"To the baddest girl I know."

I took a sip from my glass.

"Oh no," I laughed. "I'm messed up in the head. Remember that."

"Yeah, well so is the girl they talkin' 'bout in this song. First, she loved Skip, then Pierre and on and on. She just like you. Don't know what she wanna do. I was worried about you Bae. I spoke to you that way because I wanted you to snap out of that fairytale world you was caught up in. You need to quit chasin' them 'bougie' men and get wit a real man, like me. I don't know when you gon' realize that."

"You don't think Darnell is right for me?"

"Hell no! He's a punk and a cheat!"

"I cheated too."

"Yeah, but you did it because you were lonely."

"So if you have a good reason for cheating that makes it right?"

"No! It just says somethin' diff'rent 'bout yo' values that's all. I don't think you wanted to sleep around Bae. I think you felt you had to in order to get what you needed. Darnell does it because he likes to do it."

I leaned back against the sofa feeling a little relieved by Mark's words, which gave me confirmation that I wasn't the slut I'd come to regard myself as.

"So what's all this about joining the church?" I inquired wanting to find out exactly where Mark's head was after hearing his insightful comments. The door buzzer rang before he could begin his reply.

"Hold that thought!" I told him as I jumped up to answer the door. Mark quickly pulled a twenty from his pocket and handed it to me.

"Here you go, Bae."

I grabbed the twenty and ran to the intercom to announce to the delivery boy that I would be down in a minute. I came back to the apartment five minutes later with a hot pepperoni and sausage pizza. I grabbed some napkins from the kitchen and placed the pizza on the floor in the middle of our pillows next to the wine.

Mark leaned his head back on the sofa as I rejoined him on the floor. He wiggled his foot to the music. The Dazz Band crooned my favorite ballad, *I Keep on Lovin' You*. I could tell it was a favorite of Mark's too. He was singing it with his eyes closed and his face was all tore up like he could feel the words and music deep down in his soul.

I keep on lovin' you after all that we've been through.

That was the hook and he sang it over and over again along with the background vocalists with great tenacity. When the song was over, he sat up and looked into my eyes again. This time I felt myself melting a little

what you do in the dark . . .

as Mark took my chin in his hand again and told me, "I keep on lovin' you, Bae, after all that we've been through! Do you know that I've loved you since the day I met you, which had to be when we were about five years old."

I smiled and looked away, then I picked up a slice of pizza and began to eat it hungrily.

"I couldn't tell, the way you used to talk about me," I answered after a few bites of pizza.

"Now, I know you know that a boy always teases the girls he likes, but when he becomes a man, well, you know." He looked at me intently.

"Want some more wine?" I asked.

"Sure," he answered looking slightly disappointed that he couldn't get me to hold our gaze for more than a few seconds.

"So, you were going to tell me about your decision to join the church."

"Yeah. A lot has happened to me in the last few months. I took my mother's death really hard and I started drinking more and smoking a lot of weed. I was selling bud for this guy named JD and I kinda lost it when Ma died. I wasn't takin' care of business. I smoked up a lot of his weed and I wasn't workin' nowhere, so I couldn't pay for it. JD got mad and pulled a gun on me. You know, I've always hung with a pretty rough crowd, but I ain't never had nobody pull a gun on me before. He had the gun right up to my head. He was talkin' much smack too! He kept yellin':

'Man don't be messin' wit my damn money! I'll kill you Man! I'll kill you!' He was like, 'Man, if we wasn't boys, I'd kill you right now! And you can't sell no mo' of my damn weed!'

Then he popped me upside the head with the butt of that gun and walked the hell off. I had to be rushed to the hospital and treated for a concussion. There was a big gash in the back of my head. I got twelve stitches. I'm lucky to be alive. Blessed to be alive, blessed."

Mark started rubbing his hands together nervously as if just talking about his near death experience put him right back at death's door again. He was sweating. I looked up at the air conditioner to see if it was running. I could hear it, but it didn't really feel much cooler in the room.

"I don't know Bae," he continued, "that experience really scared me. I knew I needed to make some changes in my life after that. I started thinking about my mother. What would she want me to do? You know? Did I tell you how she died?"

"No. I don't think so," I answered softly.

He looked at me pointedly. I knew the look came from a brief revelation that I hadn't been concerned enough to ask. Then, as if he told himself he had to let go of the anger and resentment, he went on with his story.

"She had a heart attack. Stayed in intensive care for about two weeks. I stayed with her as much as they would let me. She told me before she died, her last words as I sat at her bedside cryin', she said, 'Boy, don't you be cryin' 'bout me. I'm gon' be just fine. You need to be tryin' to go where I'm goin'. You need to be tryin' to get closer to the Lord. Then, when it's yo' time, I'll see you when you get there.' Bae, she said it like she really believed it. 'I'll see you when you get there. I'll see you when you get there.' Her last words, her last wish for me, her only child. Bae, I wanna make her proud. I didn't do nothin' she could be proud of when she was livin', but if there's really a chance that I can see her again, then I want her to be proud of me when that time comes. I wanna do whatever I gotta do so I can see her again."

A tear fell on his cheek and I put my arms around him.

"I wanna see her again Bae. I wanna see her again."

"You will. If she said you will, then you will."

He sobbed in my arms for several minutes before he regained his composure.

"I thought about when you asked me if God would forgive you for having an abortion and Mama always told me that God forgives you if you ask him in prayer and believe that He has forgiven you. I thought about all the crazy mess I've done that I need forgiveness for and I knew I had to start tryin' to make a change. I think that's what you need too, Bae. I think you and me are two of a kind. I think we need each other. I think we can do this thing together. Lord knows we both need forgiveness."

I was so moved by Mark's story that I didn't dare mention my reconciliation with Darnell. I could feel that he needed me now and I had never been there for him before. I knew I had to be there for him now.

"Bae, I need you to keep something for me."

"Okay," I responded eagerly.

I wanted to do anything I could to make up for how I had failed him before. He pulled out a small gun he had hidden in his jacket pocket. I jumped.

what you do in the dark . . .

"Don't be scared, Bae. I just want to put it in a drawer somewhere. I got it to protect myself from JD or really to get him back for what he did to me. I realize I don't need it anymore. God's got my back now. I just don't want it around me until I know I've got my head on straight, 100%. I don't trust myself with it right now. I know it'll be safe with you."

I didn't respond. I just nodded my head. He got up, placed the gun in one of my dresser drawers and then returned to me on the living room floor.

"I don't care what it takes Bae. I'm gonna do whatever I have to do to convince you that we belong together."

He took my chin in his hand once again, forcing me to look into those penetrating eyes. I looked down and he took his hand away from my chin and put his arms around me.

"It's okay. There's no rush," he assured me. "So what did you have to tell me?"

Having decided already that now was not the time to talk about Darnell, I responded, "I've been having a lot of bad dreams lately."

"Oh yeah. 'Bout what?"

"A little girl who looks like me is in trouble. She's drowning and I can't save her. I can't swim. At first, I would just have dreams about tiny footsteps that I couldn't catch, but last night I dreamed that they were the sound of the little girl's feet kicking against the water as she drowned."

"Hmmh. That's interesting."

"I feel really bad when I wake up, you know, guilty."

"Wasn't you supposed to have your baby around this time?"

"Yeah," I admitted reluctantly, "but why are you bringing that up?"

"Bae, I know it's had to be on your mind."

"Yeah, but I guess I just didn't want to say it out loud."

"Keepin' it in the dark, doesn't make it go away. It happened Bae. You was pregnant and you had an abortion. Didn't that counselor recommend anybody for you to talk to or anything to help you deal with this?"

"No. Her main concern that day was to get me through the procedure, not to worry about what effect it would have on me later. I've told you how she's been hounding me at work. She won't let me forget it and she's trying to use her knowledge of it to expose Robert."

"That's messed up. Maybe it *should* be a law against having abortions."

"Well, they're just bad dreams Mark. I'm sure they'll go away and I'll be fine."

"I hope so," he said guiding my head gently to his lap so he could stroke my hair. We sat there quietly for a few moments as he stroked my hair softly, easing me into a relaxed and comfortable state. I still felt hot and sweaty.

"The air isn't working," I complained finally.

"Here, this will cool you off." He took some ice from the bucket and slid it gently over my face, arms and thighs and then another piece down my tank top. I was reminded again of **Do The Right Thing** as he slid the ice in circular motions under my tank top and around my breasts in much the same way Spike Lee did to Rosie Perez in the movie.

I made no move to stop him. He let the ice fall inside my shirt and began to caress my breasts gently. He repositioned himself so that he sat behind me and I laid with my back against his chest and my bottom between his legs on the floor. He touched, caressed and massaged each and every part of my body until I relaxed into a deep sleep.

"Mommy! Please don't let me die! Help me!" The little girl was calling from the window of my apartment building. Flames were consuming the building quickly. I got out of my car in the parking lot and ran toward the building as I looked up at the little girl in my window.

"Oh my goodness!" I screamed. "Somebody call the fire department!"

I ran toward the door, but when I tried to open it, a burst of flames forced me out and knocked me to the asphalt pavement. I scrambled to my feet and tried to find the girl in the window again. Thick, black smoke was all around her. Her soft jet black hair was caressing her face and falling softly to her shoulders like mine. She hung out the window, reaching for me.

"Mommy, please! Don't you love me? Please don't kill me. Please don't let me die."

"I'm not killing you!" I stomped around on the pavement throwing a small temper tantrum. "Stop saying that! I'm not killing you! It's the fire! It's not my fault!"

what you do in the dark . . .

"Of course it's not your fault Mommy." She smiled at me hauntingly. "If you come in to save me, then you would die and mommies are much more important than little girls, aren't they?"

"No! No! That's not what I meant!"

"Well, come help me Mommy. Please Mommy, don't let me die."

I stormed determinedly to the door again, but when I touched the handle it burned my hand. I jerked away quickly and I looked inside at the flames that were waiting to engulf me if I dared to enter.

"I can't save you! Somebody please help me! Somebody please call the fire department!"

"I love you Mommy." The little girl told me softly as she disappeared into the flames and smoke. "I love you." I could hear her tiny footsteps move away from the window. I ran toward the door again, but I couldn't get in. I couldn't catch up with those footsteps.

"Wake up Bae!" Mark was shaking me gently. "Let me put you to bed."

I got up drowsily and walked with Mark to my bed. I caught a quick glimpse of the clock before my head hit my pillow, which told me I'd been asleep for little over an hour. Mark laid down beside me and let me lay in his arms just like we used to do when I needed comforting. Things felt different now though. I wasn't quite sure if it was right or wrong. It was still hot and I wiped sweat from my forehead and complained again to Mark.

"It's hot in here," I moaned.

"Maybe you should take off some of these clothes," he whispered as he began to help me out of my tank top.

I pulled a sheet over me and Mark resumed touching, caressing and massaging me again. This time he kissed me on my neck and it felt right. It felt good and for the first time in a long time, I felt wanted, needed and truly loved.

"Tell me if you want me to stop," he whispered as he started to kiss me gently all over my body.

I realized that stopping was the last thing I wanted him to do. His tender foreplay gave me so much pleasure that I screamed out in ecstasy three times. I shook and held him tightly as he made love to me.

"I've waited so long for this Bae," he whispered. "I'm not sure how long I'll last."

He made love to me for so long that I thought I would pass out from exhaustion. When he reached his climax, he shook the whole bed

Deborah Marbury

and grabbed the sheets in a frenzy until he finally went limp. I felt like he had released his whole soul into my womb and we both fell into a deep slumber.

A couple of hours later, I groggily awoke to the sound of my frantic door buzzer. I jumped from my bed and ran to the intercom.

"Yes!" I answered.

"Red! What are you doing? I've been ringing this buzzer for fifteen minutes! Let me in. I forgot my key," Darnell yelled at me.

"I was asleep. I didn't know you were coming back."

"Just buzz me in. I look like a fool down here ringing this buzzer like a maniac!"

I had already hit the buzzer when I turned to face Mark.

"Mark!"

"He's been here today. What's goin' on with you guys?"

"We worked everything out. We're back together."

"And what about us? We just made love." Mark had his shorts on, his shirt was in his hand.

"We have to talk about this later. You gotta get out of here before the elevator gets to the second floor. Take the stairs."

"You're still screwed up!" he yelled. His eyes burned through me.

"Mark please. I just need time to think. I didn't expect this to happen."

Mark went to the living room for his shoes and slipped out of my door without saying another word. I watched him disappear onto the stairwell as the elevator doors opened to spew out Darnell.

"Anxious to see me, huh?" Darnell teased and I realized I was standing there naked. "Why you walkin' 'round with no clothes on?" he asked.

"It's hot!" I responded irritably.

"Naw, you just want some more of me. You startin' to get insatiable, Girl," he said pulling me close to him and kissing me on my neck.

"I want to take a cold shower. I think that will cool me off."

I pulled away from Darnell and went quickly to the living room to grab up the wine and glasses before Darnell could notice that there were glasses for two.

"Just sit down for a minute. Let me pick up a little in here and change the sheets. You can wait for me in the bed while I take a shower."

"How about if I take one with you? I like when we do it in the shower."

My heart sank at the thought of having someone else inside me again. We already had sex several times that morning and afternoon in addition to the lengthy session with Mark just less than an hour ago.

I put on my thin, short robe and changed the sheets. I headed for the bathroom with Darnell right on my heels. I grudgingly let him make love to me in the shower and once again when we got into bed. He pulled out early both times for fear of getting me pregnant just in case he hadn't done so already.

"Mommy, I'm burning! Please come get me! Please don't let me die!"

Flames and smoke were engulfing the little girl with eyes like mine again. I was still in the parking lot looking at her in the window.

"I'm coming Sweetheart. I promise. I'm going to get you out!"

I ran to the door again, but before I could touch the hot handle, a gloved hand appeared where I was about to place my own. I looked up into Mark's face.

"I'll get the baby. You stay here."

I ran back out into the parking lot where I could look up at the window, but the little girl was gone. Mark wouldn't be able to save her. I was sure. I sat in the middle of the parking lot with my legs crossed and began to cry until Mark returned with a baby in his arms. I wasn't sure if it was the little girl. I didn't see her as a baby in the water or in the fire. I reached out to hold the baby, but Mark pulled away.

"The baby is safe with me," he told me and walked away.

I sat up straight in my bed feeling that same pang of guilt. I looked at my clock. It was 8:10. Monday morning. Darnell had gone to work. I had fifty minutes to shower, dress and make the commute to the **AA Times**. I jumped out of bed and sped through my morning routine at twice the normal pace.

I ran down the stairs instead of taking the elevator and rushed out into the parking lot to my car. As I positioned myself behind the steering wheel, I turned to look up at my apartment window. It was empty. I started my engine quickly and applied my make up in the rearview mirror as I sped out of the parking lot and onto Interstate 271 to 480 heading toward 77 into downtown Cleveland.

I barely acknowledged Jackie's, "What's up Girl?" as I signed in and headed into the City Room. The reporters were finishing their morning coffee and starting to sit down to their computers. I started to feel my composure returning when I noticed Jessie hadn't arrived. I certainly wasn't up to dealing with her yet. I sat down to my computer and opened my e-mail.

Caren,

We need to talk. See me in my office at 10:30 sharp.

Marge

The message sounded like trouble and I had the sinking feeling that Jessie Bassett was somehow involved. I tried not to think about what it was that Marge wanted to see me about and I checked my log for the day's assignments. I didn't have any. That was strange, but I was relieved. Now, I would be able to catch up on editing news releases and writing the stories I had already covered. Everything had to be ready for press by Wednesday.

"Ssso, did Marge send you a notice about a meeting for 10:30?"

"Do you have to know everything that goes on around here?" I snapped at Jessie.

"I was just trying to warn you. Excuse me for trying to help."

"Warning? Help? Why would I need help? I haven't done anything wrong."

"I'll say you have." Jessie smiled slyly.

"Okay Jessie, let's have it. What are you talking about?"

"I tried to get you to tell the truth, but you wouldn't cooperate. Now your job may be in jeopardy."

Infuriated at Jessie's taunting and frustrated that I didn't have a clue as to what she was talking about, I stormed full speed into Marge's office and busted in on a private meeting between Marge and Mr. Caldwell. Frozen in their positions sitting across from each other at Marge's desk, their eyes widened with expectancy. I halted suddenly realizing the stupidity of my abrupt entrance.

"May I help you?" Marge asked sternly.

Mr. Caldwell settled back into his seat and looked at me searchingly.

"I'm sorry, Marge. It's Jessie. She just drives me crazy. She says my job is in jeopardy!"

what you do in the dark . . .

Marge and Mr. Caldwell gave each other a knowing glance and then Mr. Caldwell got up from his seat, the infamous 'chair.'

"Here, sit down young lady," he said holding 'the chair' for me.

I sat down cautiously and looked back and forth from him to Marge questioningly. I don't think Mr. Caldwell had ever spoken to me directly before. He walked over to the big window in Marge's office that looked out over the city of Cleveland and showed off the city's skyline.

"It seems some information has fallen into our hands that could be harmful to you, but is quite newsworthy," Marge started.

I took a deep breath as my mind raced over all the confrontations I'd had with Jessie about Robert and me since I had gotten my abortion in January. I knew she wasn't going to let it go.

"What information?" I asked nervously.

"Jessie's been investigating Councilman Turner because he's running for state senator and it seems that there are a couple of people from your apartment building that saw you making love outside your apartment door with him the night of his dinner dance fund raiser in November. There are also some former patients of a nearby abortion clinic who say they saw Councilman Turner sleeping in the waiting area in January. They say they saw him leave with a woman who fits your description. There are some protesters who believe they recognized the both of you there too. Jessie says she's sure it was you, but she won't say why. Knowing her background, I'm sure she knows it was you too. It's a hot story and we have to give Jessie the go ahead on it. Was the young lady at the abortion clinic you?"

"Marge, how can you do this to Councilman Turner after the positive relationship we've built with him when he started the community center?"

"I don't want to do it Caren, but it's going to be one of the hottest stories in Cleveland, in Ohio! You know Jessie is a well-known writer. She can sell this story to anyone in a New York minute. We need this break Caren. The story is going to come out whether we print it or not. Just tell me that it wasn't you at the abortion clinic with Councilman Turner."

Marge looked at Mr. Caldwell for support. He was standing quietly by the window trying to give us the allusion of being alone, but probably wanting to hear everything firsthand for himself like a fly on the wall.

"What difference does it make who the woman was? The story isn't about the woman. It's about Turner and his stand on the abortion issue, isn't it?"

"Well yes, Caren, that's true, but once it's reported that a woman aborted his child with his collaboration, what do you think is the next thing everyone will want to know?"

I held my head down. There was no use. The truth was going to come out.

"My mother just can't read something like this about me Marge! My fiancé will leave me for sure. Robert is his first cousin. You can't let anyone know it was me!"

Marge and Mr. Caldwell gave each other an affirming look and Mr. Caldwell started to pace behind 'the chair.'

"Listen here, young lady, we don't want you to get hurt, but our hands are tied. Maybe you should take a leave of absence until this thing blows over. Once the story breaks, you're probably not going to want to be out covering stories anyway. Other reporters will be asking you questions about Mr. Turner while you're trying to get the story at hand. Also, I assume that things will be pretty tense between you and Jessie for a while. It'll do you good not to have to see her every day."

"I've just about had it with Jessie myself, Will!" Marge interjected.

I was startled to hear Marge call Mr. Caldwell by his first name.

"I just like her nerve threatening to sell the story to someone else. She has no loyalty Will and you know how I feel about that!"

"I've built a good reputation as reporter at this paper, Mr. Caldwell. I've done a good job for you since I was a college student. I can't believe you'd just throw me out for Jessie Bassett who would sell you out at the drop of a hat. I care about this paper. I care about the people who work here. All Jessie cares about is Jessie! How could you do this to me? I've worked hard Marge! I've worked hard! Where's *your* loyalty?"

"Look Caren. I've tried to talk Jessie out of doing this story, but she's determined. It's a big break for her and why would we risk her selling the story to someone else when we've paid her salary for her to get the story. Caren, the story is going to come out. People deserve to know the truth about Turner before they go to the polls in November. We have a responsibility to our readers. If we don't run the story, it will look like we can't be trusted to tell the truth when one of our own is involved. Our credibility is at stake. I'm sorry Caren. We're between a rock and a hard place. We have to run the story."

what you do in the dark...

Tears streamed down my face. I felt hurt, embarrassed, confused and scared. I felt like the weight of the world was on my shoulders.

"My goodness Caren." Marge walked over to me and laid her hand on my shoulder. "How could you get yourself into something like this? Haven't I always told you that what you do in the dark is sure to come to the light?"

Anger started to build as I began to try to assess who was the blame for the way my life was coming apart and my resentment grew toward Marge the moment she used that infamous catch phrase to judge me.

"Where did that stupid saying come from anyway?" I snapped as I wiped tears from my cheeks.

I concluded that the whole thing was Marge and Mr. Caldwell's fault because they could stop this from happening and they were refusing to use their influence to help me. They were too concerned about their precious paper.

"It's a biblical truth," Marge answered, "and from the way things are going for you now, you might want to spend some time in God's word for comfort. You're about to go through an ordeal unlike anything you've ever experienced and you're going to need more strength than you've ever needed in your life. I'll be praying for you Sweetheart."

Mr. Caldwell was standing beside Marge now. They looked so united against me. I thought about all the times Jackie and I had kidded about the two of them having an affair. It seemed more believable to me now than it ever had before. My anger raged as I stood up and gave them the most disgusted look I could muster.

"You know what you can do with your prayers! How dare you judge me. How dare you talk to me about the word of God. The both of you can just kiss my Black behind! I can't wait for the day when Jessie decides to put *your* story on the front page of somebody's paper! AA Times Publisher and Editor Making Out and Making News!"

I got up from 'the chair' and slammed the door behind me without giving them a chance to utter a single word. I stormed to my desk and began packing my things hurriedly. The more I packed, the more I cried and the more I pushed away any rational thought or feeling that tried to tell me I was overreacting.

"Ssso, you're leaving us, huh?" Jessie inquired.

"You'd just better get the hell away from me before I kick your nosy behind all around this City room!"

"Alrighty then," she said mimicking the Jim Carey character from **In Living Color**. "I was just trying to see if you were okay. You've really misjudged me Caren. I've tried to help you. You just wouldn't let me. Turner isn't worth what you sacrificed for him. He'll screw this city and this state the same way he screwed you. It's best for everyone if the truth comes out. Sure, it'll hurt you for a little while, but maybe the state of Ohio will be saved from at least one crooked politician."

"Go to hell Jessie!" I shouted rolling my teary eyes at her as I started on my way with all my belongings in a duffle bag. "You don't give a damn about saving Cleveland or Ohio. All you care about is making a name for Jessie. You could have found another way to support the other candidate if that was your real concern. You didn't have to ruin lives to prove that Robert wasn't the best man for the job."

I stormed out of the City Room as all the reporters watched me in wonderment, sure to ask Jessie what happened as soon as I was safely out of sight. I busted through the door that led to the lobby where Jackie was typing on her computer. She looked up when she heard the door.

"What's going on?" she asked.

"I'll have to tell you later. Call me."

I passed her and headed out the door to the stairway that led to the parking lot and left the **AA Times** for the last time.

what you do in the dark . . .

september harvest

Oh, when will there be a harvest for the world?

"The fruit is always so good this time of year," I said to Darnell as we walked through the produce aisle in the supermarket.
"Yeah," he responded absently pushing the cart while I inspected nectarines and peaches. "It's harvest time."

I was in a good mood. It was Labor Day. Darnell and I were shopping for a few items to have an intimate cookout on my apartment balcony.

I had told Darnell that I quit my job because I couldn't get along with Jessie. He gave me a long lecture about how I shouldn't let other people interfere with my personal goals. He also made a point of telling me that I, of all people, should know that you don't leave one job until you have another one.

He suggested I take the postal exam scheduled for sometime within the next few weeks. So I applied and he seemed relieved that I was finally going to work in the real world.

It had been a week since I'd left the **AA Times** and I was enjoying every moment I could with Darnell. I knew our days were numbered. Jessie's story would be hitting the newsstands soon. Darnell and his whole family would know that I'd slept with Robert. My mother would know that I had an abortion. I had gone over countless explanations, excuses and reasons that I could give everyone, but none that I thought might gain me forgiveness and a wedding ring.

I started to pray for God to intervene, stop them from printing the story. Let Jessie get struck down by lightning. Let Jessie's sources be unreliable. Mrs. Bagley across the hall probably told Jessie about Robert and me making love in the hallway. I should have been more careful. Maybe Mr. Caldwell and Marge would take pity on me and somehow convince Jessie to ditch the story. None of these options were likely. I knew it.

Darnell and I drove back to my apartment in silence. He looked very pensive as he drove through the streets of Bedford Heights. I wondered what was on his mind. Had someone already told him about the story? Finally, as we were nearing my apartment complex he uttered, "We need to talk."

My heart stopped and quickened. I tried to anticipate what he wanted to talk about. Those words, 'we need to talk' reminded me of Marge's e-mail on the day I left the **AA Times**. He *knew*, my thoughts alerted me. I hadn't checked the paper this morning. Maybe it was in the **Plain Dealer** instead of the **AA Times**. I couldn't rule out the possibility that Jessie might sell out. This was probably D-day and I didn't even know it. I thought I might have until Thursday when the next issue of the **AA Times** came out, but if Jessie went to the **PD**, the story could come out any day.

"I never wanted you to find out about this, but this is something you can hide for only so long," he started.

"What is he talking about?" I asked myself. "Find out about what?" I asked him.

"I have a son," he announced. "He was born last week."

I was stunned. My heart dropped and broke into millions of little pieces and floated to every part of my body. I was crushed, shattered. I didn't even know how to react. My mind kept revisiting memories, trying to make sense of what Darnell had just said. It returned to July when I found the letters from Mercedes Jackson in his room. He had a son with that tramp after I had given up my daughter for him! I screamed in my mind.

"With Mercedes Jackson?" I muttered.

"Yeah," he answered softly giving me a brief look of surprise at the realization that he had already lied about the depth of their relationship. Then, he shrugged it off as if he thought it irrelevant at this point. "I

what you do in the dark...

tried to save you from all of this, but I couldn't. Mercedes got pregnant on purpose. She told me that she was on the pill, but she wasn't. I tried to get her to have an abortion, but she refused. She wants to get married."

"And you?"

"Red, Mercedes doesn't mean anything to me, but our child means everything to me."

"So, you're going to marry her?"

"I don't know, maybe."

"So what has all this time we've been spending together been about? What about the promises you made about our new commitment to each other?"

"Just my way of trying to hold on to something I knew I was about to lose."

I sat quietly as Darnell pulled into the parking lot and parked the car.

"I told her that I was in love with you, but she insists that there is no future for us. She thinks if I really loved you, I would have married you by now."

"Is she right?"

"Red, you know how much I love you. I can't even imagine not having you around. I've tried to distance myself from you, but nothing works. I still want to be with you. I'm just not satisfied with you and I can't get over the things I read in your journal."

"Is that why you slept with her without using any protection?"

"Why did you sleep with the guy you were with and not use protection?"

"I was lonely. It wasn't planned."

"I was lonely too."

"Darnell, I've always been there for you. How could you have been lonely?"

"I never felt like it was me you wanted."

"What? That doesn't make any sense. I wanted to spend the rest of my life with you. I wanted to be your wife. *I* wanted to have your children."

"You definitely wanted to get married and have children, but I don't think it necessarily had to be me that you did those things with."

"How could you say that? I've been faithful to you for almost ten years. You're the only man I've ever been with except for that one mistake."

"Yeah, but you don't think I'm good enough for you. I bet that other guy was a college graduate, probably what you would consider successful. You think you deserve better than me because you graduated from college and I'm just a postal worker."

"Darnell, I just applied there myself. You're just not making sense."

"It's a career for me, Red. For you, it's a temporary setback."

"This conversation is stupid. I'm not like that. I don't think I'm better than you. I love you just the way you are."

"You're not being honest with yourself."

"So, what's going to happen to us now?"

"I don't know. What do you think should happen?"

"What is it you see in this Mercedes?"

"That's what I mean. You don't think she's good enough for me, do you?"

"No, I don't. She's a tramp."

"She's a person."

"So, what attracted you to this *person*?"

"It's the sex if you must know. She's good in bed."

"You don't think *I'm* good in bed?"

"You always want me to make love to you. Sometimes I just want to have sex! I just don't think we're compatible sexually. I'm a carnal lover and you're a spiritual lover."

"You sound crazy! I thought you enjoyed being with me. I don't understand what you want."

"I'm not sure what I want sometimes either, but I do know what I don't want. I also know what I want right now is to go see my son."

I fumed with anger at the sounds of those words, 'my son.' He said it like he was proud, even happy. I felt left out, alone. I got out of the car and started taking the grocery bags out of the trunk of Darnell's Nissan 300x.

He got out and grabbed the bags I couldn't carry and followed me into my apartment building. Once inside my apartment, we put the bags on the kitchen floor. I went to my bedroom and flung myself onto the bed. Darnell followed me and stood over me quietly.

"I have to go. I'll call you."

And he was gone.

My heart was aching so much I didn't know whether to cry, scream or call someone to just talk it out. I wanted to call Mark, but I knew he was angry with me. I thought about calling Michelle, but she would just

what you do in the dark . . .

make light of the situation. She didn't like Darnell anyway. Jackie would lecture me. My mother or sister would pity me.

I just wanted someone to hold me and tell me that even though the man that I had loved for an entire decade had betrayed me, I was still beautiful, still desirable, still worth having. Only Mark could do that for me, but would he? I picked up the phone and dialed his number. The phone just kept ringing.

"Damn!" I shouted as I slammed down the phone. "Doesn't he know anything about answering machines?"

A couple of hours passed. It was six in the evening. I was beside myself with grief. I imagined that Darnell had gone to be with Mercedes and their baby. Was she in the hospital? Was she at home? Was she at Darnell's? Why didn't anybody in Darnell's family tell me? I'd been a part of their family for years. Didn't his mother care about me at all? Didn't she at least sympathize with me as another woman? Thoughts of all the holidays and special occasions I spent with Darnell raced through my head.

Everyone always said I'd be a Jennings one day. It was just a matter of time. Darnell and I would marry, have children and live happily ever after. Now, he was with someone else. He said he might marry her. They had started a family. I had killed my baby in hopes to fulfill a dream that would never be.

I picked up the phone and called the community center. It was Robert's campaign headquarters. Even though it was Labor Day, I knew sometimes Robert liked to work when no one was around.

"Councilman Turner here. Can I help you?"

"Robert. It's me."

"Caren? Hi. How are you? You sound upset."

"Robert, I need to talk to you."

"Talk? About what? I don't think it would be a good idea to see you until the election is over. What's up? You miss me?"

His voice softened. My heart was soothed somewhat by the sound of desire in his voice.

"You're married now, Robert. I called because I need to talk to you. I need a friend and I had no one else to call. Besides, I have some news that might affect your campaign."

"I'll be at your apartment in fifteen minutes."

Deborah Marbury

I hung up the phone and then I called Mercedes Jackson whose number I had committed to memory since the day I looked it up in Darnell's phone book.

"Hello!" she screamed in my ear. The baby was crying in the background.

"Mercedes?"

"Yeah, who 'dis?"

"This is Darnell's fiancée, Caren. He told me about the baby and I just wanted to let you know that it doesn't change anything. He loves me and we're still getting married."

"I thought I told you not to call me no mo'! Here, you better tell this tramp somethin'!"

"Caren, why are you calling here?" Darnell yelled.

I hung up the phone and began to pace the floor. I wanted to do something, but I didn't know what. I was so hurt and angry. I imagined Darnell comforting Mercedes, telling her I was crazy or something. I paced the floor for what seemed like hours. I was so mad. I could have just spit!

Robert finally rang my buzzer. I took a glance at myself in the bathroom mirror. I looked terrible. My eyes were red and puffy. I had been crying and rubbing them and I hadn't even realized it. Somehow my hair had gotten all messed up. It was flying every which way.

I followed the trail of clear blue plastic grocery bags from the kitchen to the living room door. I buzzed Robert in and opened the door for him to enter once he got to my floor. I saw my neighbor's door crack as I stood in the doorway, then close again quickly. Mrs. Bagley, I thought.

Robert stepped off the elevator looking as smooth as usual in an expensive suit, silk shirt and tie and a pair of very stylish shoes. His hair was neatly trimmed and faded. Jet-black waves laid nicely on the top. He was sho' nuff fine!

"What's up Sweetheart?" He kissed my cheek as he walked into my apartment. "You look like you've been crying. What's going on?"

"Robert," I said leading him to the sofa. "I have some bad news for you." We both took a seat.

"Okay." He took a deep breath.

"Jessie has found witnesses to corroborate her suspicions about us. I quit my job about a week ago. The story is coming out soon. Has anybody questioned you?"

what you do in the dark . . .

Robert looked stunned for about five minutes and then he answered, "No. Why'd you wait so long to tell me?"

"We haven't exactly been on speaking terms these days, Robert. The only reason I'm telling you now is because I'm really alone and I don't have anyone else to turn to. I don't know what to do."

"What does Jessie know? How did she find out?"

"Marge said neighbors, probably Mrs. Bagley across the hall, told her that they saw us making love in the hallway in November. The night of the dinner dance. Former patients from the abortion clinic told her that they saw you sleeping in the waiting area and that you left with me when I had the abortion in January."

"I knew we hadn't been careful enough. I had no idea that night of the dinner dance or the day I took you to the clinic that I'd be running for the state senate."

"Robert, what made you decide to run? What does Veronica and her family have to do with it?"

"Veronica!" he shouted in panic. "Veronica," he said again softer.

"Well Robert! What's going on?"

"Look Sweetheart. It's really quite simple. Veronica and I dated when we attended law school together at Ohio State. She got pregnant. I was going to marry her. She had a miscarriage and I called off the wedding. She broke up with me, of course. I graduated and came to Cleveland. I hadn't seen or heard from her since. When she read in the **AA Times** Columbus edition that I was starting a community center in Ward One, she called me. She wanted me to come to Columbus for a visit. I went to see her when I returned from Florida, my grandmother's funeral. She told me her father and uncle wanted to help me. They had connections, power and influence. They were sure they could get me elected to the state senate. I talked to them about it and it seemed like a good career move. The next thing I know she's telling me how much she still loved me, regretted leaving me. Said we could have it all, together. So I bought into it and here I am married to her and running for office."

"Why marry her now?"

"It was part of the deal. Besides, Veronica is really special to me."

"So, what do you think her reaction will be when this story hits?"

"I'm sure Roni will understand. This all happened before we married. Everything will be fine. I just need to adjust my political strategy a little."

"That's fine for you, but I'm losing everything. I lost my job. Darnell is already halfway into the arms of another woman. When he finds out about us, he'll leave me for sure."

Robert gazed at me intently with a look of pity mixed with concern and desire.

"You're still hung up on Darnell, huh?"

"He's all I've got Robert!" I started to cry again.

Robert pulled me into his arms and held me.

"It's gonna be alright. Talk to me. What's going on?"

"Darnell's a father. He had a son last week with some girl named Mercedes."

"Yeah, I know about Mercedes. Don't know what Darnell sees in her. According to the family he's been seeing her for about a year or two now. I know about Darnell Jr. too. We all kept telling Darnell to tell you, but I guess he didn't want to deal with it."

"Darnell Jr.! Robert, why didn't *you* tell me?"

"I tried to tell you on Easter. You weren't ready to accept that you and Darnell were over. It wasn't my place to tell you anyway. You're too good for Darnell or me. Give yourself some time to get over this. The right man will come along. How could any man resist you?"

He gave me a light kiss on the lips and squeezed me tight.

"I have to go now. I need to call a press conference for tomorrow morning before Jessie goes to press with her story. I wish you had told me about this when it first happened."

"I'm sorry, but before you leave will you promise me something?"

"Anything Sweetheart. What's up?"

"Talk to Darnell for me. Explain things. Tell him I love him. Convince him that I'm better for him than Mercedes. Tell him he doesn't have to marry her just because of the baby. We can work something out."

"I'll do what I can Sweetheart, but you're better off without him."

He kissed me again and headed for the door. I followed him slowly to see him out. He opened the door to camera flashes, microphones and TV cameras.

"Councilman Turner! Is it true that you and Caren Boogerton conceived a child together that you aborted in January of this year?"

"Councilman Turner! Is Ms. Boogerton your own first cousin's fiancée?"

what you do in the dark . . .

"Are you and Ms. Boogerton still carrying on this affair even though you're married to Veronica Kirkland now?"

"Do you have any morals, Mr. Councilman?"

"Is Ms. Boogerton getting dressed now, Sir?"

"No! I am not getting dressed. Councilman Turner and I were just discussing some business!" I yelled and tried to slam my door shut.

"Ms. Boogerton, how can you and Councilman Turner possibly have any business to discuss when it's been reported that you no longer work for the **AA Times**?"

"Ms. Boogerton, are you still engaged to the councilman's cousin?"

"Yes I am! Darnell Jennings and I are set to be married before the end of the year and there's absolutely nothing going on between Councilman Turner and me. He escorted me to the clinic to abort *my* baby, not his own."

"So it was you at the abortion clinic in January?"

"Yes. I aborted for medical reasons."

"Ms. Boogerton had your abortion been for medical reasons, you could have done it with your own private doctor."

"My doctor doesn't perform abortions for any reason. It's against his religion."

"Your neighbors say that they've seen you making love with Councilman Turner in this very hallway? Are you sure that the baby was not fathered by Mr. Turner?"

"Sssooo, Mr. Councilman, what do you have to say now?" Jessie Bassett stepped out from among the crowd of reporters. "Does your wife know you're still sleeping with your cousin's fiancée? Will her father still finance your campaign when he finds out? Or is it all worth it to the Kirklands just to have another Ohio state senator in their pockets? That is, *if* you're elected."

"No comment," Robert answered sternly. "I'll be happy to make a statement at my press conference tomorrow morning at the Ward One Community Center."

Robert pushed through the crowd of reporters and to the staircase exit. Some reporters followed him down the stairs. Others fled to the elevator. Jessie stood there for a moment smirking at me.

"Ssso, Ms. Boogerton. It seems the grits have finally hit the fan. I told you this day would come."

I glared at Jessie without saying a word. I noticed she was wearing a Plain Dealer badge. I closed my door and went to bed.

Pounding on my apartment door awakened me at about 3 a.m. I jumped out of bed and opened the door without even asking who it was.

"What's up? Sista-in-law," a drunk, staggering David Jennings slurred as he stumbled into my apartment.

"David! What are you doing here? And at three in the morning? How'd you get inside the building?"

"Came to you see you Sista-in-law. Came in with the rest of the bar-closers who live in this building."

"What's wrong? Why are you drunk?"

"I thought we could consooole one another. I got a bottle of Seagram's in the car. You want some?"

"You've been driving in your condition?"

"Darnell is a punk! He slept with Linda and he cheated on you with that tramp, Mercedes!" he announced.

"I'll go make you some coffee. You're not making any sense."

I went into the kitchen and left David sprawled across my sofa. I boiled some water for instant coffee. I made him a nice strong cup, black with just a teaspoon of sugar. When I brought it to him, he looked a little more alert. He sat up straight. I gave him the coffee. He drank it in silence. I made a few more cups. He started to sober a little.

"How much have you had to drink?"

"Not that much. I don't really drink. I just can't believe my own brother would do this to me."

"I *don't* believe it. Darnell wouldn't sleep with Linda."

"He did."

"How do you know?"

"I caught her at his condo yesterday."

"There must have been a reason."

"Yeah, they've been messing around. That's the reason."

"Did you ask him what happened?"

"Talked to him earlier today."

"What did he say?"

"Said he was sorry. It just happened. Said she was just using me anyway. Tried to act like he was protecting me or something."

"I'm sorry David."

"Thanks. I'm sorry for what he did to you too. I just don't know what's gotten into Darnell. It's like he just don't care about nobody but himself. If it's any consolation to you, that statement you made on the

what you do in the dark...

news tonight really pissed Mercedes off. She thinks Darnell is really planning to marry you instead of her."

"What do you mean think? How did Darnell react to what they said about Robert and me?"

"He was quiet. You didn't really sleep with him, did you?"

"You better get some sleep. We'll sort this mess out in the morning."

"Thanks Caren."

"No problem David."

I gave David a pillow and a blanket and then I turned in for the night. It only took me a few minutes to drift off. I was exhausted. My whole world had been turned upside down and inside out. I had no idea what I was going to do next. I was hurt beyond belief. I was angry and I felt helpless and hopeless. Sleep was my only comfort.

The telephone awakened me around noon.

"Hello," I answered groggily.

"Sweetheart. It's me, Robert. I have bad news."

"Oh, your press conference. How did it go?"

"I cancelled it. Darnell's been shot, murdered."

"What? Robert, what are you talking about? I just talked with Darnell yesterday."

"I shouldn't have given you this news over the phone, but I can't come see you right now. I'm with the family. Everything's a mess. They're holding Mercedes for questioning."

"Mercedes? What's going on Robert?"

"All I know is that Darnell was shot on his route at about 8 this morning in the projects where Mercedes lives. I think the police believe she may have seen or heard something."

"I'll get dressed and come over. Where are you? At the Jennings?"

"Yeah, but I don't think it would be a good idea for you to show up here. The family's all upset about the news reports of our affair last night. Veronica's here with me too. She's not happy either. The baby is here with Aunt Mattie and they expect Mercedes to come back shortly. They don't want any fighting between the two of you."

"Okay," I agreed reluctantly and hung up the phone.

I got out of bed and went to check on David. The blanket was folded with the pillow on top of it. I checked the bathroom, but David was gone. I guessed he was embarrassed to face me sober.

I was relieved he had left. I didn't want to be the one to have to tell him that his brother was dead. I still couldn't believe it myself. Darnell dead. Murdered. What happened? Killed on his route. Who would have done such a thing?

It was Tuesday, September 2, time for the first of the month checks to come out. Maybe someone tried to rob him. That had to be it. Why were they holding Mercedes? Was she a witness?

Darnell was dead. I kept telling myself. The anger I had been feeling toward him the day before was fading. I was numb. I didn't know what to feel. It was like losing him twice. I called my mother.

"Ma," I said when I heard her answer.

"What the hell was you messin' 'round with that damn Councilman Turner for?" she yelled.

"Damn!" I whispered to myself. I had forgotten about the news reporters last night.

"I can't believe you had no abortion! I know I raised you better than that! I'm just too embarrassed to leave the house! Everybody all over town is talkin' 'bout how you all caught up in this mess! What possessed you to sleep with that man and then kill the baby? Lord, have mercy! What you gon' do now? Lord, have mercy! Lord, have mercy! Please have mercy on my child!"

I hung up the phone. It rang again immediately. I stared at it for about twenty minutes as it just rang and rang, then I turned on my answering machine. My mother was just a preview of what I was in store for if I dared step out of my apartment or make any contact with the outside world. The phone stopped ringing for about ten minutes. Then, it started to ring again. This time the caller left a message instead of hanging up on my answering machine.

"Caren. It's Michelle. Girlfriend, what in the world is going on? You've been in the news all morning on the radio, on TV, in the paper. Girl, this is major drama! Call me."

Next. There was a message from Jackie. "I was afraid this was going to happen. Marge is worried sick about you. She wants you to know that she's sorry about everything. Call me. I'm worried about you too."

Then, there was just ringing and hang-ups.

Next, my door buzzer started ringing every thirty minutes or so. I had become a prisoner in my own home. I couldn't answer the phone. I couldn't answer the door. I couldn't call anyone. I couldn't go anywhere. I just sat in my room, thinking.

what you do in the dark...

I didn't know what to do about Darnell. I didn't know what was going to happen with Robert's campaign. By now, they were reporting Darnell's murder as a part of the story about Robert and me.

I wondered what Mark thought about all this. I wondered if he would speak to me if I called. I picked up the phone and dialed his number between the ceasing of rings. No one answered. I felt really alone now.

I fell asleep.

After a few days of seclusion, I felt better. I was determined to face the world and attend Darnell's funeral. I got dressed and headed to the Jennings' house. When I arrived, Mattie Jennings opened the door.

"Yes Caren, what can I do for you?"

"I wanted to know about Darnell's funeral arrangements."

"I'm sorry, Honey. We buried Darnell yesterday."

"Oh."

My knees weakened a little. The life seemed to drain from me just hearing that Darnell had been buried. I stumbled.

"I'd like to come in to offer my condolences. Why didn't anybody notify me? I'm his, I mean I was his fiancée."

"Someone tried to call you, but there was no answer."

"Why didn't they leave a message?"

"Look Baby. I didn't make the calls. Other family members did that. I'm really sorry that you missed the service, but as you know Darnell left a child here. His mother is here right now and I don't think it would be a good idea for you to come in. I'll tell everyone you were here, okay?" She smiled at me nervously.

"Alright Mrs. Jennings."

As I turned to leave, Robert and Veronica were approaching.

"Robert!" I exclaimed, so happy to see someone who might be nice to me. "What's been going on with the campaign? Is everything alright?"

Veronica grabbed his arm and through clenched teeth, I heard her say, "Don't you dare say a word to her."

Robert looked at me nervously. He nodded at me as they walked past me without speaking. Mrs. Jennings welcomed them and I headed back to my car. I drove to Mark's house. I got out and knocked on the door. There was no answer. I wasn't quite ready to discuss this whole mess with Michelle or Jackie, so I went home.

Once I was inside the lobby of my apartment building, I checked my mailbox. It was full of handwritten letters. I opened one. It had the

Deborah Marbury

words, 'Baby killer,' sprawled across it in big black letters written in with a magic marker.

I dropped the letters to the floor and there in the midst of my hate mail was an official post card from the United States Postal Service. I picked it up, stepped over the other letters and pushed the elevator button. When the elevator opened for me, I stepped in; turned around and let the doors close me in. I pushed two and I read the post card. It said that my exam was scheduled for Wednesday, September 17 at 9:00 a.m.

what you do in the dark . . .

october homecoming

A chair is not a house, and a house is not a home
When there's no one there to hold you tight

"Hey! Let's go to the Central State homecoming this weekend. That will cheer you up. They're having some great alumni activities according to the brochure they mailed me. Did you get yours?" Michelle coaxed as I sat quietly on my sofa. She regarded me carefully from the recliner.

"I can't believe Darnell is dead."

"Girl, you're gonna make yourself sick just sitting here worrying all the time. How long have you been sitting around here in that terrycloth bathrobe?"

"It's been a few weeks. I'm just lost without Darnell. I can't believe how his family just turned their backs on me just because I slept with Robert. They have a lot of nerve when they knew Darnell had fathered a child with Mercedes while he was engaged to me! I guess I am making myself sick. I haven't even had a period since the middle of August."

"Oh Lord," Michelle whispered.

"What?"

"I just get a little worried when women start missin' periods."

"I know you don't think I'm pregnant!"

"Well, are you?"

"Don't be ridiculous!"

"Am I being ridiculous?"

"Yes you are. I don't even wanna think about no more babies being born or not being born!"

She shrugged and decided to change the subject.

"How's Mark?"

"Haven't talked to him." I thought back to the last time I'd seen him. He had stormed out of my apartment because Darnell had showed up. Darnell and I had made love and now Darnell was dead and Mark was angry with me because. . .

"Oh Lord!" I exclaimed.

"What's the matter?"

"Michelle, I could be pregnant. I was trying to get pregnant in August!"

"Well here Girl!" She pulled a pregnancy kit from her purse, "Find out for sure!"

"You keep pregnancy kits in your purse?"

"Look Girl. Mind yo' business! Now go pee on this thang before you make my blood pressure go up!"

I took the kit and went to the bathroom. I came back to the living room with it a few minutes later and placed the test on top of my television.

"Now we just have to wait a few minutes."

"Yeah, I know. So what you gonna do if it's positive?"

"What can you do if you're pregnant by a dead man or a man who hates your guts?"

"A man who hates your guts? What you talkin' 'bout?"

"Mark. I made love with Mark and Darnell on the same day in August."

"Woo, you was really getting yo' groove on Girlfriend! Mark Townsend?"

"You can't judge a book by its cover. Mark's got it goin' on! He looks much better now than he did in high school."

"I never said his cover was bad! That was you always actin' like you was too good for him."

"Michelle, how will I know whose baby it is?"

"They got DNA tests to figure that stuff out now Girl."

"What would be the point of knowing anyway? Darnell's dead and Mark isn't speaking to me."

what you do in the dark . . .

"What's the point? Girl, you're trippin' as usual. Getting paid is the point. Darnell worked for the Post Office. If it's his child, you can get paid. I don't know what you gonna do if it's Mark's."

"Mark has a good job now."

"Oh yeah! Well, there you have it. Child support. It's all good."

"Does everything have to boil down to dollars and cents with you Michelle?"

"Dollars are the only thing that make sense to me in this crazy mixed up world."

I stretched out on the sofa, then curled into a ball.

"Girlfriend. You got too much drama goin' on in yo' life. I told Jackie to come over. We're gonna cheer you up. So what you think about goin' to homecoming?"

"Jackie won't go to anything like that. She didn't go to college and besides she has a family to take care of."

"Well, she can stay her Susie Homemaker butt here! We can go. Come on. It'll be fun."

"Do you think Darnell went to heaven?"

"Hell no!"

"He was raised in the church, you know?"

"And ever since he's been raised, he's been raising hell. 'Cause he knew that hell was gon' be his home! Girl, his cheatin' behind ain't hardly in no heaven. Believe that!"

"My mother said that all you had to do to go to heaven is believe in Jesus Christ. He believed in Him."

"If he really believed in Him, he wouldn't have been so damned whorish! That ain't Christ-like! People that believe in Jesus supposed to act like Jesus. That's what my mama told me."

"So, where do you think you're gonna go? You got yourself a membership in the hell raisers club too, you know."

"I know I'm going to hell, so I'm gonna have all the fun I can while I can. Girl, I know I can't be like Jesus. So I don't even try. I might as well enjoy myself now. That's the way I see it. Besides, it's so many religions out there, how could you possibly know which one is right? Muslims don't believe in Jesus. The Nation of Islam says that Jesus was just a prophet. Christianity is for white people and you know I'm down with Louis Farrakhan anyway. He can set some white folks straight! He ain't no joke!"

"Yeah, but where do they go when they die?"

"They're just dead I guess! Look, I really ain't tryin' to worry about dying right now. Go check your test."

I got up from the sofa and walked over to the television. Nervously, I picked up the test. A big blue plus sign glared at me through the plastic tube.

"It's positive."

"Damn. Pregnant twice in one year. What you gon' do?"

"I don't know. I don't wanna think about it right now. I still have to see a doctor. Maybe the test is wrong."

I sank into the cushions of my sofa again and curled into a ball.

"We can only hope," Michelle whispered.

The door buzzer rang. Michelle motioned for me to stay where I was as she got up from the recliner to answer the door.

"Yeah!" she shouted into the intercom.

"It's Jackie!"

Michelle buzzed her in, opened the door and went to meet her at the elevator. A few minutes later, Jackie and Michelle joined me in the living room. Jackie sat by my head where I was still curled up in a ball. Michelle turned on the radio and went back to her seat in the recliner.

"How you doin'?" Jackie asked stroking my hair.

"Pregnant again."

"Yeah. Well, you know Michelle filled me in on that in the hallway."

I smiled weakly and put my head on Jackie's lap. She settled back on the sofa so I could be comfortable.

"My life is so messed up Jackie. I'm so embarrassed. I can't even talk to my mother or sister. I miss Darnell. His family hates me. They blame me for Darnell's death."

"Why do they blame you?" Jackie asked. "All the reports say that Mercedes is the main suspect."

"I don't know. The police claim that Mercedes may have killed Darnell because I said we were planning to marry by the end of the year on the news that night. Darnell had promised to marry her. My comments made it look like he lied to her."

"So that's your fault?" Michelle snapped. "Is his family stupid or something? She's the one who pulled the trigger, not you!"

"I think they're mad because I slept with Robert."

"Whatever!" Michelle rolled her eyes and rocked in the recliner.

"We miss you at the **AA Times**."

"Yeah right. *You* miss me. I'm sure no one else does."

what you do in the dark . . .

"No. Marge misses you. She knows you just went off because you were hurt and angry. She's the reason Jessie's at the **Plain Dealer** now. She decided not to publish the story about you and Robert. Marge saw that you had been right about Jessie's lack of loyalty. She appreciated your warnings."

"So why hasn't she called to offer me my job back?"

"It's too soon. She still thinks you wouldn't be very effective as reporter with all this bad publicity. Have you talked to Robert? How do you think this has affected his campaign? Looks like he's still on top according to the news."

"Yeah. I think he's going to make it."

"It's that 'good boy' image you created for him that's hard for people to shake. The community center is doing well. People care about a man's work. They know people make mistakes, but his record as councilman has been great. It was you that helped people see that."

"Mark said that too."

"Mark?" Jackie looked puzzled. "Who's Mark?"

"Mark Townsend."

"Oh yeah. You still talk to him, huh?"

"She does more than talk to him."

I gave Michelle a stern look.

"What now Caren?" Jackie asked exasperated.

"Mark might be the father of this baby if I'm really pregnant."

"Oh Lord! Does the drama ever end with you Caren?"

Jackie got up and began to pace the living room floor.

"Don't get all bent out of shape, Miss Holier Than Thou. She's already depressed. Don't make her feel worse."

"You're right. I'm sorry Caren."

"It's okay."

"Now as I was saying before. We need to do something to get rid of all this gloom and doom. Let's go to the Central State homecoming!"

"I don't feel like going anywhere and I'm sure Jackie can't go."

"Ain't nothin' to it, but to do it! Right Jackie?"

"I'll go on one condition."

"What's that?" Michelle asked.

"We have to go to church on Sunday when we get back. My husband and kids are out of town this weekend visiting his family in Chicago. I can kick it with you guys all weekend just like a single woman.

Just like when we were in high school, but we have to go to church on Sunday."

"Church!" Michelle responded with pure indignation. "I don't feel like all that. I'm gon' be tired when I get back."

"Come on Michelle. Caren needs something to feed her soul. Look at her. She's in bad shape. Partying isn't going to do anything to lift her spirits like Jesus can."

"Whatever!" Michelle waved her hand at Jackie, then she looked at me and her expression became solemn. "Alright I'll do it for Caren," she conceded.

"You in Caren?" Jackie asked.

I was touched by their concern for me. True friends, I thought.

"I'm in."

"Good!" Michelle exclaimed. "Go take a shower. We'll help you get packed."

After I got showered and dressed, Michelle and Jackie helped me pack an overnight bag. We left that Friday evening in Jackie's van for Central State. My head started to flood with memories of the days Michelle and I went to fraternity parties and homecoming activities every year. I thought about all the nights Darnell and I had made love in each other's dorm room.

I cried every time I thought about Darnell, but I was glad I decided to go. We went to the football game on Saturday afternoon as usual, then to the homecoming dance that night. Michelle and I renewed acquaintances with old friends, sorority sisters and introduced Jackie to our old life. We had a lot of fun reminiscing in the dorm room we stayed in. It was just like the sleepovers we used to have as teenagers. We went to sleep late and got up early.

We headed back to Cleveland in time to make it back for 11:00 worship service at Matthias. It felt good to be there. The choir was exuberant with song. The fellowship period was warm and welcoming. I sat between Jackie and Michelle. Michelle was fidgety as if it really bothered her to be there.

Jackie just looked on at everything with a peaceful smile. She didn't really say much. I watched everyone and everything, taking in every detail. I felt like a foreigner. I'd forgotten what it was like to be part of a church. I noticed that some people were pointing and whispering about me. It didn't last long. After the collection plate was passed around a

what you do in the dark...

couple of times and the choir sang a few songs, Reverend Peoples stepped up to the podium in the pulpit and started his sermon.

"It's homecoming time saints! Several colleges have just celebrated their homecoming. They have partied all weekend. Won or lost football games. Marched in parades. The band has played and fun has been had by all. But, I'd like to take a closer look at the word 'homecoming'. I just believe that there is something about that word that should mean something to the saints today. Amen?"

The congregation replied, "Amen."

"Homecoming as defined in the dictionary is an annual event whereby alumni return to visit their home colleges or universities. My brothers and sisters, you see, I find it very strange that colleges could have this special time every year whereby alumni can come back home to these campuses, but I'm faced with the question, where are these alumni coming home from?

What I'm getting at, my brothers and sisters, is that the church or shall I say God used to be the home of some of these educated scholars who now find their homes in places of higher learning, corporate offices and entrepreneurial endeavors. They've ventured away to pursue the American dream and they go back to their college and university homes, but they haven't come back home to God.

Now, my brothers and sisters, I want to know when will our college-educated prodigal sisters and brothers come back home? When will they realize that as the Scriptures say, 'What does it profit a man to gain the world, but lose his soul?'

When will the prodigal sons and daughters of the most High God come back home? And I know you all know the story that Jesus told about the prodigal son, don't you? Well, if you don't, you can find it in your Bibles. The fifteenth chapter of Luke. When you get to it, say amen."

I looked around nervously as people began picking up their Bibles and leafing through them hurriedly to find their places until you could hear a chain reaction of amens throughout the sanctuary.

Jackie found her place and waited patiently for Reverend Peoples to read from it. Michelle was leafing absently through the church bulletin. She sat at the end of the pew with her crossed leg dangling in the aisle. Occasionally, I saw her peep over the top of the bulletin and wink at a handsome brother sitting in the adjacent pew. We were sitting in the

Deborah Marbury

middle section and he was sitting to our left. He was quite fixated on Michelle's long shapely leg.

I noticed a red Bible on the back of the pew directly in front of me. I picked it up and began to leaf through the pages. I thought I remembered Luke as a book that was in the New Testament. I flipped through the pages in the back and there it was, The Gospel According to Luke. I found the fifteenth chapter.

"Starting at verse 10 in the King James Version," Reverend Peoples continued, "the text reads as follows and Jesus says, 'Likewise I say unto you, there is joy in the presence of the angels of God over one sinner that repenteth.' And he said, 'A certain man had two sons: And the younger of them said to his father, Father, give me the portion of goods that falleth to me. And he divided unto them his living. And not many days after, the younger son gathered all together, and took his journey into a far country, and there wasted his substance with riotous living. And when he had spent all, there arose a mighty famine in that land; and he began to be in want. And he went and joined himself to a citizen of that country; and he sent him into his fields to feed swine. And he would fain have filled his belly with the husks that the swine did eat; and no man gave unto him. And when he came to himself, he said, 'How many hired servants of my father's have bread enough to spare, and I shall perish with hunger! I will arise and go to my father, and will say unto him, Father, I have sinned against heaven, and before thee, and am no more worthy to be called thy son, make me as one of thy hired servants.' And he arose, and came to his father. But when he was a great way off, his father saw him, and had compassion, and ran, and fell on his neck, and kissed him. And the son said unto him, 'Father, I have sinned against heaven, and in thy sight, and am no more worthy to be called thy son. But the father said to his servants, 'Bring forth the best robe, and put it on him; and put a ring on his hand, and shoes on his feet, And bring hither the fatted calf, and kill it; and let us eat and be merry, For this, my son, was dead, and is alive again; he was lost and is found.' And they began to be merry."

Reverend Peoples paused, took a deep breath, and then announced, "I'd like to take for a thought today, A Homecoming for the Prodigal Sons and Daughters of the Most High God."

The congregation closed their Bibles and everyone seemed to settle in to listen to what he had to say. I followed suit. I was genuinely

what you do in the dark...

interested. I was also touched by how that father had received his son back home after he had left and blew all his money.

"By show of hands," Reverend Peoples continued, "how many of you are college graduates?"

I looked around as I raised my hand. A little less than half the people in the pews raised their hands in a crowd that looked to be about four hundred strong.

"Now, I'm not going to ask how many of you have accepted Jesus Christ as your personal Lord and Savior or how many of you used to be a member of a church before you went to college and are not members anymore. I'm a shepherd, I know my flock and I can safely assume that some of you have not made this church or any other church your home. So I'd like to say to you who have not accepted Christ or who don't have a church home, welcome home!

I know a lot of you know what the prodigal son of Luke 15 experienced when you were in college. You know what it's like to leave home, squander your money and discover that there's no place like home. I know a lot of you know what it's like to have spent all the money your parents sent you at the first of the month by the 12th of the month and you had to survive until the 30th of the month before you could get anymore. A lot of you fasted without having any desire of sacrifice for the Lord in mind."

The congregation laughed.

"And you couldn't wait to get back home for that good ol' soul food dinner that Mama cooked so well. You'd go home for the weekend so you could wash your clothes and get your Sunday dinner, and for you, that was a great homecoming.

But oh, my brothers and sisters, what a great homecoming it is when you can come back home to your heavenly Father who is waiting for you with open arms. And instead of a soul food dinner for your homecoming, He has a homecoming feast for your soul! Somebody knows what I'm talking about!"

People started to shout hallelujahs, amens and thank you Jesus! Jackie jumped to her feet and started clapping. Michelle started to pay attention.

"Oh just check out verse 10 one more time saints. 'Cause you oughta be excited! It says that there is joy! Joy in the presence of the angels of God over *one* sinner that repents! Oh Hallelujah! So that means that if just one of you repents from your sins and turns to Jesus today, then the angels in heaven will start a party! They'll be partyin' harder than you were last night at that homecoming dance. They'll be partyin' harder than you were at that frat party. They'll be partyin' harder than you were at that nightclub last night!

The angels will rejoice because just *one* sinner has come back home. You see, my brothers and sisters, those of us who have been like the prodigal son and know what it's like to lose the comfort, security and provision that we have in our Father's house are clapping and rejoicing right now because they can say and mean what that Psalmist David said, 'I was glad when they said let us go into the house of the Lord!' Many of us who are back home today know what it's like to be a prodigal son or daughter out there starving in our sinful ways. We were out there just crying, 'Oh if I could just find someone to love me for me!' Can I get a witness somebody?"

The congregation was on fire now. People were running up and down the aisles screaming, "Thank you Jesus! Thank you for letting me come back home!"

"How many of you are out there just crying at night and worrying the Lord? Saying Father please, just send me somebody to love me for me! And you're still starving in your sinful ways! Oh, I need some help up here this morning!"

"Thank you Jesus!" A young woman shrieked.

"You're jumping from bed to bed trying to find love, trying to find someone you can call your own, but after you gave all you've got to give, you get up and you're still starvin'. Some of you lookin' for love in a bottle of Jack Daniels, in a crack pipe, rolled up in an E-Z wider, but when you get through drinkin' and smokin' you're still starvin'! Some of you eat all day and all night, butts just as wide as a house, but you're still starvin'!

You're hungry and you're thirsty and you know you could have that hunger satisfied and that thirst quenched if you could just find love. Someone to love you for you! And you go home to your Mama and Daddy's house, but you're grown now and they're tellin' you or they *should* be tellin' you that it's time for you to be on your own. You see, because your mother and father were never designed to satisfy the hunger or quench the thirst of your soul. They should have told you how to get your soul filled and a lot of you had parents that did that for you. But, you went to college, to the military, to a job, to drug dealing, to stealing and everywhere else you went when you left home. And you

what you do in the dark . . .

think you're rich now because you have inherited the world. You got a new car, a new house and a pocket full of money, but you're still starvin' and thirstin' and you just wanna be filled.

Well, my brothers and sisters, you might ask me, Brother Preacher, what is it that I'm starvin' and thirstin' for and how can I be filled? How can I find someone to love me for me. And lastly, Brother Preacher, where is my home if it's not with my parents and how can I come back to it? And I say to you, my brother and sisters, I'm glad you asked.

First of all, it's not food and wine that you're starvin' and thirstin' for. It's the broken body and shed blood of Jesus. Now, I'm gonna show you in a minute that man cannot live by bread alone. It's not a lover that you need, at least not one that loves your body or your personality. It's your soul that needs to be nourished and loved and God is the lover of our souls."

Humans are not even capable of the kind of love our soul needs. If you do one thing we don't like, then we've got a problem with you. We want you to fix it. And the only time we can love you for you is when you is a whole lot like us. Can I get a witness?"

The congregation shouted, "Amen!"

"You gotta be careful, too, about the places you call home. 'Cause a job is not a home. A place of learning is not a home. Your mama and daddy's house shouldn't even *always* be called *your* home. 'Cause like the song says,

Mama may have and Papa may have, but God bless the child that's got his own!

And then sometimes you can have your own house, but even your own house is not a home, when the right person's not there. Now, I know you all know that song,

A chair is still a chair, even when there's no one sitting there
But a chair is not a house, and a house is not a home
When there's no one there to hold you tight
And no one there you can kiss goodnight

So, for all of you who have a house, but you're still looking for someone to love you for you, you're still hungry and thirsty for something, then I think it's safe to say that your house is not a home.

So, I say to you now, my brothers and sisters, you ain't gonna find no home on earth. You can search this old world over and you won't find what you're looking for outside of the Word of God.

You see if you pick up the Word of God, you'll find that this place is not our home. We're just passing through and what you hunger and thirst for is righteousness. And you can get filled when you break the bread of life, which is the Word of God with other believers in the house of God, which is the church.

Because it's Matthew 4, verse 4 that says man shall not live by bread alone, but by every word that proceedeth out of the mouth of God."

Reverend Peoples held up his Bible and announced,

"I present to you, my brothers and sisters, your homecoming feast for your soul. If you want someone to love you for you, then just order some John 3:16 which says that 'God so loved the world,' and you can just slide your name in there where it says world, 'that He gave His only begotten son. And whosoever believeth in Him shall not perish, but have everlasting life.'

Now what man, woman, boy or girl can love you like that. Love you so much that they would give their only child for you. You can't even borrow sugar no more from most people.

Now if you're still hungry maybe you need to order some Romans 5, verse 8 where it says, 'But God commendeth his love toward us' (and that means you and me) 'in that, while we were yet sinners, Christ died for us.' That means you can come to Jesus just like you are. Don't waste no time trying to get cleaned up for God, 'cause he knew you were messed up when he died for you. And how does God know this, you ask?

You're still hungry, huh? Let's order a little Romans 3:23 which says, 'For **all** have sinned and come short of the glory of God.' So I guess 'all' would include me and it would include you! Some of you are still hungry! I hear your souls grumbling now. 'What about Moses? What about Abraham and all those good saints in the Bible?' Take a bite off of Romans 3:10, 'And it is written, THERE IS NONE RIGHTEOUS, NO NOT ONE.' That means Moses, Abraham, me and each and every one of you! None of us are all that without Christ. We're all sinners.

Are you still hungry? Souls still grumbling? But how can I receive the love I need for my soul if I'm so bad? It's time for the main course now. Let's take a bite out of Romans 6, verse 23. 'For the wages of sin is death, but the gift of God is eternal life.'

And how can you get your gift of eternal life? Your soul still rumbles. Take a chunk out of Romans 10:9-10, 'That if thou shalt confess with thy mouth the Lord Jesus, and shalt believe in thine heart that God raised him from the dead, thou shalt be saved. For with the

what you do in the dark...

heart man believeth unto righteousness; and with the mouth confession is made unto salvation.'

Your Father in heaven is saying to you now, 'Come back home just as you are. I've demonstrated my love for you while you were sinning, I sent my son to die so you could come back home to me.

He says when you come home, he won't leave you any more messed up than the father of our text today did for his son in Luke 15. He'll clean you up and dress you in fine robes. His blood will wash away all the dirt of your sins and He will present you to the world just as the prodigal son was presented to the father's servants.

God will say this about you, 'This is my lost son or daughter who was dead and now is alive.' Because without Christ in your life, you are spiritually dead and your soul is lost as you are physically dying. But the gift of God is eternal life in Christ Jesus our Lord.

So I say to you, my brothers and sisters, you've partied all weekend. Let's start a party in heaven! Luke 15:10 says that if just one sinner repents, if one of you says Father I have sinned against you, and I'm not worthy to be called your son or daughter, then the angels of God will rejoice in heaven. There's a party going on in heaven right now as sinners turn to God and away from sin on this the Lord's day in churches all over the world. Let me hear the church say, It's a party up there!"

"It's a party up there!" The congregation responded enthusiastically.

"Now let's start one down here. Is there *one* here today who wants to start a party in heaven? Is there one?"

The choir stood to sing and the whole congregation stood to its feet clapping and praising God.

I realized that I had been hungering and thirsting for righteousness. I was ashamed of the person I'd become. I was pregnant for the second time in a year and I didn't even know who the father was. I wanted to come back home to God. I wanted to know Him better than I had as a child. My heart was yearning for someone who would love me for me. Reverend Peoples had convinced me that I could find that love with Jesus.

"The doors of the church are open," he appealed. "If you're starvin' and thirstin' for something more meaningful in your life, the God we serve says in the bread of life, Philippians 4:19, 'He shall supply all your needs according to His riches in glory in Christ Jesus.' He is Jehovah Jirah, the Great Provider. If you're looking to be rescued from the meaningless life you've been living Our Lord Jesus Christ is the Great Redeemer. He will save you, wash you with His precious blood. There is nothing too terrible that you may have done that you can't be forgiven for except if you continue in unbelief. Make Him your Lord and Savior right now. He'll never leave you or forsake you. When you need someone to talk to or someone to console you and you just don't know which way to go, the Holy Spirit is the Great Comforter, and the Great Counselor. He will lead you into all truth.

Come on down and confess the death, burial and resurrection of our Lord Jesus Christ right now and believe it in your heart. Come on home to Jesus. He's gone to prepare a place for you. A home for your soul. And he's coming back for all those who believe. Is there one?"

I could feel the presence of the Lord as I sat there wondering if He could forgive my sins, if He could clean me up. But there was another presence, something that kept saying,

"No. You can't turn away from everything the Lord wants you to turn away from. You can't feel the Lord's arms around you at night when you're home alone in bed. The Lord can't make you feel beautiful and desired. And he sho' can't make love to you the way Mark did that night. You need a husband first. And who is going to marry you if you don't have sex with him first. Especially if you've got a child. You know you can't abort this one. God's already mad at you for what you did to the other one. No one is going to marry you and take care of some other man's child and they don't even know if you're good in bed. That's why Darnell left you for Mercedes because she was better in bed. Do you want a man, a husband? Or do you want the Lord? If you go up there now, you're not going to have anymore fun. You'll be just like Jackie minus the husband. Just church and loneliness. No sex. No men. And wouldn't you just love to have someone make love to you the way Mark did that time in August? Hell, maybe you could get Mark to make love to you again if this is his child you're carrying. You better wait until you get a husband, then you can come to the Lord with your whole heart."

People were starting to come down the center aisle of the church moving toward Reverend Peoples who was standing with his arms outstretched at the altar. There were about four young women who came. They were seated in front of about five deacons.

Jackie was shouting, "Hallelujah!"

Michelle was crying softly.

I was frozen in my spot.

what you do in the dark . . .

Then, a medium build man with a reddish brown complexion, a sharp haircut faded in the back and on the sides, dressed in a stylish black suit approached Reverend Peoples. They hugged each other and shook hands. He turned to face the congregation and I saw those sparkling hazel eyes. He kept looking down, but finally those hazel eyes rose and met mine. He turned away quickly to focus on Reverend Peoples.

"And what do we hear concerning our dear Brother Townsend?" Reverend Peoples asked the deacons after the ladies had been accepted into the church on their Christian experience. "Wait a minute," he said before they could answer. "I just want to say something about this young man. His mother, Sister Gladys Townsend, has been a long-standing member of this church. Most of you probably know, she passed away earlier this year. I do believe it was Easter Sunday. But like a true saint, her last words were sharing the Gospel with her only son. She told him that the only way he was going to see her again was if he accepted Jesus Christ as his Lord and Savior. He took his mother at her word and here he is standing before us today, ready to give his life to Christ. I know the angels of God are really rejoicing today. Hallelujah saints!"

The congregation echoed, "Hallelujah!"

"Deacons?"

"I move that Brother Townsend be accepted into Matthias Fellowship Christian Church by way of baptism."

"Second."

"Any questions or discussion? There being none, let's use the usual sign for voting around here. All in favor?"

"Hallelujah!"

"All opposed? There's nobody angry but Satan. Welcome home to all of our new members. Everybody, let's give the Lord some praise!"

The congregation stood to their feet and clapped.

Mark did it! He said he was going to turn his life over to the Lord and he did it!

"Hey, that's your boy Mark." Jackie nudged me.

"So that's Mark?" Michelle nudged me from the other side. "He does look better than he did in high school."

I squeezed past Michelle into the aisle and rushed out of the church to wait for Michelle and Jackie in the van. I told them I wanted to be alone when we got to my apartment, so they left.

I went to my bedroom and started to undress. My feelings were starting to overwhelm me. I realized when I saw Mark today that I truly missed him. I loved him and he hated me. It was his child I was carrying. I just knew it. What was I going to do? I thought back to the time in August when we made love for the first and only time and I thanked God that I had finally known what it was like to truly be loved and cherished by a man even if it was a sin.

I wanted to be with him so badly, but the way he looked away from me told me that there was no chance of that. I looked around for something to hold that reminded me of him. Something that would make me feel close to him again. Something that would prove that we really did share something special that day. I remembered the gun he left in my drawer. I opened the drawer, but the gun was gone.

"It was David," I whispered.

Yes, that journal entry, that night and that year had changed my life. It was that night when I started to look for love in all the wrong places. I began to make decisions that year that took me on the road to spiritual death.

It's been ten years and even though Satan kept me from giving my life to Christ that day in church, little did I know, it was that day when I started a ten-year journey back home to God.

It was my search for true love that Satan used to lead me away from God, but God used that same quest to bring me back home to a Provider, Savior, Comforter and Counselor who loves me for me.

Praise you Lord! Miss you Daddy!

about the author . . .

Deborah Marbury, born and raised in Cleveland, Ohio, is a child of God, mother, teacher, playwright as well as a first-time novelist. She is a member of Mt. Olive Missionary Baptist Church. She obtained her Bachelor of Arts degree in English and a Master of Education degree in adult learning from Cleveland State University. She teaches English for the Cleveland Municipal Schools. She lives on the east side of Cleveland with her son, Calvin Kelly (a.k.a. CK), who graduates from Benedictine High School in June 2002. He plays football, basketball, and runs track.

She plans to take **What You Do In The Dark . . .** to the stage in the fall of 2003. Her first stage production, **Diary of Black Women at the University of Anywhere: How Do You Love a Black Man?** was produced and performed in 1989 at Cleveland State University. She also plans to write a novel every other year and adapt each one for the stage. Caren is a character Ms. Marbury would like to stay with for a while. She desires to develop the character into an amateur sleuth for a mystery series that will start with the solving of the murder that occurs in **What You Do In The Dark . . .** Although this first effort is not a mystery, Ms. Marbury is hoping to make the mystery genre her writing home starting with **Dark's** sequel in progress, **Am I My Brother's Keeper?**

Printed in the United States
1251100004B/259-363